THE EDUCATION OF VICTORIA

ANGELA MEADOWS

Published by Accent Press Ltd – 2009
Reprinted 2010

ISBN 9781906373696

Printed and bound in the UK

Cover Design by
Zipline Creative Ltd

Prologue
Victoria is Sent Away to School

His mouth pressed against mine, his tongue squeezing between my lips. Something in me resisted his invasion although in truth I wanted to give in to his desires. Bill's left hand rubbed against my right breast and I could feel my nipple hardening under the pressure of his palm. My back was against the wall of the stable and his horsey smell added to the heady fumes of the straw. Something hard between his legs dug into my abdomen. I was giving in, my lips parting to accept his tongue. His right hand moved up and down against my left thigh, steadily lifting my thin woollen skirt. A shock like an electric spark travelled from my thigh up my back at the first touch of his rough stable-boy's fingers against my smooth skin. My mouth opened wide and his tongue explored the interior. I felt as if I was drowning in his attention.

'What is going on here? Get away from my daughter, you scoundrel!' My father's voice woke me from my swoon. Bill lifted his hand from my breast to defend himself from the blows of my father's riding crop that fell on his shoulders and back. He retreated leaving me spreadeagled against the wall watching in horror as my father raised his arm to strike again.

'No, Father, don't hit Bill. It was my fault.'

My father paused mid-stroke and turned to look at me. His cheeks were red and he was breathing hard.

'Get to your room. I'll see to you in a short while. Go on, off with you.' I picked up the hem of my skirt and ran from the stables into the big house. Tears filled my eyes as I ran up the stairs to my bedroom overlooking the stable yard.

I stood at the window and watched as Bill emerged from the stables with my father behind him. I couldn't hear what was said but I could see my father's mouth working. I turned away from the window and watched the door, waiting fearfully for my father to arrive. It was not long. He flung the door open and stood there in his full hunting clothes, his boots still carrying mud from the yard. He took a few steps into the room and sat on my bed.

'Come here, Victoria. Bend over.' I did as I was bidden. I stepped up to him and bent over his knees. He pushed on my shoulders and I almost toppled forward as my feet left the floor. I balanced across his lap. He tugged at my skirt until he had bared my bottom. It had been some years since he had last punished me this way but I knew what was coming next. The full weight of his hand fell on my buttock drawing a gasp and a cry from me. I struggled but his arm held me firm.

'How dare you let that boy, that guttersnipe, that peasant, touch you.' Another slap ignited the other side of my rear.

'Don't you have any respect for me, for your place in society?' Another open-handed stroke.

'Are women so feeble-minded that they give themselves to any and every eager young rogue?' Yet another smack. A few others followed but they became weaker and weaker. Finally my father rested his hand on my naked buttock. A finger moved in a circle producing a not dislikeable sensation. Father seemed to be musing.

'Ah, but I see now it is all my fault. For too long I have allowed you to mix with the village folk and the estate workers. I have been blind to your friendships with the young lads and lasses. I have failed to prepare you for your

2

future as a lady.' He lifted his hands from me and started to rise to his feet. I rolled onto the floor and struggled to get up.

'Look at you, dressed like one of the gleaners.' I looked down at my old rough-weave skirt which I wore because it was light and comfortable. 'Now you are sixteen, my girl, things will have to change.'

'Oh, Father, please,' I appealed, against what I was not sure.

'I must take you away from temptation by that young whelp.'

'Oh, please don't dismiss him, Father. I was leading him on.'

'I don't believe that for one minute. But no, I won't dismiss him. I promised his father that I'd give him a job and he is a good stable-hand. He will stay here while you and I return to London.' I was half relieved and half disappointed; relieved that Bill would not be thrown out of his livelihood but disappointed that I would be leaving my beloved Berkshire and shut up in the city in August.

'Oh, Father. Must I come to London?'

'Yes, Victoria, you must. I see now that I must take you away from the influence of these simple country-folk. You are of an age when you must learn to act like a woman, like a lady. You must dress and behave as befits your station in life.'

Two days later I was indeed dressed as a lady in waist-cinching corset, layers of petticoats and a linen dress that scratched at my chin and brushed against the floor. I sat in the hot stuffy drawing room of our town house, flicking over the pages of a novel and already bored. I missed the countryside and my young friends with whom I ran through the fields and played hide-and-seek amongst the barns and haylofts. My father arrived home from his business at supper

3

time and over the meal he talked at me.

'I have been giving your situation some consideration. While your tutors have done a reasonable job instilling in you the rudiments of education, before you can enter society there is more that you must learn.'

'Such as, Father?'

'I don't know. What women need to know. Cookery, stitchery, that sort of thing.'

'Oh, I see.' I didn't really but I don't think Father did either.

'A business acquaintance has mentioned a school on the continent where you can finish your education, Victoria. I have contacted the headmistress of the Venice School for Young Ladies and I await her reply.'

The thought of travelling across the continent to be schooled appalled me. I didn't want to leave my familiar and comfortable home. Nevertheless the thought of Venice was quite appealing. I had read of the city in the sea with beautiful buildings and waterways for roads. It sounded exciting and romantic. Perhaps if I had to go somewhere to complete my education, then Venice would be one place I would not mind.

Chapter 1
A Lesson for Victoria

My carriage jolted and lurched up the rough alpine track making me uncomfortable as well as angry. I didn't want to leave home, but I did understand my widowed father's reasons. Finding me in the arms of his stable-boy was not what he expected of his 'little girl'. My lips still tingled with the memory of Bill's kiss and my nipples hardened at the thought of his hand pressed against them with just a thin layer of cotton in between. No, the real reason I was so upset was finding that the Venice School for Young Ladies, as Father had called it, was miles from the city of canals – and up a mountain.

The sun was sinking behind the peaks at the end of a late summer's day as we drew up to a large granite house with the distinctive steep roof of the Alps. The carriage door was opened immediately and my gaze fell upon a young man. He was wearing traditional Tyrolean leather shorts and his bare knees and strong thighs impressed me. It seemed that a swelling was forming in the tight leather at his crotch. I looked upwards past the loose cotton shirt, and found the blue eyes of the blond, smooth-faced young man looking at me intensely. He smiled and it did not seem a smile of welcome but more one of anticipation. He helped me step down from the carriage. His firm grip on my wrist seemed to be a signal of possession as he guided me up the steps to a heavy wooden door. He returned to the coach to retrieve my trunk. The door was opened by another handsome young man, similarly dressed but with black hair and brown eyes. He also gave me a thorough examination as he invited me to enter.

I stepped into a square hall carpeted with an old but thick Turkish carpet. A short grey-haired lady emerged from a side room and advanced towards me.

'Ah, you have arrived at last.' She spoke English with a French accent. 'It is Victoria, is it not?' I nodded. 'Named after your dear Queen, I imagine.' I nodded again. 'Come, take off your cloak and join the rest of the girls in the drawing room.'

I felt the doorman remove my cloak from my shoulders. His hands brushed my neck gently and a spark of electricity travelled down my back. The little French lady was scurrying back to the room from which she had come so I hurried after her.

I entered a large, tall room with a window at one end. The setting sun was filling the room with light that reflected off the three huge mirrors that went from floor to ceiling on the other three walls of the room. Apart from cupboards in each corner, the room was quite bare of furniture. There was a large wide couch in the centre of the room, almost the size of a double bed and covered with furs. Some feet away from the couch was a line of six high-backed chairs. Five of the chairs were occupied by young ladies of a similar age to me. They all turned their heads to look at me but there was no sign of emotion on their faces. No doubt like me they were new to the school and wondering what was going to happen.

'Sit down, Victoria,' the little French woman pointed to the empty chair. 'The principal is waiting.'

I took my place and noted that the shape of the seat and the hard straight back forced me to sit upright. I had barely adjusted my posture when a tall woman entered. She appeared to be in her early forties. She wore a green silk dress buttoned up to the neck and had cascading locks of fair hair. The other girls leapt to their feet and I struggled to emulate them.

'Good evening, girls. Please sit.' We sat down as one. 'Welcome to the Venus School for Young Ladies.' Did she really say Venus I thought, or did she say Venice in a strange way? 'I am Madame Thackeray, your headmistress, and you have already met Madame Hulot, my assistant.' She smiled and looked at each one of us girls in turn. 'Here you will learn the knowledge and skills that will enable you to take your place in society as the wives of gentlemen. You will learn cuisine; you will study arts and music; you will discover the fashions of the day; you will practice the art of conversation and you will be taught how to run a household. These studies will occupy your days. In the evenings, tuition will turn to the art of attracting a husband and how to satisfy him. Lessons will start shortly but first you will be shown to your rooms.'

Madame Thackeray turned to Madame Hulot who opened the door. Six elegant young ladies entered the room. They wore identical silk evening gowns in the fashionable new mauve dye. I gasped at the dresses as they left the girls' shoulders completely bare and revealed considerable décolletage. Their waists were extremely narrow and the skirts flared out. The six girls lined up in front of us.

'These are our senior girls,' Madame continued. 'They have a year of experience in our ways and will help you in your studies. They will now show you to your rooms.' The girl facing me stepped forward, smiled broadly and held out her right hand.

'Hello, I'm your mentor. Come with me.' She hooked her arm around my left elbow and guided me back into the hall and up a wide stairway. On the second floor we entered a landing with doors on either side. My guide pushed on one door, and we entered a comfortably sized bedroom. 'Here we are; this is our room.' It seemed that we were to share a room and a bed as there was just one ample double bed to be seen. I was surprised, but having shared a bed with a cousin, I was not upset by the prospect. My mentor sat on the bed, scooping up the hoops and silk of her dress. 'I'm Beatrice, who are you?'

'My name is Victoria,' I replied.

'Named after the Queen, were you?' I nodded resignedly. 'I expect you are hungry after your journey. You were rather late so missed dinner but a cold buffet has been prepared for you.' She indicated a tray of bread, cold meats and cheese on a side table. 'The bath is also ready for you; I'm sure you need one after your journey. I will return shortly to help you dress in your school evening wear.'

Having satisfied my hunger, I was enjoying a lazy hot bath when the bathroom door opened and Beatrice reappeared. She looked somewhat flustered.

'Good heavens, Victoria, what are you still doing there? You should be getting ready or you will be late.' I suddenly remembered that I wasn't on holiday but at a school. I was reluctant to get out of the bath and expose my naked body while Beatrice stood in the doorway glaring at me. 'Come on, Victoria. Don't be prudish. I'll help you dry yourself.'

She entered the room, picked up the bath towel and carried it towards the bath. I realised that she wasn't going to leave me alone so I decided to stand up and let her see me unclothed. The water cascaded off me. Beatrice examined me closely and I began to blush. Then she nodded with approval and I blushed some more.

'How old are you, Victoria?'

'Sixteen last June.'

'You look quite mature for your age. Your breasts are well formed and firm and your hips are broad but your stomach is suitably flat. The men will take a fancy to you

I'm sure.'

I wasn't sure that I liked this appraisal, which made me seem like one of my father's horses, but the mention of men made me think of Bill. He had paid my body compliments – the little that he saw of it.

Beatrice wrapped the towel around me and rubbed me vigorously so that I was soon dry. She tossed the towel to the floor and pulled me by the hand back into our bedroom. Clothes had been laid out on the bed, I presumed for me, but I was surprised at what they consisted of.

There was a white satin corset. My own corsets were dull cotton. Beatrice wrapped it around me and began to tighten the laces. I groaned and moaned as she constricted my waist to smaller dimensions than I allowed my maid at home to do.

'Why do I have to wear this?' I gasped.

'Because it is part of the school uniform and because men like the figure it produces.' I was standing in front of a mirror and noticed that I certainly had more shape. My breasts were pushed together and upwards so that they rested on the top of the garment, my nipples on show. The narrowing of my waist also made my buttocks appear larger and more rounded than they usually did. Beatrice looked at my image and then at me. Her eyes descended and came to rest at my exposed mount of Venus. She passed the palm of her hand over my tuft of hair. There was a tingle inside that was unfamiliar. 'You have quite a bush down there, haven't you?'

'I have?'

'Yes, we need to trim that. Men don't like too much hair you know.' She tugged my underarm hair. 'This will have to go too. It's very unsightly. Still, no time now.'

She passed me a pair of white silk knickers which barely covered my bottom and, having made me sit on the bed, pulled white silk stockings up my legs and fastened the tops

9

to clips at the bottom of the corset. She presented me with a pair of white satin slippers. As I put them on my feet she brought a long gossamer-thin gown trimmed in white fur. I put my arms through the wide sleeves. The garment did nothing to cover me but instead seemed to form a frame for my corseted figure.

'There. You are ready. No time for make-up, but that's all part of the course anyway. Come, it's time for your introductory lesson.' Beatrice tugged on my hand and dragged me out on to the landing. We almost ran down the stairs, my gown flaring out behind me. I felt as if I had no clothes on at all and wondered what sort of school I had come to.

We reached the room where we had first met. Beatrice pushed me in and departed. Like before, my classmates were already sitting there but this time they and I were identically dressed. I took my place in the uncomfortable chair at the end of the row and looked around me. The curtains had been drawn as night had now fallen. Many oil lamps had been lit so that the room was very light. A large candelabrum dangled over the fur-strewn couch.

'Ah, you have joined us at last, Victoria,' said Madame Hulot impatiently. 'Punctuality is a virtue we foster here. Gentlemen do not like to be kept waiting.' She left and a few moments later Madame Thackeray swept in, beaming at each of us new girls.

'Wonderful, girls. You now look as though you belong here and are ready for your instruction to begin. This evening you have nothing to do but watch. I want you to concentrate on what you will see and what I have to tell you. You will observe certain techniques which you will be studying during your time here so do not worry if you do not understand tonight.'

I had no idea what she was talking about but as she moved to take up a seat at the side of the room Beatrice reappeared and, without looking at Madame Thackeray, or the six of us, she went to stand by the couch and began to look at herself in the large glass mirror that was behind it. A moment later a young man entered the room. I recognised him as the blond servant who had helped me from the carriage. Now, however, he was wearing evening dress and looked exceptionally smart and aristocratic. I wondered about the meaning of his change of attire but things soon started to happen. He stepped up behind Beatrice, put a hand on her bare shoulder and spun her around. When she faced him he bent his neck and placed his lips on hers.

'For the purpose of this evening's demonstration, ladies, you must imagine that Eric is the man that Beatrice wishes to marry and that he desires her as his wife.' Madame's words seemed to provide some explanation for the deep kissing that was going on. I presumed that we were watching a theatrical performance with Eric and Beatrice as the actors. However, the manner in which they clung to each other and inserted tongues into each other's mouths did seem to go beyond the realms of acting that I was familiar with. Bill had only placed his lips on mine for moments, but as I watched I began to wish that I had responded as Beatrice was doing now.

The pair parted and Eric began to undo the buttons on Beatrice's gown which, conveniently for him, were situated at the front.

'Men often find the small buttons of a gown difficult to undo, so you must learn to assist discreetly,' Madame continued. Indeed Beatrice had assisted so quickly that the gown had slipped to the floor and she revealed not the white corset that I and the other girls wore but a blood-red garment with black lacing. Beatrice now turned her attention to Eric. 'You will also have to acquire the skill of undoing the fastenings of the male vestments.' Beatrice certainly had the skill because Eric was swiftly divested of his jacket, stiff collar and shirt and trousers. In the same time he had kicked off his shoes and stockings. He wore no underclothes.

For the first time in my life a man stood naked in front of me, but his attention was on Beatrice. His buttocks were white firm globes and he stood with his feet a little apart. He gave Beatrice a gentle push and she fell back on to the couch. Now I could see in the mirror beyond them the front of Eric's body. He had a strong muscular chest, but my eyes were drawn to his member which was as firm as a broom pole and stood out at a right angle from his body. I never knew that it could be come so large. The tip was a shiny purple and shaped like a massive toadstool.

'As you can see, it takes little to arouse a man. The skill comes in prolonging the arousal and giving satisfaction.' Beatrice had by sleight of hand unfastened her stockings so now when Eric took hold of the vivid red knickers he was able to pull them off in one swift, fluid movement. Beatrice spread her legs wide and bent her knees, pulling her feet up onto the couch.

From my position at the end of the row I had a full view of her sex despite Eric standing just a pace from her. I saw that she indeed had far less pubic hair than myself and that it was trimmed into a neat arrowhead pointing at the cleft between her legs. Without thinking my hand moved between my legs and I could feel my outer lips swelling like Beatrice's and a dampness penetrating my knickers. Her swollen crack glistened with her excitement. Eric knelt between her legs and lowered his head towards her sex. I saw his tongue stick out and lap at the juices oozing from her fanny.

'Not all men have a liking for cunnilingus, but many do. By offering herself, Beatrice has given Eric the encouragement he needs and for as long as he remains drinking at the trough, so to speak, he will retain his erection and derive great pleasure. It is important that the lady also

12

derive satisfaction from the process as she must retain her own level of arousal and lubrication.' Beatrice evidently was enjoying the experience because she moaned at each flick of Eric's tongue and thrust herself at his mouth. He gripped her buttocks, held her firmly and pushed his face hard into her groin. I almost felt as if I were Beatrice and his tongue was exploring deeper and deeper up my love canal.

Eric withdrew, drawing breath, and stood to stretch his back. Beatrice immediately slid from the couch to kneel in front of him. They slickly turned side on to their audience. Now I and my fellows could see Eric's long stiff cock (the word I recalled Bill had used for his sex). It stretched to within an inch of Beatrice's face. She poked out her tongue and gently touched the tip. It trembled and Eric mumbled something, a 'Ja' I think. Beatrice leaned forward, carefully opening her mouth to surround the red onion at the end of the penis. I gasped as I saw it slowly disappearing into her mouth. She kept her jaws wide apart as she took more and more of it in. She stopped with her small pert nose almost buried in his pubic hair.

'Beatrice is one of my most skilled pupils in fellatio. Very few ladies can take the full length of a man's erect penis but some like Beatrice are able to open their throat and avoid gagging. The heat and the softness of the woman's mouth bring intense pleasure to the man.'

Eric was indeed moaning and there was a tremor in his knees. Beatrice rocked back slowly and the shining wet penis re-emerged, but that was not the end. Now she started moving her head to and fro, in turn enveloping and revealing the member. As the glowing tip emerged from her lips her tongue played around it before it disappeared again into the depths of her gullet. Steadily she increased the frequency of her movements. Eric sighed and groaned and began to shake. His testes in their sac wobbled and swung from side to side. Beatrice reached up and grasped them in her hand, holding them firmly as her head now oscillated up and down the shaft. My hand was now pressed hard against my sex, rubbing in time with Beatrice's movement. I was hot and perspiring so much that I felt rivulets of sweat running down the clefts between both my breasts and my buttocks.

'Stamina is needed for this stage in the act. Some men reach satisfaction very quickly but many are lucky enough to be able to withstand the agony of pleasure for some time.' Beatrice showed no sign of tiring. Her lips were now locked firmly around Eric's cock as it slid in and out. At last, when even I was beginning to feel exhausted, Eric let out a cry. I saw Beatrice gulp and swallow and immediately stop her movements. She remained kneeling, holding the penis in her mouth, sucking gently.

'Some men like to withdraw at the point of orgasm and expend their semen in the woman's face. A number of women prefer that to swallowing the fluid, but in the spur of the moment you rarely have much choice in the matter. A warning though. After orgasm the male often finds his penis rather tender. Be careful not to let your teeth cause pain.' Beatrice reluctantly let Eric pull his penis from her mouth. It flopped, shrunken and wet between his legs.

'Young men take a few minutes to recover before they can embark on further lovemaking so this provides us with a break in the proceedings. I was pleased, girls, to see that you were watching intently. I noticed also that one or two of you were driven to pleasure yourselves by the excitement of what you saw. I hope you are able to remain dispassionate and observe the skills that Beatrice displayed. Over the next two years you too will learn these techniques. That is our objective here at the Venus School for Young Ladies.'

Now that I realised that my new school was named after the goddess of love and not a watery city I wondered how my darling father could have gotten so confused. Did he have any idea of the curriculum I was to study? Reflecting

14

on the emotions I had felt as I had watched Beatrice give and receive pleasure, I was excited by the prospects that lay ahead. I thought of what I could offer Bill or any other eligible young man once I had completed my education.

'Now as Beatrice has had a chance to draw breath we will continue with the proceedings. As Eric has been temporarily incapacitated we will have a substitute.' Beatrice had relaxed onto the couch and Eric gathered up his clothes and left. As he departed the other young man that I had met entered. He made his entry naked with his cock already pointing the way forward. He moved towards the couch. I sat up straighter and peered avidly at the pair. My fingers slipped inside my knickers and felt the slick wetness between my pussy lips. I looked forward with gleeful anticipation to what scenes of lovemaking would unfold before my eyes.

Chapter 2
Victoria Learns the Arts of Pleasure

I sat on the bed unfastening my silk stockings and thinking about the evening's events. I wondered what was in store for me at the Venus School for Young Ladies. It looked unlikely to be the demure training for married life that my father had imagined when he sent me away from my beloved Bill.

The door opened and my room-mate Beatrice swept in. Her lace gown was undone and I saw at a glance that she hadn't replaced her knickers after her exhibition of lovemaking.

'I don't know about you, Victoria, but I'm exhausted,' she said. She did indeed look tired. Her hair was wet and straggly, but there was a rosy glow to her face.

'I am quite tired,' I admitted. Beatrice jumped on to the bed and knelt beside me.

'Did you enjoy the demonstration?' she asked. I really did not know how to answer. I had watched her pleasure two young Austrian men in turn while our headmistress explained their actions. I blushed as I recalled how excited I had become watching them perform extraordinary acts upon each other.

'Y-yes,' I stammered, 'it was, uh, exciting.'

'That's good. I really wanted to be the one that Madame selected.'

'Didn't you mind being watched while you, um, uh ...'

16

'While I fornicated do you mean, Victoria?'

'Uh, yes, I suppose so.'

'Well why not. If you've been trained to do something well, why not show off your skills?'

'Do the other girls think the same?'

'Oh yes, I think so. There was quite a competition for tonight's show, but Madame says I'm the best at fellatio, and I do adore having a man lick me really deeply.' I blushed again at the memory of Eric kneeling between Bea's legs and lapping at her sex.

'Do you love Eric or Hermann?' I asked innocently.

'Eric's a dear and Hermann has the most wonderful cock. It is so broad that it really stretches you. But you mean love in the sense, am I going to marry them, don't you?'

'Well, yes.'

'Of course not, you silly. They're just for training, like the other boys. I'm going to marry a rich man and keep him happy for as long as he lives.'

'Who is he?'

'I don't know. I haven't met one yet – but I will.'

'Oh. Did you say there are more boys here?'

'There are five, or is it six? No, it's five. Madame employs them around the house but they are really here to help us girls practise the arts of love. Look, I'm ready to sleep, can you undo my corset?' She turned her back to me.

'Yes, of course.' I started to undo the lacing. 'Perhaps you could do the same for me. I've never worn one before.'

Soon both of us had pulled off the tight garments and our stockings. Beatrice pulled the bedclothes over herself while she was still naked.

'I can't be bothered with my nightdress. Come and cuddle up with me, Victoria.' It was another new thing after a day of surprising events but I did as she said and for the first time in my life felt my body touching that of another, skin to skin.

17

Lessons began the next day and soon I was learning the knowledge and skills necessary to please a man, or at least Madame Thackeray's vision of what men wanted in a wife. I studied art, improved my French and began a course in cookery. In the evening I joined my classmates in the drawing room dressed as we had been on the first evening, in white corset, stockings, bloomers and a light dressing gown. For our first lesson Madame told us that if we were to give pleasure to a man then we must know what gives us pleasure. That meant 'getting to know ourselves' as she put it. She put up pictures of the female anatomy and got us to recite the names for the various parts of our fannies. Then she explained about the clitoris. I didn't even know it existed before but apparently it is what gives women that wonderful experience of climax. She gave us each a small hand mirror and told us to return to our bedrooms. We were to examine our own sex, find our clitoris and stimulate ourselves until we managed an orgasm. It was the strangest homework I had ever been set.

I sat on the bed with my knickers off, my legs apart, holding the mirror at an angle so I could see what was going on down there with just the oil lamp for illumination. I soon found the hard little knob at the top of my slit which I presumed was the fabled clitoris. I twiddled it and rubbed it. I felt a pleasant sensation but I certainly wasn't experiencing raptures like Beatrice had when Eric licked her. I was getting a bit fed up but then Beatrice came in.

'Oh, you're here, I thought you would be in the lesson with Madame,' she said as she slipped off her gown and joined me on the bed, 'but, I remember now, you are having your first lesson at getting an orgasm.' I blushed and squeezed my legs together. She laughed at my modesty.

'Any luck yet?' I shook my head. 'It's all in the touch.

Look, let me help.' She wriggled closer and took the mirror from my hand. Then she caressed the inside of my right thigh.

'Come on, open your legs.' Reluctantly, I parted my thighs a little. Beatrice lifted my knees and pushed them wider apart. I rested my head back on the pillows.

'There's no wonder you had trouble. Your bush is so thick I can barely fight my way through to your little knob. It's time we did something about it.' Beatrice leapt off the bed and into the bathroom, leaving me confused. A moment later she returned with a bowl of lather and a fearsome blade – a razor. She knelt between my legs and covered my mound with soapy suds.

'Now keep still.' I was too scared to move a muscle. The cold, sharp blade slid over my most sensitive parts but Bea was so skilled that I felt no nicks. In a very short time she wiped the remaining foam away with a towel and sat back to look at her handiwork. I too looked down between my legs and saw a sight I had never seen. My hair had been reduced to a narrow arrowhead pointing at my cleft. My vulva was revealed in its pink, crinkled nakedness.

Beatrice licked the fingers of her right hand. The next moment I felt a spasm of electricity pass through me as her fingers touched the lips of my fanny and slipped inside. I had felt dry but with that one touch I immediately began oozing juices. Beatrice's fingers slowly moved up and down. My swelling lips parted and revealed the dark depths of my sex. Then she moved up until she found the little hooded tip. Her fingers circled it and teased it. Each movement, each touch, each new sensation sent shudders of pleasure through me.

'Is this it?' I asked breathlessly.

'Not quite. You'll know.' Now she had two hands at work, one massaging my clitoris and the other delving deeper and deeper into my crack. Her fingers worked their way into my vagina, rhythmically moving in and out. Now I could feel a change occurring inside me. A wave of emotion seemed to start in my toes and set my legs quivering. It entered my stomach and rose up to my breasts and finally burst through my skull. I clenched my hands and cried out. On and on it continued. I thought I was trapped on a pinnacle of pleasure, but gradually, reluctantly, it faded and passed away. I sobbed and shook. Beatrice gently removed her hands and put the covers over me.

'Now that was an orgasm,' she said smiling.

As the days passed I discovered how to give myself pleasure but never did I match that first explosion of feeling that Beatrice gave me. Our evening lessons moved on, however, to consider the male anatomy. I was sitting next to Natalie. She was a petite French girl with piled ringlets of jet-black hair. We had made friends because I was able to speak French quite well while the other girls were German or Italian speakers. Although Natalie was as innocent as me about the art of lovemaking she found our lessons most amusing. She giggled and whispered rude asides to me as Madame described to us the workings of the penis. Then Madame opened a small leather case. We all leaned forward to get a peep at what was inside. There nestling in padded purple velvet were three items made of glass. Madame lifted one out and held it up for us to see. It was in the shape of the male member, about six to seven inches long, an average size so Madame said. The others were the same, exact in every detail. They had a flat end so that they could rest on a horizontal surface and stand up proudly.

'This evening, ladies,' Madame announced, 'your task in pairs is to take one of these fine dildos to your rooms and practise inserting it in each other. I want you to learn how to accept the object into your bodies and to position yourselves for the greatest satisfaction.' I gulped as I looked at the dildos. Only one or two fingers had so far penetrated me and these objects looked so huge. I hesitated but Natalie was eager. She grabbed my hand and pulled me from my seat. She took the first dildo that Madame proffered and dragged me up the stairs to the room that she shared.

Natalie flung off her robe and leapt onto the bed.

'Please help me remove this corset. I cannot follow Madame's instruction with my breath being squeezed out.' To be truthful there was little of Natalie to be squeezed as she had the smallest waist I had seen in a girl of seventeen years. I agreed with her as I too found the corset restricting of movement. We took it in turns to divest each other of the garment and then sat side by side with our stockings sliding down our calves. Natalie held the dildo between her palms, warming it. We both looked at it for a moment. Then Natalie jumped up, tugged her bloomers down and handed the dildo to me.

'Come, I will try first. Let us see if it fits.' She lay back on the bed and pulled her knees up, revealing her sex. I could see at once that she was excited because her lips were swollen and glistening pinkly. I knelt facing her and slowly advanced the tip of the dildo towards her gaping crack. She jerked when it touched her flesh.

'Sorry,' I said, withdrawing it.

'Non, the first touch was surprise. Allez.' She pulled her knees back further. I took a breath and leant closer. This time she did not flinch as the end of the dildo touched and then passed between her lips. The oval knob slid easily into her and then the shaft disappeared inch by inch. She gasped as I gave it a final push. Now only the flat end was visible surrounded by her engorged labia.

'Oh, oui,' she sighed, 'I am full. Do you think a man will feel the same?'

'I don't know,' I replied, 'I cannot imagine any penis being as hard as glass. What do I do now?'

'Make it move, like a man would.' I gripped the end of the dildo and slid it out a couple of inches, then pushed it back in.

'Yes, yes, faster,' Natalie urged. I moved it backwards and forwards. It slid easily with Natalie's secretions lubricating it. I quickly found a rhythm and was soon pounding the dildo into her. She screamed, urging me to ever greater exertions. It seemed to go on and on. I was perspiring profusely and my arm was tiring when she let out a piercing cry.

'*Oui, oui.* Aah.' She trembled violently then released her thighs at last. I sat back leaving the dildo embedded in her. My arm was tired and stiff.

'I think I will prefer it when the man has to exert himself,' I said. Natalie sat up, still panting, and pulled the dildo from her vagina.

'Oh but it was worth your effort, my dear. Now it is your turn.'

There were no lessons on Saturdays, so most weeks, if the weather was good, we would go out for walks in the mountains. By late October, winter was approaching and already there was snow on the peaks that surrounded us. Natalie and I decided to visit the nearest village to purchase some fresh fruit. We walked down the rough track. The village was poor and there were only a handful of stalls in the marketplace. The villagers did their best to ignore us. Did they shun us because of what we got up to at the school? Did they even know? Or was it merely distrust of strangers? No one offered us fruit for sale.

There was a boy standing by the last stall. He looked to be about the same age as us but was quite short and dressed in very rough clothes.

'You want?' he said vaguely and beckoned us to follow him. Thinking that he might know of a store of fruit we heeded him as he hurried up a narrow alley between two buildings. At the rear there was a wooden shack leaning against the stone building. He opened the door and entered. I ducked my head and joined Natalie in the rough shed. Sunlight entered through the many cracks in the walls and roof. The boy turned to face us.

'Me, Albert,' he said. 'You get me job at school?' With that he lifted up his torn and grubby smock and revealed a huge penis. I gasped and covered my mouth with my gloved hand. Natalie giggled. Albert gripped his member with his right hand but he could barely reach around it. He waggled it at us. The pink glans sparkled in the sunlight.

'You want?' He waved his immense cock at each of us.

'No, no, put it away,' I insisted and waved him away. He let the hem of his smock fall, but now that he was fully excited, it did little to hide it. Natalie began to question him and through a mixture of broken English and poorly interpreted German we gathered that he was an orphan, completely destitute and without any means of support now that he was past sixteen years of age. We agreed to pass on his request to Madame Thackeray and said that he should present himself at the school on Monday.

That evening I waited for Bea to return to tell her about Albert and ask her advice. It was gone midnight when she returned. A look of surprise greeted me.

'You are still awake, Victoria. I was sure you would be asleep at this time.' She climbed gingerly onto the bed and lay face down.

'What's the matter, Bea? Where have you been? Are you ill?'

'I'll be all right, Victoria, don't worry. I have been having an extra lesson with Madame Hulot.'

'What kind of lesson?' I asked innocently.

'What do you think? Lessons in what men like from a woman. There is much more to learn in the second year, my

23

dear.'

'More than we saw you do on that first evening?'

Beatrice turned her head towards me and gave me a thin smile. 'Far more. Now we are learning the dark arts of lovemaking. Look.' She pulled up her gown, which I noted was now black lace. Underneath was a black satin corset but her buttocks were bare. I was astonished to see that both white globes were criss-crossed with red marks.

'Madame Hulot did that? Had you done something wrong?'

'Not at all, I performed perfectly.' There was a pride in her voice. 'She held me down over her lap while Eric wielded the cane. I cried but did not struggle. Then with Madame Hulot pressing down on my shoulders he knelt behind me. I thought he was going to enter me from behind but he forced his way into my forbidden passage.' I had no idea what she was talking about. 'But forget what I have told you, they are secrets for your next year of tuition. Why are you not asleep?'

I told her about Albert, his desire for a job and his immense attribute. Bea agreed to put the matter to the principal and then bade me to put the light out and get to sleep.

A few evenings later the six of us were sitting in pairs in the drawing room with the candelabrum and oil lamps fully lit. Madame placed the three glass dildos in their padded box and said, 'I think that is enough of the artificial. Now for the real thing.' She clapped her hands and immediately the door opened. Three young men entered wearing knee-length smoking jackets. At the front were Wilhelm and Heinrich who worked in the yard chopping wood and stoking the fires in the kitchen. Behind them was Albert. Albert saw Natalie and me and immediately came and stood in front of us. The other two boys went and stood in front of our classmates.

'Welcome, gentlemen,' Madame said, 'now you may disrobe.' The three boys flung off their jackets. All six of us girls gasped at the sight of three naked men. Albert's body was completely white except for his arms and lower legs, and he looked and smelt a lot cleaner than when we had last seen him. What had not changed, however, was his long, thick penis. It was considerably bigger than the glass dildo. It stood out proudly, quivering slightly, its root buried in a mass of brown curls, with a fist-sized sac dangling below.

'Now girls, you may caress the shaft and lightly touch the glans.' Natalie leaned closer and reached out a hand. Albert was staring down at the two cherries in the centre of the small moons that rested on the white satin of her corset. She placed a finger on the shaft about halfway along its length and slid it first one way then the other. Albert groaned and at once a fountain of milky fluid burst from the tip of his cock and hit Natalie between her breasts. She recoiled with a cry and fell backwards. Madame strode over to see what disaster had occurred.

'Really, Albert, I must teach you some measure of control.' Albert looked as unhappy and embarrassed as he possibly could. His penis had shrunk to a quarter of its erect size and hung limp and forlorn. 'You must restore it quickly, Albert. You are young and should not need to waste time,' Madame whispered kindly to him and leant down to take his penis in her hands. She massaged and caressed it and in but a minute or two it began to swell and stiffen once again. Madame turned to me.

'Now, Victoria. You feel it. I am sure we will have no more intemperate accidents.' Albert took a step towards me and I slid off the chair to kneel in front of him. Now his penis was at the level of my breasts. Albert looked down at them, his eyes wide with the delight of seeing my full bosoms exposed above my corset. I saw his penis stiffen and rise another inch or so, beckoning to be fondled. The foreskin had pulled back completely, revealing the door-knob-sized glans pierced by a small hole which now gaped open. I placed the palm of my right hand on his abdomen, lowered my fingers into the shrub of pubic hair and then, bending my wrist, slid my fingers slowly and gently along his shaft. My thumb rubbed along the underside feeling the tight, smooth skin. When I got to the point where the pink glans began I stopped and squeezed gently. Albert moaned softly. I looked up into his face and could see his eyes wobbling in their sockets. His knees started to buckle.

'I think you had better lie down, Albert,' I said quietly. He needed no second bidding and he subsided to the floor, soon lying flat on his back with his legs apart on either side of my knees. I had not let go of his penis and now with it pointing towards the ceiling I began to massage it up and down. The skin moved easily. On each down stroke, the skin of the glans was pulled taut so that it glistened with the reflected light of the candles. On the up stroke, the foreskin slid over the tip. Albert groaned with pleasure on each movement. I was so intent on my actions that I found myself becoming excited as well. I slipped my left hand into my bloomers. Already my pubis felt hot and moist and I found my little knob hard and erect. I rubbed it in time with the vibrations of my right hand on Albert's cock.

'Harder, harder,' Albert muttered between gasps of pleasure. I increased my frequency of movement, both hands working hard, the right on Albert and the left on myself. I began to wonder if Albert could be brought to orgasm so soon after spraying Natalie with his semen. I need not have feared, however, for just as my arm began to ache, Albert stretched out his legs and arched his back, and another fountain of white fluid shot from his penis. The shock pushed me to the point of orgasm too. The spasms of pleasure made me cry.

'Oh, bravo,' cheered Natalie, clapping her hands

26

gleefully. 'You have done him for sure, and yourself too.' I sat back on my heels, holding my hands up in front of me and stretching out the fingers to relieve the stiffness of the exertion. Albert lay on his back panting.

'Very good, Victoria.' I hadn't realised that Madame had been standing nearby watching me perform, 'but you must learn that when you are servicing a man, his pleasure is paramount and you should not divide your energy by pleasing yourself as well as him. You will go to my office and wait for me to come and teach you some lessons in the etiquette of lovemaking. Now, Natalie, your turn to work on Albert.' I rose to my feet and turned towards the door. I was upset that I had apparently transgressed and earned Madame's displeasure. What punishment had she prepared for me?

Chapter 3
Victoria Learns Discipline

The oil lamp gave me a ghostly appearance in the long mirror due to my white-stockinged legs, white satin bloomers and corset, the white skin of my face and exposed breasts. The only contrast was my brown hair and my small red nipples.

For the first time since I had arrived at the Venus School for Young Ladies some six weeks earlier, I stood in the study of Madame Thackeray, the principal. Why I was there I wasn't sure. Somehow I had displeased her while pleasuring young Albert during the evening's lesson. Now I stood patiently awaiting her, standing beside her desk and looking at my image. To my right was a large bed as this was Madame's bedroom as well as her office. The bed had heavy wooden head and foot-boards with pineapple-shaped knobs at each corner. At the foot of the bed was a strange, waist high stool. It was in the form of an elephant standing on four sturdy legs. Its trunk and two curved tusks pressed against the bed and it had a broad, padded leather back.

I turned my gaze to Madame's desk. It bore just four items, two of which were framed photographs. One showed two ladies whom I recognised in the dim light as being Madame Thackeray herself and Madame Hulot, her companion and assistant. They were dressed in light blouses and dark skirts and carried parasols. The other photo was a different style entirely as it showed a naked woman facing

28

the photographer with a fine scarf suspended lazily from her right hand. She appeared to have no body hair whatsoever. I peered closely and was a little astonished to confirm that the figure was Madame Hulot.

The other two items on the desk also seemed rather incongruous for that of a school principal. One was a black leather riding crop and the other a magnificent ebony phallus. I bent to look at the latter more closely. It was broader and longer than the glass instruments that Madame had given us to practise with, and it had a pair of fist-sized testicles at one end. The other end was a helmet-shaped knob so large that I thought I would barely be able to get my hand around it. I could not imagine what use such a tool could be put to, but further examination was prevented by the scrape of the door opening. I stood up straight.

Madame swept in, circled me and sat at the chair behind her desk. Although surely in her early forties, she was a handsome woman with her long fair hair piled up on her head. She rested her hands on the leather desktop and looked up at me.

'What is your purpose here, Victoria?' she asked curtly.

'To study the arts and sciences required to manage our future husband's household and affairs and to satisfy him in any way that he desires.' I recited the oft-heard catechism of Madame Thackeray's school.

'That is correct, Victoria, but you disappoint me. You have shown great aptitude for the arts of love but it seems that you cannot resist taking pleasure yourself.'

'But, Madame,' I protested, 'you taught us to find pleasure in being touched and how to arouse excitement in our private parts.'

'I did indeed and valuable lessons they are, but what you have not yet learned is that there is a time to indulge your own pleasure and a time to devote to servicing your lover. Caressing and coaxing the male member requires all your attention, not least in preventing him from reaching a climax too soon. Instead of using both hands on your man you had one hand up your fanny.'

'I am sorry, Madame.'

'You will be, Victoria. However, there is another matter and that concerns Albert. He has a marvellous attribute and will be a great asset to us here, but he is inexperienced and spurts far too readily. As well as learning your own lesson you must teach him restraint.' I was nonplussed; what did Madame mean? She answered my unspoken question immediately.

'You will spend an hour each day before supper handling Albert's magnificent cock. You will ensure he retains his erection for the whole hour without ejaculating and you will refrain from fingering yourself in that time. A senior girl will observe and record transgressions. Next Sunday you will report to me at three of the clock and we will examine your progress. Each failure will be rewarded with a stroke of this.' Madame raised the crop and brandished it at me. 'And now I will give you a taste of what to expect if you fail.'

My heart beat faster as I realised that she intended to beat me.

'Remove your bloomers if you please, Victoria.' I had little choice but to obey Madame. I tugged on the ribbon at my waist. The bow undid and the garment duly dropped to the floor. I stepped out of it.

'Now bend over the elephant.' The purpose of this strange stool had become apparent. I stepped slowly and fearfully towards it. When my thighs rested against the cool leather, Madame pushed against the small of my back with the riding crop. I bent forward until my stomach was resting on the padded back of the elephant. My arms and my hair dangled down.

'Further,' Madame urged. I raised myself up on the tip of my toes and found myself delicately balanced on the elephant's back. I felt Madame's slippered foot slide between my ankles and push my legs apart. My feet lost contact with the floor and I really was lying across the stool. I was very conscious that my buttocks were as exposed as they could be, as were my most private parts. I lay there listening to Madame's soft breaths as some moments passed. Not even my dear but strict father had given me more than a spanking before so I had no idea what to expect. I trembled in anticipation. There was a fizz through the air and my left buttock burst into flame. I yelped, but before I could take a breath there came another screech of the crop and my right buttock exploded.

'Please, Madame,' I appealed, but to no avail as the crop scorched across my left cheek a second time. I tried to struggle off the stool.

'Be still, Victoria.' She was breathing deeply now, but her energy was barely expended as the crop came down again on my right buttock. I screamed out, as it felt that both my cheeks were aflame.

'That is enough for now,' Madame said soothingly. I remained thrown over the whipping stool like a sack of potatoes over a donkey. I sobbed but the pain began to subside a little.

I felt a pressure in the small of my back, a finger that began to slide between my cheeks. It lingered, circling around my arsehole. Despite the smouldering fire on my buttocks the touch was like an electric shock. It became the centre of my attention. The finger moved on, parting my lips and slipping inside. I realised that my juices were flowing. The finger delved deeper and was joined by its neighbours and by a thumb that felt for and found my swelling button. I groaned as the pleasure competed with the pain of the beating. In fact the pleasure seemed greater than I had ever experienced. In a few moments I was moaning as pulses of indescribable desire rippled through my abdomen. My thighs shook uncontrollably and I came with a gasp and cry. The hand withdrew.

'There, that will teach you something, Victoria. Pain and pleasure complement each other, the former raising the latter to a new plane of sensation. You may dismount now.'

A little wriggling shifted my weight so that I slid off the elephant and onto my unsteady legs. I turned to face Madame. She was standing holding the door open, my bloomers dangling from an outstretched finger.

'Don't forget – five of the clock each evening, in the drawing room. Return to your room now.' I grabbed the undergarment and fled from the office and up the stairs.

When I reached my bedroom I flung myself face down on the bed. My bottom still burned but my thoughts were of the ecstasy that Madame had given me. Barely a few moments passed before there was a knock on the door, and a whispered voice asked, 'Victoria, are you there?' I recognised the French accent of my friend Natalie.

'Come in,' I called, my voice breaking somewhat. The door opened.

'Oh, Victoria, what has happened to you?' Natalie approached me and I could see her wide eyes staring at my bottom. 'Has Madame beaten you? You have a cross of red marks on your smooth, white bottom.' I explained what Madame had said and the punishment I had received. Natalie laid her hand gently on my bottom.

'Ooh, I can feel the heat still,' I said. Then I began to describe how Madame had caressed me.

'Do you mean like this?' Natalie's finger traced out the same path as Madame's and again my loins trembled with the delectable pleasure.

'Yes, just like that,' I moaned. Natalie pressed her hand between my swollen lips.

'You are indeed excited, Victoria. I am sure that just a

little movement like this,' her fingers rubbed in and out of my vagina, 'will make you come.'

'I, I think you are correct,' I gasped as the tremors increased to a climax.

Afterwards we lay together on the bed and discussed the strange way that the beating I had been given seemed to make me quicker to achieve orgasm.

'Perhaps Madame will find occasion to use her whip on me,' said Natalie almost wistfully.

As the clock in the hallway struck five, I entered the drawing room. Beatrice was sitting on a couch, sewing in the light of the sun that was about to set beyond the mountain peaks. As I stepped towards her I heard footsteps behind me and turned to see Albert joining us. Bea put down her work and looked at each of us.

'Good afternoon, Albert.' Albert nodded his head in greeting. 'Hello, Victoria. You know what you have to do.' I turned to face Albert and pressed a hand against his groin. His cock was already hard and straining at his lederhosen.

'You are not going to do it in those clothes, are you, Victoria?' Bea's voice carried a note of authority. I looked down at my long grey woollen skirt and high-necked, long-sleeved, white linen blouse. 'You do not want to get semen on your day uniform. Take it off.' I had no argument to put to Bea, so unbuttoned my blouse and slipped it off my shoulders, then unfastened my skirt and let it drop to the floor. I stepped out of it and stood somewhat self-consciously in my slip.

'And the rest,' Bea ordered. I looked at her questioningly. 'Yes, I said take off your slip. Don't waste time.' Bea seemed to enjoy giving me orders. I grasped the hem of my slip and pulled it up over my head. For the first time in my life I stood unclothed in front of a man, well, a boy, as that was all that Albert was really. His eyes widened as he took in the full sight of my naked body. His adoring look immediately excited me and I felt my nipples swell and perk up. I began to sway from side to side feeling extremely sensuous. My breasts swung in response to my movement and Albert's head followed them.

'Now release him, and get down to work.' I came to my senses and remembered what I was supposed to be doing. I knelt in front of Albert and undid the buttons of his flies. Before I had finished, his erect penis pushed through the suede leather and throbbed a few inches from my face. He pushed the braces from his shoulders and his shorts slid down his legs. He pulled his smock over his head and then stood naked but for his knee-length woollen socks and the slippers that the men wore inside the house. The rays of the sunset streamed through the window and illuminated his body. His skin seemed to give off a golden glow. I gazed at his marvellous tool, so long, so broad, so firm. There was a tingling between my legs and I lowered my arm so that my hand could find its way between my thighs. My fingers found my crack.

'Victoria, I can see what you're doing. That's one black mark against you.' Bea's sharp words wakened me as if from a dream. I remembered Madame's command that I must not pleasure myself but concentrate on Albert. I resolved to do as I was told.

I placed my right hand under Albert's testicles and felt their weight on my palm. I caressed his scrotum with my fingers, the coarse curly hairs like a nest. I encircled my left hand around his shaft, my fingertips just meeting my thumb. I pushed my hand away from me, pulling back his foreskin. His shiny, purple knob appeared and the tiny hole in the tip gaped. Albert moaned. I looked up to see that he had thrown his head back and had clenched his fists on either side of his thighs.

I closed my right hand around his balls and pulled my left

hand towards me. The glans disappeared in the folds of the foreskin. I repeated the movement just once but that was enough. Albert moaned again and shuddered and thick white semen gushed out of the penis and covered my bosom. It dribbled down between my two breasts. I released Albert's penis and testicles from my grip.

'That's hardly a good start, Victoria.' Bea's sneer indicated her low opinion of my skills. 'It hasn't been five minutes yet. You've got to hold him at the edge for an hour. You had better start again.'

Albert had sunk to the floor and was lying stretched out on his back on the thick carpet. His penis, though still three or four inches in length, flopped flaccidly against a thigh.

'What should I do?' I appealed to Bea.

'Caress him, his whole body, not just his cock. Use your bosom.'

I knelt beside Albert and allowed my fingers to wander over his smooth hairless chest. He murmured with satisfaction. I lowered myself further until my nipples touched his skin, and then I moved from side to side so that my breasts made random curved patterns over his abdomen. The movement gave me pleasure too and my nipples become as hard as acorns. Albert opened his eyes and stared at me with a look of utter amazement. I glanced at his groin and saw his penis stir. I continued to move but watched in fascination as his cock unfolded and grew. It rose higher and higher, straining towards the ceiling. The purple head forced its way through the foreskin and emerged like the fruit of some tropical plant. I was surprised by the light touch of fingers on my breasts. I looked round and saw Albert's hands cupping and caressing my pendulous bosom. The touch sent a thrill to my stomach and beyond. I could feel my lips swelling and parting. I was in a dreamy state of pleasure and unable to think as my hand slipped between the folds of my vulva.

'Victoria! That's twice.' I withdrew my hand and awoke with a start. I knew that Bea would report my misdemeanours to Madame Thackeray and my buttocks tingled with the anticipation of another beating.

Albert continued to massage my breasts while I leaned over him. He was stretching his legs and pointing his toes. I reached out my right hand to grasp his erect tool, but as I did he was convulsed with a spasm and another glob of semen spurted from the hole.

'Well, I suppose that was a bit better. At least he lasted fifteen minutes that time,' Bea sighed. 'You still have forty minutes left, Victoria.'

It took a little longer to revive Albert after his second ejaculation but allowing him to play with my breasts and nipples kept his attention. I ran my hands all over his young, taut limbs and trunk, exploring a man's body for the first time. It was so much firmer than a female's, the muscles hard beneath the silky skin. He explored my body too, his supple fingers tracing the marks of the crop on my buttocks. His long, eager cock trembled and waved as we embraced and moved over each other but I succeeded in restraining him from another orgasm. My resolve only slipped as the clock struck six. He was kneeling over me and I reached between his legs to grasp his tool with both hands. Albert groaned and arched his back. White drops of semen dripped onto my stomach.

'Your time is up, Victoria. You can dress now, Albert.' Albert stood up and pulled on his lederhosen while I lay back exhausted.

The next day at the same time, Albert and I met again in the drawing room. We undressed and got to work caressing each other. Today it was Helga who was supervising us and waiting for me to make a mistake. Helga was a big, fair German girl whose conversation seemed to consist of shouted commands. Albert and I had been busy for about twenty minutes without mishap when my hand slipped between my legs. Helga was vigilant.

'*Nein*, Victoria. You must not,' she bawled. Albert paused in his manipulation of my breasts and spoke to Helga in German. They proceeded to have a conversation. At last he turned to me and smiled broadly.

'I have explained your task to Albert,' Helga explained loudly. 'He now understands that you are not allowed to play with your own private parts but he asks if there is any reason why he should not touch you there.' Helga shrugged, 'If he wishes to do so I see no reason why he should not.'

Albert reached out, took my hand and guided me to the couch. He beckoned for me to sit down. When I had done so he knelt at my feet. I lay back and he pushed my knees apart and gazed adoringly at the wonders that I kept between my legs. I could not see much of what was happening from my reclining position but I imagined that his penis was still firm and wobbling gently. Albert placed his hand on the softest skin at the top of my thigh and wound the short curly hairs around his forefinger. Then he used both hands to peel my lips apart. He lowered his head until his hair and ears touched the skin of my legs. I was waiting for something but I was not sure what was to come. The muscles in my buttocks were tense and my fanny throbbed. When the touch finally came I let out a gasp. His tongue touched my clitoris then slid down into my crack. Warmer and softer than a finger, the feeling was exquisite. He lapped at my hole which I knew was oozing my juices. He had started slowly but steadily he increased the speed of the rhythmic movement. I knew that I was trying to teach Albert restraint but I could not stop myself from being carried away on the wave of orgasm. I sighed and arched my back as the pleasure took me. He sucked greedily on my fanny, gripping my buttocks in his strong hands, then gently allowed me to subside panting onto the couch.

Albert stood up and I was delighted to see his penis still proudly erect. I slid from the couch onto my knees in front of him and eagerly caressed the magnificent tool. I took care not to grip it too hard but touched and flicked my fingers up and down the shaft, under and around his balls and the crack between his cheeks. I was torn between wanting to give him satisfaction and achieving my task. I am afraid to say that the former won and in a few moments he too shuddered and a fountain of white foam spurted over me. Albert laughed.

'We start again,' he said while Helga harrumphed in the background.

The next day, Friday, we again had just one accidental orgasm and on the Saturday we reached the chimes for six of the clock with not even one. Bea was again watching over us and had shown considerable interest in Albert's eager exploration of my bosom and fanny. Now I was ever so carefully caressing Albert's erect member and touching the tip gently with my fingertips. At the end of the hour he was begging to be allowed to come and his penis almost trembled with impatience. As the hall clock struck six Bea left her seat and came towards us.

'Well done, Victoria, you can stop now.'

She pushed me gently but firmly to the side and knelt in front of Albert. She opened her mouth and leant forward so that her lips surrounded the glowing head of Albert's penis. Albert groaned as his knob disappeared into Bea's mouth. Although I considered Albert's penis to be exceptionally long and thick, still Bea inched forward taking more and more of it down her throat. Albert staggered and steadied himself by placing his hands on her head. His hips jerked as if to thrust his manhood further into her. I could not believe it when her nose finally rubbed against his pubic hair. Almost immediately Albert shuddered and his hips vibrated rapidly. I thought Bea would choke but she held onto his thighs while he shot his load straight down her gullet. Moments later he edged backwards, and his penis emerged shrunken and wrinkled. Bea gasped and took quick, deep breaths. She licked her lips and looked at me triumphantly.

'There, that's how you avoid getting semen on your clothes.' She laughed while I still looked at her in wonderment.

'How do you do that? How can you swallow a huge cock and not gag?'

'I don't know, Victoria. It's just something I can do. I know that very few girls can do it even if they have tried. But the boys like it.' I looked at Albert still standing and swaying slightly with a blissful expression on his face. I began to pull my slip over my head.

'Tomorrow I have to face Madame,' I said sadly.

'Don't worry, Victoria,' Bea replied kindly, 'while you had some misadventures earlier you have shown today that you can keep Albert excited for an hour without allowing him to reach orgasm. That is a very great skill. I am sure you have already discovered that though Madame sticks to her word she likes to mix rewards with punishment.' She gave me one of her knowing smiles and I wondered if she too had been disciplined by Madame Thackeray. I looked forward to the next day with curiosity as well as apprehension.

Chapter 4
Victoria Pleases the Headmistress

For the second time in a week I stood in Madame Thackeray's study bedroom but today being Sunday I was dressed in my finery. I wore my hooped green silk dress with several layers of starched petticoats to make it stand out and a low neckline that made my breasts prominent. On my feet were matching green silk slippers. Although it was just an hour after lunch, the light coming through the window was a dull grey. It was snowing again and already the mountains surrounding the Venus School for Young Ladies were capped with white. While it was surely cold outside, a roaring fire in the hearth kept the room more than comfortable given that I was fully dressed. My fellow pupils were either in their rooms or in the drawing room engaged in quiet pastimes, but I knew I was to experience more energetic activity.

I stood patiently while Madame read from the report presumably written by Beatrice and the other senior girls who had observed me. They had watched as I had entertained young Albert. For an hour each day for the last week my task had been to excite him, draw him to the edge of an orgasm and keep him there in delicious agony of anticipation. I had not been successful in every respect. I knew I was going to be punished but I hoped the girls had been charitable to me.

Madame laid the papers on her desk, took off her

spectacles and looked at me.

'Well, Victoria, I see that you disobeyed my instructions,' she said sternly.

'I did?' I enquired, uncertain of what response was required.

'I told you not to touch yourself and yet you did, on three occasions.' I recalled the three times that the senior girls had called out as my hand wandered between my legs.

'Yes, Madame,' I acknowledged sadly. My colleagues had not spared me from my fate.

'For those lapses you shall be punished. I also see that you failed to control Albert five times. Five times he ejaculated when you were charged with merely keeping him excited.'

'Yes, Madame, I am sorry, but he is so, ah, high-spirited.'

'Nonsense, girl, it is your skill that is wanting.' Her stern expression softened a little. 'However, I note from Beatrice's report that on the last day you succeeded in keeping him erect for a whole hour without orgasm. That certainly suggests that you have some talent. Beatrice also notes that you used your initiative in utilising your whole body to retain his interest.' My memory was that Albert's hands and mouth were all over me, caressing my bosom, my buttocks and especially my feminine parts. He gave me intense pleasure while also ensuring that his interest was maintained.

'Thank you, Madame.' I curtsied in acknowledgement of her praise.

Madame's hand stroked the large ebony phallus that lay on her desk then moved to lift the leather crop. She gripped the handle in her right hand and caressed the supple leather at the other end with her left.

'I think that under the circumstances I will lessen your punishment to six strokes.' I felt a little faint and gulped saliva.

'Yes, Madame, thank you,' I said weakly. The memory of the four strokes she had given me earlier in the week was all too fresh in my mind and imprinted on my buttocks.

'Now, Victoria, undress if you will.'

'Yes, Madame, but could you assist me with the fastenings, please?' Madame Thackeray rose and came around her desk to stand behind me. She deftly undid the buttons of my dress and helped to pull it from my arms and over my head. The dress was followed by the petticoats, one after another. At last I stood in just my slip. I pulled that off too and stood before my headmistress completely naked. The smallest hint of satisfaction seemed to pass across her face. It was the first time she had had a full view of my body. Her eyes looked me up and down, alighting on my ample bosom and perky nipples that now hardened under her gaze. Her eyes descended to the bush of dark brown hair that covered my mound and a small smile passed across her face. Then she picked up the crop and pointed to the elephant stool that stood at the foot of her large bed. I took the steps towards the stool slowly and reluctantly.

The padded leather seat of the stool came up to my waist. When my pubic hair was just touching it, there was a prod in the middle of my back and I was forced to bend right over so that my head and arms fell forward over the other side of the elephant. I balanced with my bottom elevated. The first time that Madame had beaten me I had just rested over the stool like this, and so I waited for my beating to begin. I was surprised when Madame gripped my right wrist and wound a black silk cord around it before tying it to the nearest leg of the elephant. She repeated the action with my other arm and my ankles. I struggled a little but found that I could not move neither arms nor legs or shift my position on the stool even an inch. The cords, though soft on my skin, were as strong as ropes of flax.

'There is no point in trying to move, Victoria. You are

bound tight. I do not want you shifting while I select the site for my stroke.' Immobile, I felt completely defenceless and exposed.

Nothing happened for some time except for rustlings behind me. I wondered if Madame was moving my clothes from where they had fallen. With my legs secured wide apart and my hands also tied firmly I was not comfortable but knew full well that my comfort would decrease considerably very soon. Then I heard Madame's soft breathing behind me and knew that my punishment was about to begin. I tried to clench my buttocks but with my legs forced apart knew that my crack was wide open.

'I want you to know, Victoria, that what you are about to receive is not a punishment.' Madame spoke quietly and calmly. 'It is a part of your training. You will acquire the skills that we teach here at the Venus School for Young Ladies but you will also learn that pain and humiliation are powerful tools in the arts of sexual pleasure. Today you will suffer the pain and humiliation; soon you may be administering it yourself.'

I had no idea what Madame was talking about. I had thought that our lessons were to give us skills for pleasing the men who would be our husbands. Did some men like to beat their wives or even be beaten by them? These thoughts were swept from my mind when the first blow arrived. The air screamed and my right buttock exploded in a foot-long strip of pure pain. I yelped; in fact, I more than yelped, I shouted, not words, but an animal noise that I did not know could emerge from my mouth. The heat began to subside just a little before the second stroke came, this time on my left cheek. I screeched again and sobbed and begged.

Madame was an expert. She knew just how long to wait between strokes to build up the anticipation and terror and she had the skill to place each line exactly where she wished. Every stroke of the crop extracted the full measure of response from me. When she was done, my bottom and upper thighs were ablaze with the six stripes she had administered and my throat was raw from screaming. My wrists and ankles pulled involuntarily and ineffectually at the bonds but I knew that Madame would not release me yet.

I recalled what had happened after my previous beating and suddenly my body was desperate for her touch and I knew that my sex was swelling. I imagined that Madame was waiting and watching, observing the growing pinkness of my lips and perhaps the first drips of moisture running from my vagina. It seemed that an eternity passed before that first exquisite contact; the lightest of touches; a fingernail against the top of the crack between my buttocks. Gently, tantalizingly, deliciously, the finger travelled down, over the puckered skin of my arsehole and then between my swollen lips. It explored between them, each movement making me shudder with pleasure. I expected her to enter me but the finger withdrew. I was sad and nonplussed. I wanted her touch; my body needed her touch. While my beaten buttocks still burned my desire burned even hotter.

But then something round and smooth and cool pressed against my fanny. Fingers parted my lips and the object slid into the vestibule to my hole. It felt like a vast hard ball was pushing against me. Then with a little more force, it entered me. I gasped as my canal opened to receive it. I realised that it was the huge ebony dildo that lived on Madame's desk. I was horrified. It was so large, surely it could not enter me; I would be torn asunder. Nevertheless, slowly and skilfully Madame introduced it into me. It felt as if I was being impaled on an admittedly blunt and smooth but nevertheless immense stake. It threatened to pierce my whole body and emerge through my throat. Each thrust pushed it a fraction of an inch up my tunnel and each movement sent spasms of pleasure through my clitoris. While my head swam with delirious ecstasy I realised that Madame really knew how to use a dildo. She didn't just force it into me, she withdrew it a little way and twisted it, and each re-entry renewed the feelings that rippled through me.

At last it seemed that no more of the long black instrument could be forced into me. Now Madame began a repetitive oscillation that made the whole of my insides vibrate in unison. If I had been delirious before now I was raving. I moaned and screamed as wave upon wave of orgasm passed through me. At the end I think I did swoon because the next I knew was Madame untying the bonds around my ankles. The dildo had been removed, but my vagina, like my buttocks, burned with the memory of what it had experienced; the vastness of the rod and a vacancy where it had been. Madame pulled on the cords binding my wrists and the silk fell away.

'Get up, Victoria.' I slid off the elephant, my legs like jellied eels. I had to rest my hands on the top of the stool to steady myself before slowly turning to face the headmistress again.

I gasped with surprise when I saw her. Madame Thackeray was naked. I couldn't help but examine her body, and she stood calmly while I looked at her. For a woman past her youth she was extremely handsome. Her breasts were not large but were firm, and her nipples pointed upwards. They and the aureoles were a deep red. Her stomach was flat and her thighs smooth and strong. Her skin was smooth and unblemished. My eyes were drawn to her sex. Her pubic hair was neatly trimmed and formed in tight blonde curls. Her skin glowed pink and showed a sheen of perspiration from her exertions. A few moments passed, and then she smiled and held out a hand.

'Come, Victoria.' She took my hand and guided me around to the side of her bed.

'Get on,' she urged and while I struggled to climb onto the high mattress she slid her bottom onto it and lay back on the pillows resting against the headboard. I found myself kneeling facing her. She parted her legs, and then bent her knees, raising her thighs. As she did so her sex appeared, a glistening pink gash beneath the fair wisps of hair. She slid down the satin covers and pulled her knees up to her shoulders. Her lips gaped open.

'Now, Victoria, your education continues. I know that Albert showed you how a mouth can pleasure a woman. Let us see if you learned from the experience.' She pulled her thighs further apart so that her crack widened. A long, swollen clitoris peeped from its hooded nest.

Her words recalled the delight that Albert had given me as his lips and tongue worked at my sex. There was a heat coming from her mount and a sweet odour filled my nostrils with desire. This woman, who had beaten me and had excited me so, sought pleasure from me. It seemed to me to be a great honour. I tipped forward, lowering my face towards her vulva. I extended my tongue and it touched the hot, taut skin. I felt her body tremble through the tip of my tongue. Slowly I licked up her crack tasting the honey that was oozing freely from her vagina. The sweet, musky flavour excited me and I pushed my tongue between her lips searching for the source of her juices. My lips met hers and my nose touched the firm but silky clitoris. She sighed and groaned and shifted her grip on her thighs to give me even greater access. I pressed my face hard against her fanny, my cheeks against her groin, my lips pushing her labia apart and my tongue questing deeper and deeper.

My tongue was inside her hole, lapping at the flowing juices. I shifted an inch or so and now my mouth closed around her clitoris. I nibbled with my teeth, pressed my lips against it and rubbed my tongue up and down in a sucking motion. She moaned and began to thrust her abdomen against my face. I wrapped my arms around her thighs, not stopping her movement but ensuring that I did not become dislodged. She began to scream and shout and wriggle but I held on and kept on sucking and licking and biting and chewing on her sex. All my being was focused on her cunt; all my desires were directed to her orgasm; time meant nothing. She let out a huge cry and a great convulsion passed through her. A great gush of fluid flowed from her vagina and I drank it thirstily. And then she subsided, I let go of her thighs and her limbs sagged on to the bedcovers. I backed away panting because for the last few minutes I had barely been able to catch a breath as my mouth was so closely locked to her sex.

I looked up to see her watching me, her head raised from her pillow.

'You do have talent, Victoria. With training you will be a fine cunnilinguist. Next week you will begin to study fellatio – the art of using your mouth to pleasure a man. I have no doubt that you will succeed at your studies. You may go now.' Her head fell back, her eyes closed and her muscles relaxed. I slid off the bed and retrieved my slip. Then I gathered up my dress and petticoats and left Madame snoring softly.

I returned to our bedroom and found Beatrice sitting at her dressing table in her slip, writing a letter. She turned towards me as I entered the room, my arms full of clothes.

'Oh hello, Victoria. I presume you have had your interview with Madame.' I dropped the clothes in a heap by my wardrobe. I was suddenly aware that my buttocks were still stinging quite severely.

'Yes, Bea. Madame beat me.'

'I knew she would. How many?'

'Six.'

'Let's have a look, lean over the bed.' I did as I was told and bent over the edge of the bed quite grateful to rest my torso on the mattress. Bea stood up and came to stand behind me. She lifted my slip and I could feel her gazing at my maltreated buttocks.

'Oh yes, she's given you six good ones there. Do they still hurt?'

'I'll say they do. My buttocks feel as if they're on fire.'

'Let me see if I can help. Stay there.' Bea went into the bathroom and returned a few moments later. She sat on the bed beside me and pulled my slip above my waist. Once again I felt exposed with the weals on my bottom throbbing painfully. Then there was a feeling of cool moistness. Bea put cold cream on my bottom and gently spread it over each of the six burning marks.

'Did anything else happen while you were in Madame's study?' Bea asked, continuing to apply the cream. Her caressing movements and the coolness of the cream were having a welcome effect. I began to tell her all that had happened after the beating. My penetration by the immense wooden dildo and then Madame's wish that I use my mouth to pleasure her.

'Ah, yes, Madame's delights.' Bea sounded wistful. I realised that I was obviously not the first of the pupils to bed the headmistress.

'Have you, uh, been with –'

'Oh yes. There were many times last year and earlier this term when she sought my services. Rather like you, a bit of punishment, a bit of pleasure.'

'Does she get all the girls to make love to her?'

'Oh no, only her special ones.'

'Her special ones?'

'Yes, the girls that she thinks have a talent in lovemaking. Me, you, perhaps one or two others. You'll have been selected for special training.'

'Is the punishment part of it?'

'Most definitely. Madame knows that pain heightens pleasure. You will have more opportunities to learn that fact from now on.' Bea's hand had lingered on my buttocks, her fingers tracing a pattern around each of the stripes, then slipping between my legs to caress the soft skin of my inner thighs. I didn't want to move as I was enjoying her touch so much.

'She said that I had talent with my mouth.'

'You have more than just that, Victoria. Don't forget I watched you with Albert. You have the potential to become a great lover.'

'But I failed. Albert came five times.'

'As he was bound to. He is so young and inexperienced. You had him dangling time after time. Considering you didn't suck or fuck him you couldn't have done more.'

'So my punishment –'

'Was an excuse. An excuse for Madame to get you into her room, an excuse to beat you, an excuse to play with you and an excuse to get you into her bed to give her what she wanted.'

'What should I do?'

'Relish the opportunity. Madame is a wonderful woman, is she not?'

'She is very fit and handsome.'

'And she will teach you, as she has taught me, everything there is to learn about enticing men.'

'Is that what it's all for?'

'Isn't that enough? With the skills that we learn here we can enter society and achieve all that we desire.'

'A husband?'

'If that is all you want. But the arts of pleasure can bring you fame, fortune and power.'

'Power?'

'Yes. Men may think they rule the world but a knowledgeable woman can manipulate them to do anything that she wishes. Men are guided by what hangs between their legs.'

'I think I understand. But why are we permitted, encouraged even, to pleasure each other, and women such as Madame herself?'

'Why not? If we have the techniques why not also take pleasure for ourselves when the opportunity arises. Talking of which, the sight of your beautiful buttocks has got me excited. How about using your talent on me.' Bea pulled the slip over her head revealing her white skin and ample bosom. She slid further onto the bed, tugged my slip off me then threw herself into the middle of the mattress and lay back.

'Come on, get over me, I want to taste your cunt while you're licking me.' It sank in what Bea wanted. I clambered onto the bed and straddled her, facing her feet. She took hold of my hips and pulled me back until I felt her nose touch the crack between my buttocks. She pulled harder and I gasped as her tongue slipped between my lips. Her mouth worked away sucking my lips and licking up and down my dripping crack.

I bent forward and buried my head between her thighs. She raised her knees and pushed her sex towards my face. I lapped at her vulva, running my tongue from her clitoris to her arsehole, each long, slow stroke creating ripples of movement in her thigh muscles. With her mouth firmly locked in my fanny and my head deep in hers we moved together, rocking back and forth. Because we were both working hard, concentrating on each other, we couldn't give ourselves up to our own excitement. Our orgasms were delayed but the pleasure went on and on and when we came, we came together. Our arms tightened around each other, we thrust our tongues and mouths deeper into each other's fundaments and the waves of orgasmic convulsions paralysed us and locked us together.

Gradually the trembling passed and I regained control of my muscles. Bea subsided and I fell off her and lay by her side.

'You're becoming quite an expert,' Bea sighed.

'Madame says we will learn how to suck a man tomorrow.'

'Ah, now that's a talent I enjoy,' Bea smiled as she drifted into a doze.

Chapter 5
Victoria's Oral Lesson

The glistening, purple head wobbled an inch from the end of my nose and the single dark eye winked at me. My eyes were drawn down the length of Hermann's shaft. It seemed to recede at a great distance into the brown matted bush at his crotch. All my attention was focused on the immense rod in front of me. I was mesmerised by the sparkles and glints of the oil lamps and candles reflecting off the great knob. I opened my mouth wide to engulf it.

'Victoria! What are you doing?' I was shocked out of my trance by Madame Thackeray's voice. I looked up to see the headmistress standing over me, her face dark and angry. I was mortified to be the subject of her displeasure. I shifted uneasily on my white stockinged knees and Hermann took a small step back, his penis visibly wilting.

'When will you ever learn to listen?' Madame went on. 'You do not allow the male member to enter your mouth at the start of the proceedings. It is the male instinct to thrust once the penis has entered a warm, moist enclosure. He will take control and force it down your throat and in a few quick movements will reach a climax.' I bowed my head in shame that I should have forgotten Madame's instruction, but she went on, 'You, yes, you, must be in charge. It is your responsibility to make fellatio last as long as possible, to extend the pleasure for your partner until he is almost begging you to release him. You must tease him, encourage and entice, but never ever let him take over and force it into you. Nibble his testicles, lick the shaft, touch the tip of your tongue to the glans, kiss the tip. Only when he is quivering with pent-up excitement do you allow the knob to enter between your lips. Then hold it, use your tongue to press it against the roof of your mouth, rub your teeth against it – but on no account ever bite. Suck on it, draw on it as if it were a cigar, circle it with your tongue. If at the last you feel ready to allow the culmination then take it deeper, grip the shaft with your lips and suck and blow, until at last he ejaculates for the ultimate in relief.'

'Oh Madame,' Natalie said, clapping her hands and giggling with delight, rocking on her knees beside me, 'it is exciting.'

'Well, Victoria, let us see you do it.' Madame was still looking intently at me. 'Oh, I think you will have to start again with Hermann.'

The young man was still standing naked in front of me, but his penis had now flopped against his muscular, white thighs. I glanced around. There were two other naked boys in the drawing room each having their cocks sucked by my classmates. They seemed to be doing it correctly since it was me that Madame Thackeray had picked on for her lecture.

Hermann stood tall, proud of his nude body. His stomach was flat and his pelvic muscles made a V that pointed to the drooping but still large member and the weighty sac in its nest of brown hair. I crawled towards Hermann, encircled his thighs with my bare arms and buried my nose in his pubic hair. My breasts, enclosed in the white satin corset, pressed against his legs. There was an immediate stirring from his penis. I leaned my head back and watched as it unfolded and expanded. In moments it had extended to its full length and elevated to the angle of the bowsprit of a man of war. It had the girth of my wrist and the length of one of my hands with my palm and fingers fully stretched out. I crouched lower and ducked my head beneath the cantilevered beam. I ran my tongue along its length from the sac containing his two jostling testes to the head. The skin felt like silk on my tongue, silk that hid a steel rod. It quivered and from high above me I heard a moan.

'That's it, Victoria. You have the idea. Carry on.' I had been unaware that Madame was still watching me but now I felt her move away. I was intent on my task and no longer concerned by what she had to say. There was a tingling between my legs and I could feel a moistness seeping into the crotch of my silk bloomers. I felt that to achieve my own satisfaction I had to bring Hermann to the peak of pleasure.

I shifted slightly to one side and nibbled along the length of Hermann's shaft and then gobbled his left testicle into my mouth. It was mobile in its bag and I playfully rubbed my teeth against it. At the same time I gripped his buttock in my right hand, feeling the muscle tense. Then I moved around and repeated the movement on his right side. Hermann giggled and shifted on his feet but did not attempt to withdraw himself.

Now I moved once again to face the taut purple globe. There was a drip of liquid at the entrance of the narrow but gaping tunnel. I pushed my tongue out as far as it would reach and leant slowly forward. The tip of my tongue touched the end of his penis and I tasted the salty fluid. Hermann thrust forward but I withdrew. Then I reached out my tongue again and circled around the hole. The penis flinched and then returned for more. I heard another moan from above me. Now I widened the radius of my licks, encircling the whole knob until the tip of my tongue ran around the ridge where the glans joined the shaft then underneath where the two arcs of the ridge came together. At that touch the penis leapt up and Hermann let out a sigh of pleasure. I too felt a tingle of excitement deep in my abdomen.

I was ready, at last, to take him inside me. I gripped his thighs with my hands again and leaned closer. For a second time I opened my mouth wide and slowly edged forward until my lips made contact with the penis. Pressing my lips against the thin, stretched skin, I moistened the tip with my saliva and pushed my tongue against the hole. Then ever so slowly I pushed forward allowing my lips to slide up and over the ridge of his glans. It felt as if an exceedingly soft leather ball, a hot ball, was filling my mouth. With my jaws wide apart and my lips pressed against the shaft, I paused, breathing noisily through my nose.

'*Bitte, bitte,*' Hermann muttered. I hardly needed my German to interpret his need for me to proceed. I began to suck and move my head back and forth. On each movement I pushed my lips further down the shaft so that more of his penis entered my mouth. The tip touched the back of my throat and for a moment I gagged.

I had seen Beatrice take the full length of a man and I hoped that I could emulate her. I wanted Hermann's penis deep inside me and the throbbing between my legs incited me to ignore the reflex. I forced myself to open my throat and accept the hard intruder. In front of my eyes were the matted curls of brown hair. My teeth raked gently along the shaft as it moved in and out. Each thrust took it further and further inside me, and I was unable to breathe but now Hermann was crying out and screaming, '*Ja, ja, ja!*' It felt as though the penis was forcing a path all the way down to my fanny.

All of a sudden I felt the penis judder and as it pulled away from me a wave of fluid poured into my mouth and down my throat. At that moment contractions rippled inside me and I gasped for breath. Hermann's legs began to buckle but I held firm and sucked eagerly on the softening penis, licking around the glans to extract every last drop of his semen. Only then did I release him. He fell to his knees and then sank back onto the carpet, utterly spent, his penis already shrunken and flaccid.

My chest heaved, restoring my breath, and my cheeks burned with heat. I tasted the fishy saltiness of his semen in my mouth and licked my lips. I sat back on my thighs, satisfied with myself.

'Oh yes, Victoria,' Natalie yelled with delight, 'you have drawn every last drop from him.'

'Very good.' I looked up to see Madame once again standing over me. I had not realised that she had returned to observe the dénouement. 'An excellent first effort.'

'Thank you, Madame,' I said, bowing my head.

'Now, Natalie, it is your turn,' Madame continued. Natalie looked aghast and pointed to Hermann who was still prostrate on the floor.

'But, Madame, he is finished. Victoria has sucked all the juice from him.'

'Ah, but now, Natalie, you can demonstrate your skill in reviving him. In addition to using your mouth, utilise your hands as you have already learned. He is young so he will soon be rampant and ready for more. If indeed he requires more encouragement, Victoria may remove her bloomers and show him her maidenhead. Now, begin.' Madame strode off to deal with another altercation that was occurring. Natalie looked at me and I shrugged.

'Madame says you should start,' I said, not particularly helpfully.

Natalie knelt at Hermann's feet and spread his legs apart. She crawled forward and leaned down pressing her face into his crotch.

'*Nein, nein,*' he complained and started to push her head away with his hands. I hurried to kneel at his head and took hold of his hands in mine. He did not resist as I pushed his hands to the side of his hips. Natalie teased at his penis with her lips and nibbled with her brilliant white teeth. Then she held the penis up with a hand and licked at his scrotum and chewed his testicles. Already Hermann was beginning to stir. His penis was thickening and starting to harden once again. It already was stiff enough to support itself and Natalie licked up the shaft, lingering at the tip of the glans.

Hermann was moaning again but made no attempt to get out of my grip. I released his hands and he pressed them against the floor while Natalie administered to his manhood. I remained kneeling with his head between my thighs. Now the penis was restored to its magnificent fullness. It pointed to the ceiling, a glowing beacon of readiness. Natalie sat back on her thighs.

'It is too big,' she said. 'It is impossible for it to fit into my mouth.' Natalie was indeed small and had a very delicate mouth with thin deep red lips. Hermann's penis was however extraordinarily broad. I could fully understand Natalie's difficulty. I had an idea.

'Use your hand to grip the shaft and just move your lips and tongue over the head,' I suggested. Natalie took the penis in her hand barely able to encircle it with her short fingers. She lowered her head again and touched the tip with her tongue. Then she started a rhythmic up and down movement with her hand which she mirrored with her head. Her lips moved over the shining skin of the glans and Hermann began to thrust his pelvis in unison with her hand movements. He was soon groaning and panting and bucking like a horse.

'Go on, Natalie,' I urged, 'he is almost ready.'

She increased the pace and violence of her movements, struggling to keep her mouth in contact with the oscillating rod. Hermann let out a cry and arched his back. His white fluid burst from the end of his penis and hit Natalie full in the face. She let go of the penis in surprise and fell back. Hermann sank to the floor exhausted once again.

Natalie sat on the floor licking her lips and wiping the

semen from her cheeks.

'Urgh, I do not like to taste semen,' she said, screwing up her nose. I was surprised.

'Oh, I enjoyed it,' I said. 'Give me more.'

During the remaining two weeks of term we had other opportunities to develop our oral skills. I was delighted to invite all six of the young men to place their cocks in my mouth and I swallowed the semen of each with relish. I was interested to note that each had his own taste and was convinced that, if I was to be blindfolded during the act, I could tell which boy I was pleasuring, not merely from the size and shape of his tool, but from the flavour of his effusion. Meanwhile we continued with our daytime studies of art and literature and our practical lessons in cookery and embroidery. The days were now short and the snow was banking up around the house. The mountains were often hidden behind thick blizzards. Each day the men had to clear paths from the doorways to enable deliveries of food and fuel. We did not venture into the cold outside but warmed ourselves by the fires in our rooms.

At last we came to the last evening. Tomorrow we would depart to our scattered homes, but tonight Madame Thackeray and Madame Hulot welcomed us to an early Christmas celebration. After a marvellous supper the six young men joined the two women and us twelve girls in the drawing room. The men wore their finest linen shirts, leather breeches, woollen socks and leather clogs while the women were dressed in fine silks and satins of every colour. The entertainment began quietly with Madame Thackeray singing songs from various countries to Madame Hulot's accompaniment on the pianoforte. Madame certainly had a fine, sensuous voice. Then we pushed back the chairs and chaise longue, Madame Hulot struck up a jolly tune and we all began to dance. We whirled and twirled and the men flung their arms around our waists to swing us off the floor. We sang and cried and laughed.

I cannot recall how long the festivities continued for as I was having so much fun that I lost track of time. But I began to notice that our numbers were thinning as the candles and oil lamps began to go out. The older girls were first to leave in the arms of one boy or other. Then my classmates departed, followed by Mesdames Thackeray and Hulot arm in arm. At last it was just Natalie, Albert and me left in the room. We had fallen on the floor in an exhausted heap.

Albert was the first to get up. He stood by my side and placed a hand on his crotch.

'You want?' he said in his thick Austrian accent. I looked at Natalie and grinned.

'Tomorrow we will leave and there will be no more cock for us,' I said sadly.

'I know,' she replied. 'I shall miss it. Shall we give it to Albert?'

'Yes,' I said eagerly, 'but let us go upstairs to a bedroom.' We had not had a boy in our rooms before but I guessed that that was what all our classmates were doing. Natalie jumped to her feet and offered a hand to pull me up. Then each of us took one of Albert's hands and dragged him out of the room. He did not resist and willingly accompanied us up the stairs. We came to Natalie's room first and found it empty. A single oil lamp produced a yellow glow which cast shadows around the room. We hurried inside and closed the door.

'Quickly, help me remove my dress and then I'll help you,' I requested of Natalie. We fumbled with each other's buttons, eager to be free of the restricting garments. Albert watched, his eyes wide with wonder, until we got down to our slips. Then he burst into action pulling off his shoes and socks, dropping his lederhosen and pulling his shirt over his head.

At last all three of us stood naked and panting with the effort. Albert's magnificent cock was at once ready for business and he looked from Natalie to me with open-mouthed longing.

I jumped onto the bed and lay on my back with my head right at the edge of the mattress. I bent my head backwards and I looked at Natalie and Albert upside down.

'Come, Albert,' I said and then opened my mouth wide hoping that he would realise my intention. He took a few steps and stood behind my head. Because the bed was high and Albert short, the tip of his penis just rested on my forehead.

Natalie squealed, 'I must see what you do.' She too jumped on the bed and lay on her stomach by my side, her face close enough to mine to kiss me on the cheek.

'Forward,' I urged Albert. He shuffled forward a few inches and now his long penis rested against my nose and mouth and I was staring at his testicles in their hairy bag. I bent my neck further and reached out with my tongue. It touched his knob, which quivered with excitement.

'Natalie, help Albert guide his cock into my mouth,' I said, then opened my mouth wide. Albert was already eager to do what I wished and placed the tip between my lips. I knew that at the angle at which I was lying my gullet was in direct line with my mouth. What I hoped for soon happened. Feeling my lips around his cock gave Albert the signal to thrust but he retained enough sensibility to control his forward movement so that the knob slowly slid down my throat. I couldn't breathe and the tool filled me completely but in the last few weeks I had learnt not to gag at all when I took a penis into me. Albert stopped when my nose touched his scrotum. He withdrew a little way and then thrust gently once more.

'Oh, la, la,' Natalie cried. 'You have all of him!'

Unable to breathe I began to feel sense leaving me, but

Albert had but a few more moments and thrusts before he erupted. I felt the hot fluid shoot through my breast and then he withdrew. I rolled over gasping and panting for breath. I recovered quickly enough and licked the last drops of Albert's semen from my lips. I felt elated and proud that I had taken all his formidable length but regretted that I had not been able to savour all his ejaculate.

I sat up on the bed, still breathing hard, and beamed at Albert and Natalie. Albert had stepped back into the shadows muttering '*Mein gott*' over and over again. Natalie was wide-eyed with amazement.

'I do not know how you do that, Victoria. It would not be possible for me.' I smiled, very satisfied with myself. I was pleased to find that I had a skill that I could use to surprise and pleasure the boys.

Albert, apparently recovered from his adventure, came to the bed. He whistled softly and made signs that seemed to signify that he had found the experience pleasurable.

'I eat you now,' he said and pushed at my shoulders. I fell backwards and he immediately pushed on my knees. I found myself sprawled on my back with my legs apart and Albert staring at my sex.

'You first, then her,' he said gesturing to Natalie; then he ducked his head between my thighs. I gasped as his tongue quickly found my clitoris and licked down my crack. After the excitement of the evening and my recent exploits it did not take long before he had me cooing and moaning. Once before Albert had brought me to ecstasy by sucking my fanny and delving deep inside me with his long tongue and now I was tuned to his touch. A charge of animal electricity vibrated my abdomen and reverberated up my spine to make my scalp shiver.

Natalie sat by my head and I was aware that her hand was between her legs, but all else was a blur as Albert brought me to the peak of pleasure and held me there for moments that felt like days. I screamed and stretched my limbs and finally collapsed in exhaustion.

Albert moved immediately on to Natalie, pushing her on to her back and burrowing between her legs. In no time she was kicking her feet, waving her arms and yelping with delight. As I regained my breath once more I watched his head bobbing up and down between her thighs. He knelt with his legs spread apart and as his buttocks moved his sac swung from side to side. I could not resist crawling towards him and cupping my hand around the bulging bag. He paused in making his meal of Natalie's fanny and then resumed. I massaged his balls and watched in fascination as his penis grew once more to its full length. While continuing to finger his testicles with my left hand I reached between his legs with my right arm and slid my hand up and down his shaft.

Natalie was fast approaching her climax and Albert worked ever more urgently at her as I milked his member. All at once Natalie cried out and almost leapt into the air. At the same moment, Albert tensed and a gobbet of semen gushed out of his cock onto my hand. I withdrew it from between his leg and licked my fingers hungrily, enjoying Albert's unique flavour.

We finally lay alongside each other on the bed, sleepy, happy and replete. I reflected that it may be some weeks before I would again achieve such heights of pleasure. I knew that during the vacation I would be impatient to return to share the joys of our bodies with my friends.

Chapter 6
Victoria's Christmas Vacation

It was a bright but bitterly cold day for the start of the Christmas vacation. The snow which was deep around the Venus School for Young Ladies had a crisp coating and our breath froze on our lips. I put on two slips under my dress to help keep me warm, and my thickest woollen hose. From daylight, horse-drawn sleighs drew up to take my schoolfellows down to the valley. At last it was the turn of Beatrice and me. The men loaded our trunks onto the back of the sleigh and then bid farewell to us. Albert came up to me and said in his broken English, 'I wait for you, come back.' His sadness at my departure was not surprising. For the next few weeks neither I nor the other girls would be administering to his magnificent manhood and he would have to use his own hands to take his pleasure. Beatrice and I stepped aboard and wrapped furs around us before we set off and waved to Madame Thackeray as we moved off down the hillside. We held each other tight because despite our furs and extra clothes we both felt the cold but as a result of our layers I could not feel any part of Bea's body through the layers of cloth.

We transferred to a coach, which was a little less cold, once we reached the end of the snow. At last we arrived at the railway station. Porters transferred our luggage while Bea and I hastened to our carriage.

'That's better,' Bea sighed, relaxing on the padded seat in

the relatively warm compartment. I sat next to her and looked out of the window as we began the long train journey back across the countries of Europe to our homes.

'Well, how do you feel after a term at the Venus School?' Bea asked cheekily.

'Everything that happened is like a distant dream,' I replied. 'I've felt more excitement and pleasure, and pain, in the last three months than in all the rest of my life.'

'You've learned a few things,' Bea chuckled, 'and found out a lot about what men like.'

'And women.'

'Of course.'

'What about your plans, Bea? Do you think you will find a man suitable?'

'I'm changing my mind concerning that, Victoria. What I have learned this term has given me fresh ideas. I don't think I want a life where I have to make do with just one person sharing my bed. Just think how boring that would be. You know yourself how much fun we have with the boys at school.'

I thought about my experiences with Albert, Eric, Hermann and the others. I could see and feel the different sizes and shapes of their cocks and almost taste their semen on my tongue. I understood what Bea was saying. Perhaps one husband would be unexciting.

'So, what are you going to do, Bea.'

'I'm not sure yet, but I hope that Madame Hulot can help.'

Apart from cookery lessons I had not been taught by Madame Hulot, but I knew that she gave lessons to the older girls.

'What has Madame Hulot been teaching you?'

'Ah, that I cannot say. You must wait until it is your turn next autumn. You still have a great deal to learn this year.' It seemed to me that I had learned a lot but as we had not yet engaged in intercourse with the young men, Beatrice was obviously correct.

We continued to chat in between eating and sleeping while the train rattled and rumbled across Germany and France. We reached Calais and had to wait for some hours for a crossing because of stormy weather. The journey across the Channel was indeed vexing but at last we reached Dover. Bea left me to catch a train to Brighton and I sent a telegram to Father to let him know that I was nearly in London.

When I stepped off the train, Father was there to welcome me. He gave me a sedate kiss on my cheek and almost smiled. In the cab back to our town house in Kensington he asked after me and how my studies had progressed. I replied, quite truthfully, that I had found them quite stimulating. We did not converse much more as I was feeling very tired after my long journey so I was quite relieved to finally reach my bed.

The next few weeks were frankly a bore. Each day Father left me at home alone with the servants while he went about his affairs. In the evenings we either ate dinner alone or entertained his guests, usually men he did business with. Sometimes they brought their wives but they were much older than me and haughty. My father had not remarried since my mother died ten years ago so I was expected to act as hostess. I impressed Father with my new knowledge of cuisine and table decoration but my attempts at conversation with our guests about the political situation or art drew little response other than admiration for the efforts of my teachers.

I really was missing the fun I had with Beatrice, Natalie and the boys. I longed to feel a penis in my hand or in my mouth, and a finger in my crotch. I even felt a desire for Madame Thackeray's whip across my buttocks. Anything to relieve the tedium of the days in that house. I took to locking my bedroom door, throwing off my clothes and lying on my bed or on the carpet beside the fire, playing with my own fanny. I wished I had been able to bring the lovely glass phallus that Madame had loaned us but I had to make do with twisting my clit between a finger and thumb while I pushed the fingers of my other hand up my crack. I writhed in an agony of pleasure as I strived to reach the peak, and wondered if I was going to be denied the release I sought. Nevertheless I usually managed to achieve success and bring myself to a climax. I did have to stifle my usual cries however. After one occasion when I had forgotten myself a maid came knocking on the door asking if I was unwell. I nearly flung the door open to drag her in and ravish her.

My other disappointment was that Bill wasn't there. I dared not mention his name to Father but I gathered from the groom, a man as old as my father, that Bill was still employed in the stables at our house in the country. I counted off the days until I would be able to see him.

At last Christmas Eve arrived and my father completed his business. Late in the afternoon we set off by train to Reading where we were collected by our own carriage and taken the last few miles to the estate where I had grown up. The evening was taken up by festivities. Carol singers came from the village and, having entertained us, were given mince pies and mulled wine. Father joined in the singing with half a heart. He did not seem pleased that it was Christmas and businesses would be closed for a day or two. I was delighted of course. Many of the villagers I had known since I was a child and they told me all the gossip in return for answering questions about my schooling.

I was quite exhausted when I finally got to my bed but I was determined to be up early on Christmas morning. It was still dark when I wrapped a dressing gown around my nightdress and tiptoed down to the stable yard. I took care not to be seen by the servants in the kitchen who were already preparing the Christmas feast. The air was cold outside and the cobbles were wet and slippery but I hurried into the stables. There were boxes for the horses nearest the entrance. The horses' heads followed me when I passed by and looked on as I reached the area of the barn where hay was stored. There I saw Bill turning the hay with a fork. He wore a cap and scarf tied around his neck, a leather jerkin and brown corduroy trousers with heavy boots on his feet and he looked just the same as I had been remembering during all my time away from home. The barn was warmer than the outside because of all the animals but still his breath produced wisps of steam.

'Bill,' I whispered. He turned and looked at me with surprise.

'Victoria, what are you doing here?' I went and stood in front of him, smelling the horses and the hay on his clothes and skin.

'To see you, Bill. I've been waiting for months for this chance to come.'

'But your father ...'

'In bed. We have a little time before he starts moving. Aren't you pleased to see me?'

'Yes, of course, but after your father discovered us last time, he made life difficult for me. I thought he would dismiss me. Keeping me away from the city was bad enough.'

I stepped closer to him so that I could smell his sweat and he could feel my warmth.

'It has been a long time. Time for me to think about what you wanted back in the summer.'

'What I wanted?' For some reason Bill seemed to have a poor memory of an event that had had such an effect on my life. If Father hadn't discovered us together I would not have been sent away to complete my education. I would never have gone to the Venus School for Young Ladies, or the

Venice School as Father persisted in calling it – I didn't bother to correct him – and I would never have discovered how to please Bill.

'Yes, Bill. First you kissed me on the lips.' I leaned my head forward and stood on tiptoes so that I could place my lips on his. He breathed out gently and the warm, moist air entered my mouth. Still he did not move. 'Then you placed your hand on my bosom.' I took hold of his hand and placed it on my left breast. Instinctively he gripped it lightly. The touch after so many days without contact was exquisite and I felt my nipple harden and my heart beat faster. 'Then I felt a swelling between your legs. It's happening again now.' His cheeks flushed but I did indeed feel his cock grow inside his trousers and press against my pelvis.

Before he could respond I knelt at his feet and began to undo the buttons that held his breeches up. The garment quickly dropped to his ankles.

'Victoria! What are you doing?' he said in a hoarse whisper.

'Shh,' I replied and continued my business. He was wearing an elderly pair of long johns which I soon unbuttoned and tugged down. His manhood sprang to attention once it was released and like a signpost directed itself towards me. I grasped the shaft in my right hand and pulled back the foreskin to reveal the shiny purple head. His balls fit into my cupped left hand and I felt the hard nuts moving in the hairy sac as I gently massaged them. I rubbed my right thumb against the underside of the knob and instantly his thighs trembled and a moan crept from his lips. I smiled to myself. All Madame Thackeray's teaching had trained me to be able to extend his pleasure and not let him come too soon – but I wanted to see him in ecstasy.

Seeing and holding his tool gave me a warm feeling at the core of my abdomen. I could feel my clit throbbing and a slickness between my legs. My heart beat faster in my bosom.

I stretched out my tongue and touched the end of Bill's penis. Not only did it look like a ripe plum but the skin also had the texture of a plum. He moaned again with pleasure. I licked all around the hot swollen head, squeezing the shaft so that the hole at the tip gaped open. Bill seemed to be trying to say something but it got lost in his groans. Now I took the end of his penis into my mouth and closed my lips around the shaft. I sucked and moved my hand in rhythm. I knew it would not be long now and I was quite unable to slow down and extend our mutual rapture. My desire was fulfilled when, with a stifled cry, he came and his semen gushed into my mouth like the milk from a cow's udder. I swallowed every last drop, savouring its flavour. Then at last as his penis shrivelled I released him and sat back on my thighs. I looked at him swaying, almost insensible.

'There, Bill. Is that what you wanted?' I got to my feet, 'I must go now before Father awakens. Merry Christmas,' I kissed him on the cheek and ran off leaving him still standing with his trousers and underwear lying at his feet.

I got through the day merrily after my morning's exertions. The memory of his cock in my hand and semen on my tongue sustained me through the day of feasting and tedious games. I was relieved when at last I was able to retire and go to my room alone, but I wanted more. I presumed that Bill would still be in the stables, bedding down the horses or some such chore so I got up and again covered my nightdress with my dressing gown. I took the familiar route to the stables. At this time of night the kitchens were quiet and all the servants seemed to have finished their festive celebrations.

Bill was not in sight when I passed by the horses, and they snickered at me. A single oil lamp cast its dim yellow glow at the rear of the barn. There seemed to be some movement amongst the bales of hay. As I approached I saw

69

what seemed to be two pale moons rising and falling. I rounded a heap of hay and entered a clearing amongst the bales. There a sight met my eyes. The moons were Bill's bare buttocks heaving up and down between the legs of a scullery maid. I recognised her long dark curls framing her head. She was lying on her back amongst the hay with her skirt and petticoats drawn up and her knees next to her ears. Her feet were pointed to the roof. Bill was naked from the waist down and in the dim light, standing behind them, I could see his balls waving back and forth as he thrust his cock into her. He was grunting with each forward movement and she let out a sigh with each push. A moment later Bill cried, the same cry as I had heard in the morning, and he fell in a heap on top of her. The girl looked past him and saw me standing there but instead of looking surprised she gave me a smile of satisfaction. Some movement or whisper must have told Bill that they were not alone. He twisted his neck to look at me over his shoulder.

'Victoria!' I turned and ran from the stables and back to my room. I didn't want to hear if he had anything more to say.

I lay in bed but did not sleep for hours. I was angry with Bill for not being faithful to me but I was annoyed with myself for having supposed that I was the only object of his affections. The more I thought about our brief contact in the light of the lessons I had learnt from Madame Thackeray and the other girls, I realised that Bill was acting in a typical and predictable fashion. Men sought pleasure and women were available to please them. Marriage and morals may hold an honourable man back from seeking satisfaction but given opportunity and freedom from responsibility any man would take what was offered. I had foolishly presumed that I was the sole recipient of Bill's desires and that by giving him pleasure I was satisfying his needs. But young men, as I well knew, are almost insatiable in their hunger for orgasm.

I, however, was not prepared to share a stable-boy with a lowly servant. I resolved, as Madame Thackeray had taught, to henceforth ensure that any pleasure I provided was on my own terms and intended to achieve whatever goals I set myself. I would leave Bill to his scullery maid and seek my excitement elsewhere.

The following day, being St Stephens Day, saw the gathering for the hunt. Father dressed in his best hunting gear and set off with the other riders. I stayed behind with the other ladies, feeling somewhat tired after my sleepless night. Some commented on my demeanour, which I attributed to over-indulgence on the previous day, but in truth I was in no mood for the public pleasures.

The following morning we travelled back to our London residence as Father was keen to get back to business. I resumed my lonely existence with my fingers providing my only solace. We entertained guests on one or two evenings and attended gatherings at Father's friends' houses, but no event gave me occasion for the sport I now sought.

At last the time arrived for me to return to school. I made a show of reluctance to leave the comforts of home and the tender loving care of my father but in truth I was eager to leave. Father travelled with me to Dover and saw me on to the Channel ferry in the company of some acquaintances he had made, but at last I was able to bid him farewell.

The crossing was thankfully calm and swiftly completed, and I boarded the train that would carry me almost to my destination. There was just one other person in my carriage, a gentleman who appeared to be in early middle age. He was smartly and expensively dressed but having greeted me and helped me get settled he sat down with a magazine and said not one word further.

I was intrigued as to what publication could absorb a man to so great an extent. It appeared to be one of the regular cheap booklets that carried serialised novels such as those by Mr Conan Doyle but I could not see its title page clearly as we were sitting at opposite ends of the compartment. I gave the appearance of being deeply interested in my own book, an improving novel by George Elliot, but in truth I was watching this quiet reader. From time to time his breathing became a little more rapid and I noticed a small swelling in the crotch of his trousers. What reading matter, I wondered, could so arouse a man? I desperately wanted to find out what was absorbing his whole attention.

Thankfully, despite the obviously exciting nature of his pastime, the rhythmic swaying of the train encouraged him to nod off to sleep. Shortly he began to snore gently and the magazine fell from his hand. As quietly as I could I moved to pick it up from the floor of the carriage and at once settled back to read. The title of the publication was *The Pearl* and I quickly discovered the nature of its works of fiction. Each told the tale of a young man and handsome young lady forced, against her will and her upbringing, to service the man, the hero of the story. It turned out that despite her coercion the girl was soon an enthusiastic convert to the pleasures of the flesh and cheerfully engaged in all manner of activities at the behest of her master. In truth I did find some of the descriptions of their amorous engagements somewhat exciting. I was conscious of my nipples hardening and a heat between my legs but I was disappointed that it was the men who determined the course of the adventures. My companion appeared to be a pleasant and well-bred gentleman and not unattractive given his years. I resolved to play a game with him.

I moved as silently as possible to where he sat and then slid onto the floor to kneel at his feet. I reached up to the buttons of his trousers and started to undo them. I had barely got one undone before he stirred. I hurried to undo another before he became fully awake. He opened his eyes and started when he saw me at his feet. I put a finger to my lips and hushed him.

'Be still; imagine that you are asleep and dreaming of the situations of which you have read.' I nodded at the magazine which I had placed on the seat but out of his reach. He looked at it and the widening of his eyes showed that he realised that I had been reading it. As I expected he was not an unwilling participant in my little sport. He rested back on the couch and allowed me to continue to undo the buttons. Inside I found more buttons belonging to his undergarments. These buttons were smaller and easier to unfasten. At last my way was clear. I reached inside and found his manhood, crushed and sad, but as I released it from its confinement it began to grow. It unfolded like a flower of the tropics pushing out its pistil to attract a pollinating insect.

To be truthful it did not match in length or girth the magnificent tools of Eric or Hermann or especially Albert, but it was satisfactory for its purpose. Held in my warm hands it soon stood erect and the gentleman looked both astounded and proud of his achievement. Unlike the other penises that I had been witness to there was no foreskin for me to pull back from the livid red knob. I lightly caressed the shaft and the head with my fingers, drawing moans of delight from my subject. Holding the shaft between a finger and thumb and raising it to point to the ceiling of the carriage, I bent my head and nibbled at the testicles in their crinkled bag. Then I licked up the shaft.

He had begun to breathe in short gasps and I realised that despite my skills he may come all too suddenly and I did not want white stains on my clothes. I took the head into my mouth while playing the shaft like an oboe. My fingers danced a merry jig and as I suspected it was not long before he shot a load of creamy spunk into my mouth. I savoured it and licked the circumcised knob clean. He let out a long strangled moan and sank into the seat like a boneless sea creature.

I returned to my seat licking my lips and took a handkerchief from my handbag to dab my cheeks and mouth. Then I sat up and resumed the appearance of reading my book. That my suspicions had been correct gave me significant satisfaction. Given the chance, the subject of my attentions had willingly adhered to my plan and given himself up to my administrations with resulting pleasure for me and himself. I watched the object of my experiment surreptitiously over the top of the pages. It took a few moments for him to recover and then he looked at me with wide eyes and flushed cheeks. He hurriedly fiddled with the fastenings at his crotch and got into a tremendous muddle with the buttons. At that moment the engine's whistle blew and we began to slow as the train reached a station. The gentleman got to his feet and collected his bags. As soon as the train was stationary he opened the door and leapt out. I never saw him again but he left his book of erotic tales behind. I put it into my bag before my carriage filled with a family of travellers.

Chapter 7
Victoria Hears Natalie's Story

It was my first night back at the Venus School for Young Ladies after our long Christmas vacation. Despite being tired after my long journey through a number of the kingdoms, republics and principalities of Europe, I was delighted to see my friend Natalie again. It was snowing, adding to the deep drifts around the school, and it was cold. To keep warm we snuggled up under the blankets of the bed Natalie shared with her room-mate.

After so many weeks alone in my bed at home it was wonderful to feel the warmth of another person close to me and to feel her sweet breath on my neck. Our hands wandered under our night dresses. Each touch of Natalie's fingers on my thighs, stomach, bosom and buttocks were reassuringly familiar but gave me a thrill as if it were the first time that I had been touched. Her caresses circled the core of my being and when at last she touched me between my legs I trembled and let out a sigh of excitement.

I too fondled Natalie's slight but delicious body. I played with the prominent nipples in the centre of her small but pert breasts and slid my hands down her side, over her hips and along her thighs before heading for the thicket of pubic hair. Natalie giggled.

While we touched each other and kissed cheeks and necks we recounted the events of our Christmas vacations. I told of my exploits, disappointments and discoveries and then listened as Natalie gave her account of surprising events.

'I was so pleased to get home to see my *mère* et *père* and my five brothers and their wives. They were delighted to see me and showered me with kisses and hugs and presents of fruits and sweetmeats. But, oh, ze house was mad. Full of people, all, how do you say, on top of each other. I did not have a single minute to myself. My bed I shared with my little sister and every time I thought I was alone, the door would fly open and there would be Emilie, Ricard or Michel or someone. After a few days I was feeling quite frustrated not having had a chance to give my fanny a good rubbing. So when my Uncle Pierre invited me to his house on the other side of Paris I jumped at the chance.

'Uncle Pierre is an old man. He and my father have been friends since they were children and he is almost part of my family. He must be at least fifty years of his age and since his wife died lives alone in his big house, except for a few servants. He spends his time making, what is the word? Light pictures? Ah, *photographs*, you know, Monsieur Daguerre invented the process. Uncle Pierre proposed that I join him for a few days, as his model. He told me in the company of my mother that he was planning a series of pictures on the theme of women of the Bible. My parents agreed to Uncle's suggestion so, next day, we took a coach to his house.

'I was provided with a large bedroom all of my own although I must confess that it was rather cold and smelt musty through not having been used for many years. Uncle allowed me to settle in and that evening entertained me to dinner with wine from his cellar. Next morning after breakfast he called me to join him in his studio. This was a room at the top of the house with a glass roof. There were blinds controlled by a clever mechanism to allow light to fall from one direction or another on the subject of Uncle's photographs. The servants had set up what appeared to be a stage set of a stable with bales of hay and a crib. There were tripods and boxes of polished wood which I gathered were his machines for the taking of photographs.

'Uncle Pierre told me to go behind a screen and change my clothes for those that he had prepared for me.

'"The first subject of my great work will be the mother of the Christ, Mary herself. You will be a fine Mary, Natalie my dear. You display pure and virginal qualities like no other."

'I had to smile to myself. Little did he know that only a week had gone by since I had held a hard cock between my lips and caressed a pair of testicles with my fingers. Behind the screen I quickly removed my fine garments and hose and donned the simple blue dress and white apron that Uncle had left for me. The dress had buttons at the front and was, I noted, rather short for the wife of a carpenter, barely reaching my knees when I was standing.

'I emerged in this costume supposedly playing the part of the Virgin Mary and Uncle told me to sit on a milking stool in the middle of the set. He placed in my arms a doll of a baby wrapped in swaddling clothes and told me to look down at it with an adoring expression. There was quite a delay while he arranged his camera on its tripod and peered through it, fiddling with the brass rings that held the glass lenses. Then he had to prepare the special glass plates that he uses to record the patterns of light.

'"Now, dear, sit absolutely still while I expose the plate. I shall count to *trois. Un, deux, trois.*" I heard a click, then there was a delay and at last another click. '*Parfaitement*, soon we shall see what a delightful Mary you are. Now, dear, if you would like to undo the buttons at the top of the dress and place the doll to your breast, we shall have a picture of the mother suckling the Christ child."

'I must confess to being surprised at this turn of events

77

but thanks to a term of Madame Thackeray's teaching I immediately recognised Uncle's intentions. His tale of a series of pictures of Bible heroines was nothing more than a ruse to observe my feminine charms. No matter, I was pleased that it appeared that this posing may turn out to be more interesting than I had previously thought. I undid the buttons as instructed and accidentally allowed the dress to flop open not only giving access to my left breast for the artificial baby but also exposing my right breast to the view of Uncle Pierre's photographic equipment.

"'Ah, excellent,' Uncle exclaimed, 'your breast is like a *glacé* of purest milk and your nipple a deep red cherry." He set to work with his plates but his words gave me just the smallest thrill. In the course of over an hour he exposed four or five of the glasses, changing the direction of the light for each and asking me to adjust my pose just a little. As I twisted on the stool the dress rode up, exposing my thigh, which seemed to delight him. I became a little stiff holding the pose for so long and was thankful that my bosom is still firm. Even when I am not excited my nipples stick upwards. Eventually Uncle Pierre told me my work for the day was complete and that I could change back to my day clothes. He went off to the room that he keeps dark and said he would spend the rest of the day developing the plates and making prints.

'I spent the afternoon quite happily amusing myself in various ways. After dinner that evening, Uncle Pierre showed me the first fruits of his labours. The paper was still a little damp but the picture of me as the Virgin Mary was perfectly formed. Uncle only showed me a copy of the first of the photographs he had taken and I wondered how my breasts looked when captured for ever on the special paper.'

I too would have liked to have seen the pictures of Natalie and I wondered what other biblical characters her uncle had in mind. I urged her to continue with the story.

'The next morning followed the same pattern. After breakfast I climbed up to the studio where I found that Uncle Pierre had prepared a new set. This one was again agricultural but showed a field with sheaves of corn.

'"Today, my dear," he greeted me, "you will be Ruth, the dutiful daughter-in-law fallen into poverty and scouring the fields for ears of corn." I was quite pleased that I would not be doing the task in reality and just posing for the photograph. I went behind the screen and undressed. The clothes Uncle had left for me were those of a simple peasant, in a burnt orange colour. When I put the dress on I found it was worn and torn and barely covered me at all. I now had a good idea what Uncle's series of pictures was really about so I decided to play his game to see how much he wanted.

'When I stepped on to the set Uncle Pierre asked me to kneel and look as though I was searching for grains of corn. When I knelt the shreds of the dress fell about me. With a little coaxing my bosom dropped into view and my thighs and bottom were exposed. Uncle showed his pleasure by taking lots of plates. His camera was rather immobile so I had to shuffle round the set, sometimes presenting a side view that gave a good picture of my thighs. At other times I was facing the camera and I could see Uncle's face becoming red and hot as he peered through his lenses at my breasts. Finally he had me present my bottom to the camera. I could not see his face of course but I could tell he was pleased by the sighs and murmurs that came from under the black sheet with which he covered his head and shoulders. He had me lingering in that position for a considerable time saying that he was having trouble with his lenses becoming clouded.

'The afternoon was again spent on my own while Uncle Pierre worked in his darkroom, and at dinner he presented me with the first fruits of his labours – an attractive and modest picture of the saintly Ruth.'

'Did it excite you posing for your Uncle in such a state of dress?' I asked eagerly.

'A little, but the time went on and on so I was quite beyond excitement when Uncle had finished with me, but, Victoria, I have not finished my story yet.'

'Oh, do go on,' I said.

'The third morning I found behind my screen just a pile of scarves made of gossamer thin silk. There were seven of them attached to a fine cord. I was unsure what to do with them until Uncle Pierre called out.

'"Today, my dear Natalie, you are Salomé and you will dance the seven veils for John the Baptist's head."

'"How do I wear them, Uncle?" I asked.

'"Drape them around you, *ma chérie*. They will cover all your amazing attributes." I did as he asked and stepped onto his stage of an Arabian palace. Of course I couldn't dance while Uncle took the photographs. Instead I had to pose in strange and contorted positions, my arms raised, sometimes with my legs parted, occasionally on one leg. The silk scarves did not remain covering my private parts. They parted and fluttered away, revealing my body to my doting uncle.

'When he emerged from under his sheet he looked flushed and flustered but most of his time was spent peering through the camera directing my movements and telling me to freeze when he found a view that appealed to him.

'"You are most beautiful, my little flower," he said, "so seductive you are bound to get what you want from a king." I thought, give me a chance and I will seduce you, you old lecher.

'That evening he presented me with a most fetching picture of me trapped for ever in my dance. Somehow he had contrived to take one photograph when my parts were covered by the fine cloth but there was a hint of my pubic hair visible through the translucent silk.'

'Ooh,' I cooed, 'your uncle is a naughty old man. What does he do with the other pictures I wonder?'

'I wondered too, but the answer to the puzzle must wait until the end of my story.'

'Do go on, Natalie.'

'The following morning I looked behind my screen and there was nothing.'

'Nothing!' I exclaimed.

'That's right, nothing, no costume at all. I emerged to speak to Uncle Pierre while he was fiddling with his cameras.

'"Do you wish me to wear my own clothes today, Uncle?" I asked.

'"No, my little sparrow, today you will be Eve, the mother of mankind, before the Fall. You are innocent, without knowledge of any sin, unaware of carnal desires, unaware indeed of your nakedness."

'"Ah, you want me naked, Uncle."

'"Yes, my dear. Take your clothes off behind the screen." I did as I was bidden, not at all nervous of showing myself off. Over the last three days Uncle Pierre had looked long and hard at my charms through his glasses and I knew that was what he really wanted to do, not record these fanciful Bible stories. He had me pose amongst the artificial trees of his Garden of Eden. With an apple in my hand and drooping branches draped over my shoulders, my hand nonchalantly but artfully placed over my mount of Venus, Uncle commenced his photography. In later poses he introduced a snake made of smooth satin that wound around my thighs and breasts. Once again I was moved this way and that, sometimes seen from the side sometimes from the front.

'As before, Uncle spent most of the time under his cloth sighing and moaning. Once, when he emerged there was a definite bulge in the front of his trousers and beads of perspiration formed on his brow.'

'And, what of you, Natalie?' I asked. 'Did the posing give you pleasure?'

'I found it amusing, seeing how Uncle Pierre wished me to arrange myself, but really the time dragged and I longed for a hand to caress me or a penis to hold. At dinner, Uncle gave me the day's first print and despite my obvious nakedness one could not say that the pose with the cascading branches and the entwining snake was at all improper. However that was the last time one could say that.'

'Oh, really, Natalie. What happened next?'

'It was the fifth day of my stay with Uncle Pierre and although nothing had been spoken of the purpose behind his hobby it was clear that he knew that I realised that the stories of biblical women were a subterfuge and that my body was his principal interest. I wondered what could follow Eve, but he had an answer in store.

'When I arrived in the studio there was just a divan covered with furs on the set. There were no clothes behind the screen so I undressed and emerged naked.

'"Are we continuing with Eve today, Uncle?" I asked innocently.

'"No, Natalie. Today you are Mary Magdalene before she found the Christ.' I confess that my Bible knowledge is not what my mother would wish, Victoria, so at first I had no idea what my uncle was referring to. But it became clear soon after. He had me lie on my back on the divan which was on small wheels to allow it to be turned easily. Uncle Pierre gave me instructions.

'"Now my dear, this may be difficult for you but I want you to imagine that you are in state of excitement. I would like you to stretch out your limbs, arch your back, open your mouth. If it would help, I suggest you moan with pleasure." I did not inform my darling Uncle that I had quite often been in this state of bliss during my first term at the Venus School for Young Ladies, but instead endeavoured to put myself in the position he described.

'The camera was positioned much more closely so that I imagined that my form filled my uncle's view. He clicked away using plate after plate as he moved the bed around in a circle capturing me at all angles. He told me to part my legs, lift my knees, throw back my head. Then he paused. The camera was between my feet, the glass eye peering right up my private parts.

'"Oh, such beauty," Uncle Pierre moaned from beneath his hood, "an exquisite flower, the lips resemble the petals of an orchid, the colour of a red, red rose. But surely we can get closer, the flower can open up. Natalie, darling, please pull your knees up and apart. Use your hands." I brought my knees up to my ears and my bottom lifted from the fur coverings. I could feel my fanny opening revealing my secret hole.

'"Yes, yes," Uncle sighed, "but still, more can be done." He emerged from behind the camera and approached the divan. He knelt on the floor and leant his head forward. From behind my raised legs I could see his face just half a metre from my pubis.

'"I want you swollen with excitement, oozing with pleasure. In your innocence you will be unfamiliar with this state, but I can bring you to it." He moved closer and now I could feel his breath on the inside of my thighs. The bristles on his chin briefly abraded my skin and then his lips made contact with mine and his tongue pushed into my crack. I think I jumped as if I had been struck by an electric spark but when I relaxed his mouth was there again. His tongue explored the folds of my labia; his lips gripped the rapidly swelling flaps then his tongue delved deep into my hole. Now it was my turn to moan, shivers passed up my legs and I struggled to keep hold of my knees to keep my legs apart for him.

'His tongue slid up and found my little knob. It circled

around and then his lips gripped it and sucked. Now his tongue descended again into the depths of my vulva and his nose rubbed against my clit. He gripped my buttocks and pressed against me, rubbing his face against me and digging deeper and deeper inside me with his tongue. And now the shivers became great shudders as the orgasm took me.

'At my moment of ecstasy he was gone. There was an emptiness between my legs. But still the waves of pleasure passed through me. Somewhere in the distance I heard my uncle's voice.

'"Yes, yes, yes. Now the flesh is swollen and the juices flow. Stay still my dear, *mon amour*." As my ardour subsided I remained grasping my knees and became aware of my uncle whirling like a Dervish. He grabbed a glass plate, thrust it into the wooden box, clicked the shutter, then whipped the plate out and repeated the movement. I cannot tell how many plates he exposed as I lost count. Finally, however, he finished.

'"Thank you, my darling," he sighed, panting with his exertion. By this time, as I had recovered somewhat, I was determined that I should give Uncle a little of his own treatment by return. I rose from the divan as he was busy sealing the last plate into its protective box. I knelt at his feet.

'"I think, Uncle, that you must need some relief from your labour," I said and raised my hand to touch him between his legs. I could feel his member swollen and hot.

'"What do you mean?" he muttered as I began to undo his buttons. In a moment I had his penis in my hands and he was looking down at me with a look of such amazement on his face. I gripped his shaft in my hand. It was hard and as I pulled back the foreskin his purply red knob appeared. I gripped his testicles in my other hand and squeezed gently, then I lowered my head until my lips met the end of the tip.

'"Oh, Natalie," he groaned and swayed from side to side.

I held his cock and balls firmly in my hands and started to lick his knob. Then, as we have been taught, I encircled it with my lips and began to suck while massaging the shaft. At that moment the urge came upon Uncle Pierre. He grasped my head with his hands and began to thrust his pelvis forcing his penis further into my mouth. I held onto the shaft tightly and now the battle between us was joined. I sucked and rubbed the bottom of his knob with my tongue while he tried to force it down my throat with thrust after thrust. I held on but my arms were tiring and my jaws were aching when he cried out and a gush of semen poured down my throat. He wilted like a plant that has gone without water. As he sank to the floor I released him and ran to pick up my clothes. As I left the studio he was slumped on the floor.

At dinner that evening, Uncle Pierre sat at the other end of the table from me and was quiet.

"'No photograph for me this evening, Uncle?" He looked at me uncertainly but said nothing. "That is a shame," I continued, "for I would like to see all the pictures you have taken of me."

"'All?" he whispered.

"'Yes, every one." He put down his knife and fork.

"'You little devil," he grinned, "and there was me thinking you were the naïve little girl. Come with me. Now." He stood up, came to me, took my hand, then almost dragged me from the room and up the stairs to his darkroom. There, hanging from lines stretched across the room like washing in a laundry, were prints of his pictures. He put on a light and I saw image after image of me. There were the chaste pictures that he had already given me but they were but a few amongst many. My breasts, bottom and fanny featured in the rest. To see so many views of myself made me laugh.

"'Why, Uncle? Do these pictures make your cock swell?

Does looking at such images help you in your handiwork?"
He nodded.

"'But there are so many? Surely you do not need so many pictures to pleasure yourself." He did not say anything but put the light out and led me back to the dinner table.

Next day I did not see my uncle. I was not required in the studio. Instead I relaxed in the library. I became aware that there seemed to be an extraordinary number of callers. The doorbell would ring, a servant would answer the door, someone would enter and a short while later they would leave. After the fifth or sixth visitor had been and gone in the space of two hours or so I became curious. When the bell rang again I opened the library door a crack and peeped out. The visitor was a man wrapped up in a cloak. The maid conducted him not to the drawing room but up the stairs. I followed at a discreet distance and saw that the gentleman was shown into my uncle's darkroom. I hid behind a pillar and waited. A few minutes later the man emerged with a package wrapped in brown paper which he tucked under his cloak before going down the stairs and out the front door. I waited and a short while later another man wrapped up in a greatcoat was shown up the stairs, entered Uncle's room then emerged with a package. I needed no more evidence to prove to myself that Uncle was giving these men pictures of me. Soon my fanny would be seen all over Paris. I was both annoyed and excited. I burst through the door into the dimly lit room. Uncle was folding brown paper over a pile of photographs.

"'Is that for your next customer?" I asked in as angry a voice as I could muster. Uncle had not seen me enter and was taken by surprise.

"'What? Oh, Natalie. I thought you were in the library," he blustered.

"'No, I'm here watching you sell my body. How dare you, Uncle Pierre, dishonour me in this way."

'"Oh, Natalie. In no way do I do you dishonour. To the men who look at my photographs you are an anonymous model with a matchless beauty. My friends, because that is what they are, are great admirers of the female form and merely provide recompense for my efforts and my supplies of chemicals and paper."

'"I seem to recall that it was me that made the effort, Uncle, spending all that time posing and doing other things." I stepped close to him and ran my hand down the front of his trousers. I felt a swelling. "Don't you think I should have a share of this compensation you refer to?" Uncle gave me a look then that showed that he understood that I was not really angry but keen to share in his good fortune.

'"You are correct, Natalie, and I had not forgotten you. You shall share in the proceeds of our little endeavour."

'So that is how I have all this money.' Natalie got out of bed and from her trunk took a cotton bag from which she scooped banknotes and coins. 'And next time I go home Uncle is going to suggest another series of pictures of great women.' She giggled.

'Oh, Natalie, you are so wicked. Do you think your uncle was really going to pay you for posing?'

'I don't know, but I think he is now expecting special service whenever we are alone together.'

Chapter 8
Victoria's Lesson in Intercourse

'Good evening, girls. Tonight we come to a most important lesson in the arts of pleasure.' I sat on the edge of my chair, my classmates alongside me equally agog to hear what Madame had to say. Already the crotch of my bloomers was damp with my excitement and anticipation. It had been over a month since the six of us had sat in our white corsets, knickers and stockings waiting to see what Madame would teach us. She stood before us in a long grey dress buttoned up to the neck, her blonde hair like a lantern bestowing its radiance upon us. Despite my state of partial undress I was not chilled because a log fire roared and crackled in the hearth, banishing the alpine winter and adding its glow to that of the candelabrum that hung over the divan occupying the centre of the floor.

I listened intently to what Madame had to say.

'Last term you took your first steps on the road to discovery of your own bodies and of those of the male sex. You learned how to use your hands, your mouths, indeed in some cases,' Madame glanced at me, 'your whole bodies to entice and excite a man. This term your assignment will be to investigate the act of union between man and woman; intercourse, coitus, the penetration of the female organs by the male member.' I felt Natalie, by my side, shiver with pent-up eagerness. I too felt the same emotion and yet I surprised myself. Just four months ago I knew nothing about love, very little indeed about my needs and aptitudes. Now I longed for a man's hands on my breasts and buttocks, his cock in my mouth and his tongue on my clitoris. Yet despite all the practice I and the other girls had had in the skills of lovemaking we, or I at least, remained virgins. While my vagina had been penetrated by fingers, tongues, glass dildos and an immense phallus belonging to Madame herself, no penis had yet made an entry to my love canal. I did at least understand the purpose of intercourse. A couple of years ago my father arranged for me to have a tutor. He was a dull man of about thirty years who only seemed to come alive when discussing the natural world. Fish, frogs, birds, mammals, he knew everything there was to know about their life history including how they procreated. A bull inseminating a cow had been just one episode in my education. Thus I was able to follow Madame's next words.

'But first, girls, a warning. Intercourse is not without its dangers, not least the chance of becoming with child. An infant at your breast is the last thing that you need if you are to achieve your destiny and meet a gentleman of substance, at least until you have married the said gentleman. You must take precautions. Do not allow a man to ejaculate inside you without checking the date. The day to watch is a fortnight, fourteen days, after the commencement of your curse, your menstrual period. It is best to avoid coitus a few days before and a week after that day. That is unless you employ a barrier to the semen.' I had little idea what Madame was talking about, never having considered the possibility of having a child or preventing the same.

Madame moved to an occasional table at the side of the drawing room and opened a small valise. She lifted out a limp object and carried it back to us. She held it up and we stared at it in wonder. It resembled a child's sock but was apparently manufactured from very thin, soft leather such as is used for the finest gloves.

'This,' Madame continued, holding the object between her forefinger and thumb, 'is a sheath for the penis.' All six of us gasped with surprise. A glove for a cock!

'When rolled on to the male member it provides a barrier and a receptacle for his ejaculate. This one is made of the finest pigskin, but I have others manufactured from cowhide and fish skin.' While speaking she had returned to the case and picked out more of the tubular artefacts. She passed them to the girl at the end of the row and we took turns to examine each one. I could see the benefit of the sheath but I wondered how I would ever be able to get it onto Albert's immense tool. His length and girth dwarfed the finger-like sock.

'They are of course available in different sizes to suit the male but I do confess that they numb the feeling that the man has within the vagina and reduce the enjoyment. Nevertheless they serve a purpose, but now I must show you a new invention sent to me by an acquaintance in the United States of America.' Madame returned once more to the small table and this time returned with a very different object. It was a pale beige colour and was considerably smaller than the other sheaths, but when Madame stood in front of us she held it in her two hands and stretched it. Its length doubled instantly and it became almost transparent when fully extended.

'This is a latex sheath that will expand to fit any cock and is so thin that it almost cannot be felt by the wearer and yet it will prevent the transfer of the sperm. I am quite sure that this will become a great boon to pleasure, but alas they are in short supply at the moment.' She returned the sheaths to the case and took out a small bottle.

'This is another recourse if you fear the possibility of pregnancy. It is a tincture concocted by Madame Hulot from ancient recipes. When soaked into a piece of sponge and inserted in your vagina it will destroy sperm and prevent conception. See Madame Hulot to collect your supply.' We each turned to our neighbours to express our amazement that such medicines existed. Madame placed the bottle back in the case and stood once again in front of us.

'Now girls, that is enough of the preparations. Let us get to the purpose of this lesson.' She clapped her hands. The door opened and Eric entered wearing a loose gown. He stood facing us, a look of eager anticipation on his strong, smooth face.

'We have our male so who shall be our seductress?' She looked along our line, a frown creasing her brow. 'Olivia, I think it shall be you.' The dark, Italian girl at the other end of the row sat up abruptly and an appearance of shock passed over her face. She remained sitting. 'Come on, girl,' Madame urged, 'let us set to it.'

Olivia stood and walked slowly to the fur-covered divan. As she approached, Eric threw off his gown and stood naked, displaying his eagerness for the fray. Olivia seemed to regard his tool with distrust but slipped her bloomers down over her ample but smooth bottom. She dropped the silk garment on the floor and sat on the bed then lay back on the pillow and opened her legs. I heard a 'tut' from Madame who was now standing close to me at the end of our row of chairs. Eric seemed a little surprised but moved forward. He crawled between Olivia's legs and lowered his tool to her gateway. He thrust forward.

'Ow!' Olivia shouted. Eric tried again and again Olivia cried out in pain and pushed him away. Madame clapped her hands and strode forward.

'Stop this at once.' Eric slid backwards and stood at the end of the couch with a look of sorrow on his face. 'Really, Olivia, what do you think you are doing? Have you learnt nothing? Where was the preparation, the foreplay? You must build up the excitement in the male and also see that you are ready. Why could he not make an entry? Have you

91

not carried out the exercises with the glass phallus that I loaned to you?'

Olivia sat on the edge of the bed, her head lowered. 'No, Madame. I was afraid that I would bleed, Madame.'

'What nonsense. You have ignored all my entreaties and now you are unprepared for the most important act of lovemaking. At the end of this evening, you will be punished for your failure. Now sit back in your place and watch and learn.' Olivia trudged back to her seat afraid to look any of us in the eye. 'Victoria, you show us how it should be done.' My stomach turned over at the mention of my name and I realised that I could not afford to get the lesson wrong. My buttocks retained a memory of Madame's punishments.

I stood up and walked slowly towards Eric, rolling my hips as I moved. Eric looked at me, a small smile appearing on his lips. His penis had subsided and withdrawn into the fair curls of his pubic hair. I knelt before him and took his testicles in my hand. As I lifted them I bent my head forward and kissed the poor shrunken member. Shrunken no longer. The lightest touch of my lips caused it to stir and grow. As the tip began to emerge I licked it. It quivered and it swelled and expanded some more. Eric reached down and with both hands under my shoulders pulled me up onto my feet. He spun me around and expertly undid the laces of my corset. It dropped to my feet, quickly followed by my knickers and stockings. Then he lifted me up and carried me the few short steps to the bed. He laid me down gently amongst the furs and knelt between my thighs. His hair tickled the smooth skin of my groin but then there was the electric touch of his tongue on my clitoris. My juices were flowing and I guessed that there would be little problem of friction. Having been pierced by Madame's ebony tool I knew I had the capacity to accept Eric's manhood and now I wanted him inside me. I touched his head and he stopped lapping at my cunt and looked up at me. He slithered up my body, planting a kiss in my navel and pausing to suck both my nipples. At last I felt his penis pressing against my lips. He gave a small thrust with his pelvis and the knob slipped between the folds of my skin, opened the portal and slid in. It was a most marvellous feeling to have that warm, soft-skinned but steel-stiff ramrod poking me. Eric pushed in as far as he was able until I felt his balls against my buttocks. For a moment he rested and I relished the sensation of being penetrated. Eric's tool was certainly not small but inside me it felt immense, filling every space in my body. While Eric lay still his penis did not. It throbbed and pulsed, each movement bringing me delight. Instinctively I tried to grasp his cock with my vagina. Although wholly without practice I evidently succeeded because I heard a small groan of pleasure in my ear. Then Eric did begin to move. He retreated, the fox withdrawing from its hole. For a moment I felt a great sadness as I was left vacant, but then my joy was redoubled as he thrust in, the glorious cock filling me once again and tugging on my sensitive button. Now Eric got into a rhythm and I responded in time. On each of his thrusts I shoved my hips up to meet him, forcing his penis deeper into my womb, his testicles slapping against my perineum. He grunted on each lunge and his body gave off such a heat that I had not felt before. I clung on to him and met his every move, urging him on, crying out at every drive. And on and on he went, until I was almost insensible with pleasure. When I thought nothing could be better than this, the wave of orgasm began to spread out from my clitoris. engulfing my womb and rising up through my body until my head was ringing with the chimes of my climax. Within me Eric's tool swelled and gushed, his semen flooding into my channel. He continued to thrust in and out, slowly subsiding until with a long drawn-out gasp he sank on top of me. I think I did pass out for a few moments because when I again became aware of myself and my surroundings, Eric had taken his weight off me and was kneeling over me. And there was clapping and hooting from my classmates and as I turned my head to look at them, there too was Madame Thackeray applauding politely and smiling broadly. She came towards me as Eric retreated and sat on the edge of the bed. Madame took my hand and helped me to my feet. Naked as I was I did not feel ashamed to be standing in front of the class.

'Well done, Victoria. That was an excellent demonstration of coitus in the first of many and various positions. Thank you Eric for demonstrating your skills so well.' Eric looked up and grinned at Madame and me then picked up his gown and left. 'Over the next months you will learn the different orientations that may be used and also discover how to prolong the exercise or bring it to a swift conclusion. Now you may return to your rooms. Olivia, with me please.' The forlorn girl followed Madame out of the room while the other four clustered around me with eager questions.

'What did it feel like?'

'Could you feel him right inside?'

'Did it hurt?'

'Did you feel him come?'

I answered as best I could – wonderful, yes, no, yes – and bent to retrieve my discarded clothes. Finally, Natalie and I escaped and ran to the room I shared with Beatrice. I sat on the bed still quite breathless.

'Oh, la, la. You were most marvellous, Victoria.' Natalie hugged me and planted little pecks of kisses on my neck and cheeks. 'I cannot wait till it is my turn. I too want to ride a cock.' We lay on the bed and cuddled each other until I began to drift off to sleep.

The next day I could hardly concentrate on the more

mundane tasks of French cuisine and household finance and longed for the evening lessons when perhaps I would again feel a penis between my legs. After supper I returned to our room to change out of my day uniform. As I entered the room my heart leapt with delight for on the bed instead of the accustomed outfit in white satin was a crimson version. I rushed to pick up the smooth satin basque and clasped it to my bosom. Beatrice emerged from the bathroom, clad in her black underwear.

'I see you have graduated to the second level,' she said smiling warmly. 'Let me help you dress.' I quickly discarded the boring skirt, petticoats and blouse of my day attire and donned the blood-red garment. Beatrice tugged on the cords, lacing me tightly and pulling in my waist until I gasped. My pink breasts were uplifted and rested on their whale-boned platform, my nipples matching the colour.

'So who did you have for your first fuck?' Bea asked as I pulled on the red stockings. I was a little shocked by her use of the rough peasant word but I reflected that it was apt for the animal-like performance that I had engaged in.

'It was Eric,' I replied.

'Ah, yes,' Bea said wistfully, 'he is good, excellent control. He knows exactly when to let go.'

As I completed fastening my stockings to the suspenders and pulled up a thin pair of red silk French knickers I looked at Bea's black clad body. It contrasted with the white skin of her arms and legs and the pale, almost translucent, properties of her breasts.

'Bea?' I began.

'Yes?'

'If white signifies that we are pupils of the arts of love and red denotes that my fanny has been penetrated by a penis, what then is black a symbol of?' Bea did not reply at once but stood biting her lips.

'I'm afraid I am not at liberty to tell you, Victoria. It is something you will discover in due course but I can tell you this. While handling and caressing and kissing and sucking and fucking are all elements of the art of pleasure, there are far more principles for you to discover; many more ways to achieve release and numerous methods for bringing a man to his ultimate pleasure. You will see, don't doubt it.' She turned away and left me still wondering.

I was of course the only pupil wearing red when we assembled in the drawing room. The others gave me a green-eyed look. Olivia I noticed was standing by her chair rather than sitting in it. I presumed that her bottom alone had been awarded the red sign. We waited patiently for Madame to arrive.

'Good evening ladies,' she said as she swept into the room followed by Hermann. 'Tonight we shall continue to explore the techniques of intercourse. Freya, you shall be our subject.' The blonde Scandinavian girl blushed and got to her feet. She advanced towards Hermann as if he was an old friend. They met and kissed on the lips then Hermann lowered his head to her supported breasts and sucked on her nipples. Meanwhile his hands worked behind her, unfastening the laces that bound her. I was impressed with how he managed without a sight of the knots. In moments Freya was naked and Hermann too had thrown off his gown. They moved to the bed and sank onto it, their mouths locked together. Freya's hand was massaging his balls and pumping his cock while Hermann's fingers were delving deep into her fanny. Freya started to move onto her back and open her legs, but Hermann whispered in her ear and rolled her over. She lay on her front until Hermann straddled her legs and lifted her hips up. With her arms and head resting on the pillow Freya was kneeling with her bottom raised and directed almost towards us. Hermann moved slightly to the side and moved her knees apart. Then he spread her buttocks and thighs and I gazed into the dual openings of her arse and vagina. Hermann positioned himself between her legs and took aim with his erect cock.

'As you can see, I requested that Hermann engage in a rear entry this evening,' Madame commented. 'This is a favourite position for many men, and for women too. It affords the man a sight of his penis entering the channel and also provides greater leverage for the thrust.'

Hermann held Freya's lips apart and began to slide his thick cock into her hole. She gasped audibly but did not flinch. From my position I could just see Hermann's penis disappearing from view and his balls dangling between his legs. He moaned as his cock became fully buried in Freya's cunt. He paused for a moment sliding his hand over her milk-white smooth buttocks, circumnavigating the twin globes. Then he gripped her hips and began to pull out. His shaft appeared but he stopped with his knob on the threshold. Freya gasped again and I imagined the feeling that the absence of the penis produced. Then he thrust and like the piston of a steam engine, his cock shot forward and out of sight. Freya groaned louder this time. He repeated the movement faster and faster till he was indeed like an express train rushing into tunnel after tunnel. With each stab he grunted and Freya cried out, in pain or in ecstasy I was not sure, but then Hermann froze his whole body rigid but trembling and he let out a great sigh. He remained thus for a minute or two while Freya sobbed. When he finally withdrew, drips of semen fell from his limp cock onto the furs. Freya's knees slid until she lay flat on her stomach. Hermann kissed her neck and whispered in her ear.

'Thank you, Hermann. A most energetic demonstration,' Madame said. Hermann stood up to attention, his legs, arms, body and head stiff and straight, all except his penis which hung flaccidly.

'I am honoured, Madame,' he said in his thick German accent; then picking up his gown he left us.

'And you too, Freya. How do you feel?' The girl was sitting up now, her cheeks still glowing and her skin glistening with a film of perspiration.

'Oh, it was hard, Madame, but I liked it.'

'Well done. You have earned your crimson like Victoria. Now the four of you still in white return to your rooms. Your opportunity awaits.' The four girls, including Natalie, hurried out. Freya picked up her clothes and also walked out of the room, a little stiffly I thought.

'And what of me?' I asked Madame.

'I am sure you will find entertainment, Victoria. I am away to guide those girls.' She too left me. It seemed that I in my red lovemaking attire was to be left alone. I was about to return to my bedroom when the drawing room door was pushed ajar and a head appeared. It was Albert. He saw that only I remained and he stepped through the opening. He closed the door behind him.

'Ello, Victoria. You want fuck?' I laughed aloud at Albert's faltering but direct English.

'Oh yes, Albert, I'm ready.' He came towards me discarding his leather breeches and smock in the few steps that he took. I dropped my knickers and stepped forward to meet him. I made contact with his bobbing penis first. The immense tool came between us. I knelt and deposited kisses up and down its length and enclosed the vast knob in my hands, feeling the silky skin with my fingertips. I was wondering how best to take this monstrous phallus into my vagina and thought that the position I had experienced the previous evening would present the best orientation. Then I had a better idea. I signalled to Albert to lie on the carpet. He followed my instruction and lay on his back. His cock was like a flagpole. I stood astride him giving him a view straight up my fanny which caused him to leer at me. Then I started to bend my knees. The look on Albert's face showed that he understood what I intended.

Slowly I lowered myself, my thighs parting and my lips opening up. I made contact with the tip of the beetroot that was the end of his cock. I paused. Could I do this? What if I should fall? He would split me in two. Very carefully I lowered myself. The knob stretched me wide, there was a moment of pain, and then I was over the thickest part. I continued to lower myself, astounded that Albert's long, wide cock was being swallowed up by my cunt. Albert too seemed surprised, his eyes wide open with wonder. At last I was squatted down so my buttocks pressed on his balls. It felt as though his penis was going to emerge through my throat. I rested, savouring the feeling of the gigantic prick filling me. Then I started to rise. The cock slid smoothly but I stopped just before it slipped out. I lowered myself again. Albert's eyes were rotating up into his head and as I descended he lifted his buttocks off the floor, supporting himself on his heels and shoulders. I repeated the movement faster this time. Legs straight, knees bend. I slid up and down his cock as if it were a well-greased piston. My thighs began to ache but now my desire was driving me. Albert cried but still I continued pumping until it happened. A fountain of semen hit my cervix and Albert let out a drawn-out moan. My legs gave way and I collapsed on top of him, his softening penis still deep inside me.

'Oh well done, Victoria.' I looked up to see Madame standing in the doorway. 'You weren't due to try that position for a few weeks yet but I knew you could be inventive.'

Chapter 9
Victoria Has a Probing Lesson

'Ah, there it is,' Natalie squealed.

I looked up stiffly from my embroidery. I was trying to complete a piece using the grey February light but sitting in an upright chair by the south-facing window in the drawing room of the Venus School for Young Ladies was starting to make my neck ache.

'There what is?' I enquired. Natalie held up a book and I could see that the title was Kama Sutra.

'The position by which I had intercourse with Hermann last night.' Madame Thackeray insisted that we keep a record of all our coital experiments and that we find out what the Indian mystics said about them. As I had observed Natalie and Hermann in their tryst, I knew what she was referring to.

Natalie had spread her naked body over the side of her bed with her feet barely touching the floor. Then she had swung her legs up and caught hold of her knees. From my position sitting on a chair just a few feet away at the side of the bedroom I had a wonderful picture of her puckered anus and her orchid-like sex. Her lips glowed pinkly in the candle light and seemed to swell as I watched. Hermann, who was also naked by this time, stepped forward obscuring my view. I moved closer and sat on the floor by their side so that I could watch what they did.

Hermann knelt and lowered his head to her fanny. His tongue reached out and orbited around her arsehole then slid up to her crack, dividing the lips and finally coming to rest on her little clitoris that just poked out of the folds. Natalie giggled and her buttocks trembled but she kept pulling on her knees so that her toes touched the bedspread beside her head and she tried to open her thighs even wider. Hermann lapped at her and her juices started to flow. A drip oozed out of her crack, ran down her perineum and was trapped in her lower hole.

The young man stopped his nuzzling and stood up. As the bed was high he could stand upright while his cock sought out Natalie's crack. The head of his penis looked like that of a snake searching for the nectar in the fleshy flower. I almost expected a forked tongue to flick from the small round mouth and taste Natalie's honeydew. The head delved deeper, disappearing from view and inch after inch of shaft followed it. I heard Natalie's gasp as Hermann's thick tool penetrated deep into her vagina. He rested when his balls slapped against her buttocks. He gripped her round globes in each hand and moved his hips to withdraw. The glistening shaft came into view again and Natalie groaned, but he didn't pull out. His knob paused in the folds of her sex for a moment then his hips thrust with such force, driving the cock into the hole at speed, that Natalie screeched with surprise and perhaps a little pain.

He pulled out again bringing another sigh from his mount. Then another thrust and another cry and now gripping her small bottom with both hands he slammed into her time and time again. I was mesmerised by the reciprocating motion of his cock in her cunt. With each thrust, Natalie cried, louder and louder and sometimes intelligibly bidding him *'oui, oui'*. Despite Hermann's experience I knew he could not last at this pace and my prediction was soon justified by his own drawn-out cry and final thrust. Natalie's legs shook as her own orgasm took hold and for a few moments they remained joined together until Hermann sighed, withdrew and collapsed in a heap on the floor.

I couldn't resist Natalie's drooling sex and crawled to take Hermann's place. I knelt and pressed my face against her dripping fanny and sucked at her canal. I loved the salty flavour of Hermann's semen mixed with the sweetness of Natalie's own secretions. My ministrations kept her at her climax and she continued to moan and shake for minutes while I buried my fingers in my own sex, rubbing myself in time with my lapping tongue until I had had my fill and reached my own climax. As I rested back on my ankles, Natalie finally let her knees go and her legs rotated to the floor.

'*Sacré bleu, très bon,*' she gasped.

'Do you agree?' I awakened from my recollections to find myself back in the drawing room with Natalie questioning me.

'Pardon, Natalie, I was far away,'

'I could see. I said that it was a good position even though the female is unable to contribute much to the motion.'

'You are right,' I assented. 'It is a deep fuck and so gives both satisfaction. You certainly seemed to enjoy it.'

'And you too I imagine. Your mouth following Hermann's cock was divine.'

The door opened and Madame Thackeray entered. We stood up and curtsied politely, our crinolines rustling.

'Good afternoon girls. I was hoping to find you here, Victoria. Please come with me.' She turned and left the room, leaving me and Natalie to exchange mystified glances. I hurried after Madame with a growing fear. What had I done wrong this time? I could not recall doing anything to incur her displeasure but my buttocks carried the memory of the previous occasions when I had received punishment.

I followed Madame into her study bedroom. There was a large wood fire crackling in the hearth and the room had a warm welcoming glow. She closed the door behind me and slid a bolt into its slot.

'Undress please, Victoria.' I could not argue so began to undo the many small buttons that fastened my green silk dress up to my neck. However, I could question.

'In what way have I displeased you, Madame?' I saw her riding crop lay in its accustomed place on her desk and the sight of it gave me palpitations.

'You have not caused me any displeasure, Victoria,' she said, a smile flickering over her smooth, pale face.

'But you intend to beat me. Am I not mistaken, Madame?'

'Oh yes. I will beat you, Victoria, but do not look upon it as a punishment. View this afternoon as a further lesson in your education.' I had completed unfastening the buttons and when I pulled the sleeves from my arms the dress subsided around me. I stepped out of the hoops and continued to remove my slip and petticoats. As I did so I noticed two objects on Madame's bed, a black leatherette case almost a foot square and an instrument that looked a little like that used for making pats of butter. It was of polished wood with a handle about six inches long and a thin flat blade some four inches wide by a foot in length.

'Will you be using your crop?' I asked tentatively.

'Not on this occasion, Victoria. That instrument, as you know, is one that I reserve for punishments such as I gave Olivia a short while ago.' The Italian girl had not been able to sit for a week after Madame had disciplined her for failing to prepare herself for intercourse. 'No, today you will experience the paddle.' She lifted the wooden implement from the bed and gave it an experimental swish through the air.

I pulled my slip over my head and once again stood naked in front of my headmistress. The sight gave her obvious pleasure and her eyes roved from my ample bosom to my neatly trimmed, dark pubic hair.

'Over the elephant, please, Victoria. I think we had better use the cords because I have no doubt that you will wriggle uncontrollably.' I took up the by-now familiar position, flung like baggage over the elephant shaped stool. Madame tied my arms and legs to those of the wooden animal; then I was left for a few minutes to consider my fate while rustling told me that Madame was divesting herself of her clothes in order to assault me with complete freedom.

At last there was silence, save the crackling of the log fire, and I was aware that Madame was contemplating my buttocks and my gaping sex. I had no idea what to expect from the paddle and when the first blow came I was pleasantly surprised. It felt like a light slap over a considerable area of my left buttock. There was none of the sharp immediate pain of the crop. However, Madame did not pause as she did with her other instrument. The slaps came one after the other over both buttocks, the back of my thighs and my calves. Soon the heat began to grow. The stinging was as if I had fallen naked, arse first into a bush of nettles. Still Madame persisted with blow after blow descending on my rear. I wriggled, pulled on my bonds and cried out, to no avail. I was scarcely conscious of each individual blow, one melded into the next, but I was aware of the fire that covered the whole lower half of my body.

At last, after an eternity, Madame desisted and through my sobs I heard her panting. I awaited her next move. On previous occasions her finger had traced a delightful trail around my arse and sex. Now my cunt ached for her attention. With my hands bound and my legs fastened wide apart I was unable to satisfy myself. I longed for Madame's touch but it did not come. The ache grew until all of my mind was focused on my swollen, exposed fanny. I was quite unaware of what Madame was doing but I knew I was dripping juices in preparation for satisfaction. Still Madame made no move. At last when I felt I could take no more of the torture of anticipation she began to undo my bonds.

'Stand up, Victoria,' she said as she released my wrists and ankles. I slid off the stool and stood up shakily. I became conscious once again of the heat in my buttocks and thighs. I tentatively reached around to place a soothing hand on my sore cheeks.

'Don't touch, Victoria! Come here,' Madame beckoned me to join her by the side of her double bed. As before, I marvelled at her slim mature body. She seemed quite comfortable in her nakedness. She was leaning over the leatherette case undoing two sprung catches. She opened the lid and I looked in at a most unfamiliar object resting in folds of satin. It had the shape of a wide V with a swelling at the apex to which a number of leather straps were fixed. The object seemed to be constructed of smooth polished leather with one arm black and the other nearly white. Both arms were about eight inches long and I would struggle to wrap my hand around them. Madame lifted the object from its case and it was then that I saw that the black and white rods were fashioned in the shape of a penis.

'It is a dildo with two ends,' I gasped.

'That is correct, Victoria.' Madame turned to face me holding up the instrument in her hands for me to examine properly. 'A steel core wrapped with linen and covered with the finest calf leather.' She pressed the two cocks together and then when she relaxed they snapped back to their former position.

'But how ...? What is it for?' I was quite mystified. I had experienced, in fact enjoyed, the sensation of an artificial cock filling my vagina but could not imagine the purpose of this double tool.

'You will see,' Madame said as she climbed onto the bed and sat with her back against the pillows. She opened her legs and I gazed at her dark hole with its fringe of soft blonde curls. She gripped the bulge at the bottom of the double dildo in both hands with the tip of the black cock resting against her sex. With a groan, she arched her back and drove the knob into her slit. I watched in awe as the shaft swiftly disappeared from view. She held the leather scrotum against her fanny and slid off the bed.

'Come, Victoria, help me fasten the straps.' I took a step forward and gathered up the strips of lather. At first I was confused until the realisation came that there were four suspenders connected to a belt. I place the latter around Madame's waist.

'Pull it tight and fasten it securely,' Madame ordered. 'I do not want it to come loose.' I did as she instructed and pulled hard on the belt until it was secured. The other straps framed the V of her pubis and encircled her buttocks. She removed her hands from the tool. I stepped away from her and was amazed by what I saw. Madame had been transformed into a man-woman. I could not help my eyes flick to and fro from her round breasts and hard erect nipples to the ivory-coloured cock that thrust up and out from between her legs. She looked as eager and ready to penetrate a vagina as any of the men. Strangely, it did not occur to me to question whom the recipient of the erection was to be.

Madame raised a hand to her mouth and spat some saliva onto her fingers. Then she transferred the fluid to the knob of the jutting cock. It glistened in the glow of the fire.

'Get on the bed please, Victoria.' It was only then that the realisation dawned on me that Madame wanted to fuck me as if she were a man. I wondered what it would be like to be pierced by the leather-clad steel rod. I clambered onto the mattress and lay on my back.

'No, on your knees, please.' I rolled on to my stomach and raised myself into kneeling position facing the headboard.

'Put your head down and spread your legs.' I did as I was bidden, folding my arms on the pillows and resting my head on my forearms. I was aware that my still-stinging buttocks were now raised up and my fanny was gaping wide.

I couldn't see but I felt Madame climb on the bed behind me. There was a pause of a few moments when I was unsure what would happen, then I felt the cold head of the dildo press against my lips. Madame did not wait to see if I was open and ready for penetration but drove in with one powerful thrust. I screamed as if it were the first time that I had been entered and my maidenhead had been torn asunder. The steel penis crashed against my cervix, a feeling like a red-hot poker drilling into my torso. Madame forced the leather-covered balls between my labia, stretching wide my vulva.

Tears trickled down my cheeks as I accepted the sensation of being filled by the steel and leather tool, but, before I could recover my composure, it withdrew. It felt as if my innards were being dragged out through my cunt but then Madame slammed into me again and I cried out a second time. Madame was quite without pity and pounded into me again and again. At first all I experienced was the pain of being torn apart as each thrust bore into me. I began to swoon but as I became numb a different feeling came over me. The rhythmic thrusts seemed to be happening to another person and instead I was engulfed in electricity that tingled pleasantly. Gradually the charge increased, setting all my muscles into contractions. I was suddenly back in my own body as the orgasm took hold with Madame still fucking me, all be it at a slower pace. I groaned loudly and Madame too cried out. She froze with the steel cock rammed hard up my fanny and then it slowly slid out. My knees slid from under me and I lay exhausted on the bed, quite unaware what had happened to Madame.

I awoke still lying on my stomach with a cool, damp cloth pressed between my legs providing pleasurable relief to my sore sex. I twisted over to look at Madame who was holding the cloth. She was still naked but had removed the weapon with which she had assaulted me.

'I'm sorry if that was too hard,' Madame said in her kindliest voice. 'When I am in the masculine role an unaccustomed violence takes over.' I did indeed feel as if I had been raped by an unfeeling monster of a man but the fact that the tool was wielded by a woman seemed to make it acceptable to me. In fact the sensation of being the instrument of pleasure for my headmistress, strangely, gave me a feeling of pride.

'I hope I gave satisfaction, Madame.' Madame withdrew her hand and the now warm cloth.

'Oh yes, Victoria, and what have you learned from today's lesson?'

I considered the beating and the fucking Madame had administered.

'That the paddle, while not so immediately painful as the crop, excites a larger area and produces a long-lasting effect.' Indeed my buttocks and thighs retained an afterglow of the fire.

'That is true,' Madame agreed.

'And the double dildo is a formidable tool for one woman to wield on another and perhaps allows one to sense what a man feels during intercourse.'

'That may be the case, although one cannot tell. Lacking sensation in the cock itself and without the process of ejaculation it must surely be a pale replica of the male experience. Well done, Victoria. As a reward for a lesson well learned perhaps you would like to borrow the instrument for your own pleasure.' I could not believe that Madame was offering to loan me the double dildo but I nodded eagerly.

I hurried upstairs wearing just my slip, my dress, slippers and the case bearing the double dildo in my arms. I stopped at the door to Natalie's room and knocked.

'*Entrez.*' I pushed the door open and entered. Natalie, also wearing just her slip, leapt off the bed and closed the door behind me.

'Oh, Victoria, what has Madame done to you? It has been hours.' I dropped my clothes in a heap and sat on the bed, somewhat gingerly, as my arse still stung. I cradled the case in my arms and described all that had befallen me in Madame's study. Natalie gasped with amazement at each revelation and her eyes opened wide with wonder as I opened the case and revealed the instrument.

'Oh, it is a wonder. Do you think we can use it?' I lay the case by my side on the bed and pulled my slip over my head.

'Why not? That is why Madame loaned it to me. But have no fear. I shall be gentle. I do not think my fanny could suffer another pounding such as she gave me.'

Natalie giggled and took off her slip. She watched as I removed the tool from its resting place and slid the white artificial penis slowly and carefully into my vagina. I was relieved that there was only a hint of soreness. Like Madame I requested Natalie's assistance in fastening the belt tight around my waist. The four straps produced a constricting but not unpleasant feeling around my mound and buttocks. Now I understood why Madame had asked for the belt to be pulled as tight as possible; the weight of the two cocks was quite considerable but, with the suspenders taut, it felt secure. The cock that filled my vagina felt immense but it was the feeling of the leather testicles between my thighs and the sight of the shiny black shaft that truly excited me. I looked at myself in the long mirror noticing how my stance had changed to allow for the stiff rod jutting from my body. In fact I was standing as the boys stood when they were proudly showing off their erections.

'Ooo, it is strange to see you with a cock, particularly a black one.' Natalie had climbed onto the bed and was watching me with wide eyes. 'How do you want to do it? Do you want to enter me like Madame fucked you?' I thought about it for a moment.

'No, let's try face to face.'

'Good. I am glad. I want to see you as you enter me.' She lay on her back and spread her legs wide. I crawled between them finding the swaying heavy cock rather unweildy. I could see that she was ready and eager because her fanny lips glistened with secretion. Natalie's eyes watched me as I positioned the tip against her entrance and gently pushed. Her lips parted and the head entered smoothly.

'It's big,' Natalie commented.

'Does it hurt?' I asked, worried that I may be stretching her too much.

'No, no, *allez*.' I thrust my hips forward and the shaft disappeared into her fanny. As the cock slid in, I lowered myself onto Natalie's body, resting my arms above her shoulders. My breasts dangled. When my nipples touched hers it was as if sparks of electricity passed between us. I drove the dildo in to its fullest extent until the ball formed a plug between her sex and mine. Our mounds pressed together and my bosom was crushed against Natalie's. Our faces were just an inch apart. Natalie smiled and opened her mouth. I dropped my head, my lips finding hers. Our tongues touched, circled, tasting each other. I entered her mouth feeling her teeth, then I sensed her tongue inside me exploring.

I moved my hips and felt the dildo move in my cunt with a reciprocal movement of the other cock in Natalie's. With

110

our lips pressed together and our tongues entwined I felt rather than heard her moan of pleasure. I experimented with forwards and backwards thrusts, side to side and circular movements. Each gave me a spasm of pleasure and elicited more moans from Natalie. As I moved, my nipples rubbed against hers, exacerbating my excitement. My thrusts increased in extent as I rocked back and forth on my knees. Our mouths remained locked together but now I was bucking forward and back involuntarily; an instinct to thrust the cock up Natalie's cunt taking over. Natalie's moans were now growls of ecstasy and her matching thrusts urged me to greater effort. Her arms wrapped around my body and her legs twisted around mine so that we were one body moving in unison; an animal with two backs.

It seemed as if the dildo had developed a life of its own, thrusting and gyrating inside the two of us, and sending ripples of pleasure to the extremes of our bodies. Natalie's orgasm began in her toes, her feet banging against my calves like a rider urging her mount to gallop faster. Then her legs were shaking and finally her whole torso. With her arms holding me tight I shook with her and as she hit the peak so I too came with climax that washed through me like a river in flood.

Gradually our spasms subsided but we remained locked together as if we were manacled. Our mouths parted but Natalie strained her neck to plant kisses on my cheeks and eyelids.

'Incredible,' she muttered, 'that was at least as good as with the men. Victoria, you are my favourite lover – you and Madame's noble tool.'

Chapter 10
Victoria's School Excursion

The warm spring sun was melting the alpine snows and the track was clear all the way up the valley from the village to the Venus School for Young Ladies. The older girls had already left for their Easter vacation and the big house was quiet without them. My classmates and I were busy packing our trunks and getting excited about our trip to Venice. I was looking forward to seeing the city of canals, the place where I had expected to spend my last two years of schooling instead of here in the mountains.

At last the morning dawned when the carriages lined up outside and the young men willingly, though regretfully, loaded our luggage. I kissed little Albert on his cheek. He looked sad, as well he might knowing that it would be a few weeks before I or one of the other girls had the pleasure of handling his huge cock.

'Come on girls,' urged our headmistress. 'Make your farewells and get on board. We must not miss the train.' The six of us girls, Madame and her deputy, Madame Hulot, clambered into our seats and we set off.

Venice was as beautiful and as magical as I had imagined. When we arrived, in late evening, gondolas carried us and our bags through the maze of waterways to the grand house that Madame had hired for our stay. Natalie and I giggled as we watched the gondolier, a young man, skilfully manoeuvring us between the buildings and avoiding all the other water traffic. He wore a loose white shirt and tight black trousers which did little to hide his manhood as he strained on his pole.

Each of us was grateful for the large comfortable beds in the rooms that had been assigned to us and I fell asleep very quickly. The following day we had a tour of the attractions of the city-state. We marvelled at St Mark's Square, thrilled to a performance of Vivaldi's music and admired the glassware on display in the museums and shops. Only Madame Thackeray accompanied us. Madame Hulot was apparently on other errands. Our guide was the gondolier from the evening before and Natalie and I spent much of our time trying to catch his eye.

Early the next day, Natalie and I met outside our bedrooms and hurried down to the exit onto the canal. It was a bright, warm morning and we were relieved to find the gondolier waiting there with his boat.

'Would you take us for a ride in your boat, please?' I asked in my best Italian. He looked a little surprised but held out his hand to help us aboard. When we had settled, he cast off and punted us along the busy canals. We pretended to look at the sights but in fact our eyes were only for him. He soon became aware of our attention and we caught a smile crossing his moustachioed face.

'Is there somewhere quieter, less busy?' I asked. He nodded and steered us off the main waterway. We travelled down narrow backwaters between grand and not-so-grand houses. At last we came to a dead end surrounded on all sides by shuttered and deserted warehouses. There was no sign of any other boats or people. Our gondola drew alongside a jetty and the gondolier threw a rope over a bollard and made us fast.

'Perhaps you would like a rest, after your exertion,' I suggested, pointing to the cushions between me and Natalie.

113

Natalie giggled. The gondolier smirked and lowered himself between us. He smelt of sweat, olive oil and cheap wine; I rather liked it. Natalie placed a hand on his chest and deftly undid the buttons of his shirt. He made no move to stop her nor when she slid her hand inside and caressed his hair-covered chest. I placed my hand on the growing mound in his trousers and it seemed as if the seams in the tight cloth would be torn asunder.

'I think this needs release,' I murmured. Despite the strain on the buttons I was able to undo them with ease and his penis leapt out. The gondolier looked proudly at his erection then moaned as Natalie tweaked a nipple. I gazed admiringly at the stiff tower with its purple minaret. I parted the flies of his trousers to free his balls from their nest of long dark hair. I placed my left hand under them and felt his hard testicles in my fingers; then I slid my right hand up the long shaft. He groaned.

Without relaxing my grip on his prick and balls, I slid into the bottom of the boat, between his legs, and lowered my head to his knob. I flicked out my tongue and touched the tip, tasting the saltiness of the fluid already oozing from the gaping hole. I held his shaft firmly and let my lips slide over the head of his penis, rubbing my tongue against the ridges beneath it. He groaned again and I raised my eyes to see Natalie's head against his chest, her mouth locked on one of his nipples.

I chewed on his glans, relishing the texture of the silky skin, then lowered my head further, taking more of the shaft into my mouth. He was already throbbing and I realised that he was less experienced than the men at school so it would not be long before he came. I began a slow up and down movement revelling in the feel of his prick rubbing against the roof of my mouth. The boat rocked with my movements. My estimation was not wrong, however, for after a few seconds his legs straightened, his muscles tensed and his load of hot semen shot into my mouth. I savoured it before swallowing and then sucked every last drop from his wilting cock. At last I released it and took my seat back on the cushions. Natalie raised her head and helpfully began to do up his shirt buttons.

'We had better get back,' I said cheerfully, 'it's nearly time for breakfast.' The gondolier, flustered, hurried to do up his trouser buttons and resume his position on the stern. It was not a long journey back to our abode and as we stepped off the vessel I called, 'Same again tomorrow morning?' He nodded and grinned.

'But next time, I want his cock,' whispered Natalie in my ear.

We had another morning of sightseeing but returned in the afternoon to prepare for the evening's entertainment. Madame had informed us that we would have guests, male guests, and that we would have a chance to demonstrate the fruits of our education. We spent hours on our toilet, dress and cosmetics till we were satisfied with our appearance and then we assembled in the ballroom. A table had been laid to provide dinner for sixteen and a small chamber orchestra played pleasant music.

The men arrived and were introduced to us. They were representatives of many of the nations of Europe and a variety of ages although most appeared to be in their late twenties or early thirties. Over dinner we conversed about Venice, its history and art, the political situation and the prospects for the new century that would be upon us in just a few years. The men listened attentively but it seemed to me that their contributions were half-hearted and that they wished to move on with the real business of the evening.

The orchestra struck up a waltz and we paired off, male and female, Mesdames Thackeray and Hulot included. My partner appeared unsure as to which of his feet was which and succeeded in stamping on my toes on a number of occasions. I took an immediate dislike to his moustache that grew from ear to ear and decided that I would look the other way if he attempted to place a kiss on my lips. After the polite number of dances I made my excuses and retired to powder my nose. Upon leaving the ballroom I spied Natalie giggling as ever and dragging her young and athletic-looking quarry up the stairs.

I danced with two or three other men, one of them old enough to be my father, but not one aroused me half as much as the fit gondolier. At midnight I had had enough, especially as most of the girls and men had left the ballroom. I slipped off to my bed, alone.

I was up early the following morning but no one else was and the gondolier was nowhere to be found. I was first into the dining room and had almost completed my breakfast when Natalie appeared, yawning.

'I was waiting for you at the door,' I hissed at her as she sat down to table.

'I'm sorry, Victoria. I overslept.'

'You had a busy night, then.'

'Yes,' she giggled behind her napkin, 'he was quite sweet and very surprised when I climbed on top of him and rode his prick.'

'I'm glad you were satisfied.'

'Oh, I had sufficient entertainment.' She looked at me with a worried frown. 'But what about you, Victoria? Surely you found a cock to arouse you.'

'No I didn't. I can't say I liked any of that lot.'

Natalie shrugged, 'Oh well, there's always tonight.'

The day followed the same pattern as that previously. In the evening another party of men arrived for the evening's entertainment but again I found not one to my taste and while all the other girls paired up and escorted their partners

116

up to their rooms I remained alone, gazing across Venice from a balcony.

At breakfast on the third morning I got up to leave and return to my room but Madame beckoned me to her table.

'You did not find any of last evening's guests appealing, Victoria?'

'No, Madame.'

'Nor the evening before?'

'No, Madame.'

'You surprise me, I thought that with your enthusiasm for pleasure you would be among the first to make a conquest.'

'I'm afraid I found them rather boring, Madame.'

'The gondolier was more interesting was he?' I blushed, surprised that Madame knew of our little escapade.

'Yes, Madame, he was most forthcoming.'

'Well, there will be another set of guests this evening and I expect you to be hospitable. These men could be a help to you in the future.'

'Yes, Madame.'

'And as an extra encouragement may I remind you that I have brought my crop with me.' I gulped at the threat of a beating. She dismissed me and I hurried out of her sight.

The day's excursions did not interest me as all my mind was on the evening activities. I hoped that at least one of the visitors would excite my desire. Once again we sat down to dinner with an assortment of gentlemen. One had caught my eye when he arrived, a tall, dark-haired Englishman. I was pleased when he took the seat opposite me at table. He showed excellent good manners in conversing with his neighbours but it seemed that the focus of his attention was on me. Our conversation was of no consequence but the words came easily. When the meal was over he invited me to dance with almost indecent haste but I was pleased because he turned out to be an expert dancer and we moved across the floor as one.

After two or three pieces he escorted me outside to a balcony over the canal. We looked across the water at the moonlit towers of St Marks, then he turned to me, lowered his head and kissed me on the lips. I was surprised at the thrill that passed right through me.

'I know you have the use of a room but would you prefer to accompany me to my hotel?' he asked. I was unsure what to say. I knew that Madame expected me to exercise my knowledge of the arts of love on this man but would she mind where it took place?

'I'm not sure. I don't even know who you are.'

'I apologise. I am Gilbert Stebbings, eldest son of William Stebbings, the engineer and industrialist, presently at Merton College, Oxford.' As he spoke I examined his face and realised that he was very handsome.

'I am very pleased to make your acquaintance, Mr Stebbings …'

'Gilbert, please.'

'If it pleases you, Gilbert,' I came to a decision, 'and, yes, I would be delighted to accompany you.'

'Wonderful.' He took my arm and escorted me down to the jetty. A gondola was waiting and swiftly ferried us to his hotel, one of the grandest in Venice. I soon found myself in a vast suite at the top of the building with a marvellous view over the whole city.

'You seem to be a man of substance, Gilbert,' I said looking around the sumptuous apartment. He approached me with two glasses of champagne in his hands.

'My father is the owner of several foundries and factories.'

'So what are you doing in Venice?'

'A grand tour. I know it is somewhat outmoded but my father, being new to riches, thought it was something that his son should do. Paris, Berlin and Vienna had their interesting points but nothing like the view I have here and now.' He was looking directly at me, his eyes moving up and down my white silk dress.

I stepped close to him, took both glasses from his hands and placed them on a small table, then pressed my hands against his chest.

'I am sure the view can only get better,' I said, unbuttoning his dinner jacket and lifting it off his shoulders. As it slid to the floor I was already working on the pearl buttons of his dress shirt. He pulled on his bow tie and it unfastened and fell to the carpet. With his shirt undone I slipped my hands inside and was delighted to find a smooth, hairless chest. He reached over my shoulders looking for the hooks and eyes of my dress. Dextrously he undid them and helped the dress to slide down my body. Being prepared, I only wore a petticoat under my crinoline, so my breasts were bared to him. He gasped as my white globes filled his eyes. I did not allow him time to stare but quickly pushed the petticoat to the floor, stepped out of it and knelt at his feet. Before he knew what to do next I had lifted his feet, pulled off his shoes and stockings and was undoing the buttons of his flies. As I undid the last he was galvanised into action, dragging off his trousers and the white undergarment he had on underneath.

We stood naked together in the middle of the huge room, lit only by the moonlight that streamed through the floor-to-ceiling windows. He kissed me again on the lips but this time we lingered; our tongues met and explored each other's mouths. Our knees slowly buckled and we sank onto the thick piled carpet. He immediately diverted his attention to my breasts, pushing me down gently onto my back. Strangely, during the months at the Venus School for Young Ladies, little attention had been paid to my two fine assets. I was surprised and delighted as he first took each in his hands, caressing, kneading and smoothing them. Then he lowered his head and licked around each in turn, and between them, before returning to devote himself to my nipples. He passed from one to the other and back again, giving each its fair share of nibbling, chewing, sucking with his lips and teeth. I was in rapture. It felt that my breasts were swelling to huge proportions and my nipples growing longer and harder with each flick of his tongue. My fanny was throbbing with lust and my thighs were beginning to stick together with all the juices that were dribbling out of me.

I didn't want to move but I needed to feel him in my hands, my mouth, my cunt. While he continued to administer to my bosom I groped around until my hands found his thighs. My fingers travelled upwards, caressing the soft skin and there, there was his dangling sac and the long, hard shaft. My touch made him pause in his work on my breasts and I took the opportunity to slide out from under him and crawl around between his kneeling legs. He had a wonderful small, firm pair of buttocks. Now it was my turn to devote my attention to a part of his anatomy. My hands slid over the smooth skin of his bottom and I kissed and licked and nibbled at it. Then I pushed the two cheeks apart and licked down the crack. He tensed as my tongue found his tight arsehole. I lingered there pressing my tongue into the crinkled hole. He gasped and groaned. I wondered if I could bring him to orgasm by just playing with his arse but decided to leave that experiment for another occasion. My tongue continued its journey onwards until I reached his testicles. I opened my mouth wide and sucked in first one then the other to chew and nibble. I released his balls and twisted around so that I was under his long, smooth rod. I licked along its length drawing more moans from the distance.

I reached his circumcised knob and circled it with my tongue before drawing the whole head into my mouth.

While I had wanted to drink down the gondolier's juice I wanted something more from this young man and he was perfectly ready to oblige. He crawled backwards, his cock slipping from my mouth and sliding wetly between my breasts, over my stomach and through the patch of hair guarding my fanny. I in turn licked up his abdomen and chest until my mouth found his. He moved his knees to between my own and gently but insistently pushed my legs apart. The tip of his cock knocked at the door and found it ajar. In a moment he had entered and was travelling up my tunnel until he could go no further. I flung my arms around his back and wrapped my legs around his thighs, opening my hips wider and driving him in another inch. It felt so good to feel him deep inside me. He paused then and kissed my eyebrows and began to thrust. Each drive brought a grunt from me and an answering push. We matched rhythms, moving in harmony. I had been on the verge of orgasm the moment he started sucking my breasts and now wave after wave of pleasure passed over and through me. All sense had gone, I was solely, joyfully, a cylinder for his piston. And now he was crying out, arching his back and in one last, deep drive, spewing his seed deep into my womb.

I must have fainted or fallen asleep then because I next remember waking to find myself in a huge, soft bed. I opened my eyes to find his looking at me. He was leaning over me, the moonlight giving a pale blue sheen to his white skin. We kissed and soon we were making love again, this time with me sitting astride him and riding him as if he were my mount on a long and satisfying hunt. And so the night passed with periods of exhausted sleep interspersed with bouts of energetic and glorious intercourse.

The sun falling directly on my eyes woke me and told me it was late in the morning. I moved my head.

'Ah, you are awake.' He was standing at the foot of the bed with a tray. 'I have breakfast; are you ready for it?' I discovered that I certainly was hungry and ate ravenously before once again turning my attention to him. The taste of me on his cock was a pleasant dessert to the meats and cheeses of the meal. Despite his exertions through the night, his manhood was ready for more excitement. I drew gasps of wonder and amazement when I swallowed his knob and shaft and buried my nose in his pubic hair. He quickly pumped his load straight into my stomach and I pulled back, delighted to have given him an unexpected thrill.

'How do you do that?'

'I don't know. It's just a skill I discovered I have.'

'They didn't teach it at that school of yours.'

'Not that, but I have learned a lot of other things.'

'The only thing I learned at my school was to keep out of the way of the older boys who wanted to shove their cocks up my arse.' We laughed and chatted about life at his public school, childhood in his father's new large house and his intention of following his father into the engineering business.

'But first I have this grand tour to complete. Would you like to accompany me, Victoria?' I was tempted but wondered what Madame would say. 'We could return here before your vacation is complete so that you can travel back to your school,' he continued. The thought was certainly exciting. Not only would I see more of the continent but I would have a cock to fuck on any occasion I wished.

We dressed and returned to the house where we were staying. Madame was at first doubtful but a generous donation to the school drawn on Gilbert's bank convinced her. I went to my room to hurriedly pack my trunk but diverted to Natalie's room first. She was lying on her bed relaxing after having had an exhausting night's activity herself. She was disappointed that we would be apart for a couple of weeks but delighted with my brief description of Gilbert's lovemaking.

Soon I was back at Gilbert's hotel, on his bed and being fucked vigorously from behind. He told me that he had rowed while at Oxford and he was certainly an expert at using his thighs to drive his cock deep into my fanny. On each stroke he pulled out so that I felt his swollen knob between my lips then he drove in so that his balls crashed against my pubic bone and his shaft almost seemed to split me in two. Having come so much already it was some time before he approached orgasm but he did not tire, banging into me over and over again and driving me from one climax to another. Finally another spurt of semen sprayed my vagina and we sank into a heap amongst the luxurious bed linen.

The next day we took passage on a steamship to Rimini. We spent most of the journey in a tiny cabin. We lay together on the narrow bunk with his penis inside me. The rolling motion of the ship produced intriguing sensations as his cock rubbed against my canal. On land once again we set off for Florence, then on to Rome and Naples. At each famous city we spent two or three days idly admiring the treasures and ruins but really viewing each excursion as an interlude between sessions of energetic lovemaking in one sumptuous hotel suite after another. I got to know every part of his body and would spend hours kissing, licking and sucking on each square inch of skin. He quickly learned how my body responded to his touch and in particular how to wield his cock to bring me to extended and exhilarating climaxes.

On a hot afternoon in Naples we were lying naked on another vast bed.

'Have you had enough of hotels and trains and works of art?' he asked.

'Mmm,' I replied sucking on his cock.

'And people,' he continued, 'everywhere, crowds. Natives, visitors, servants.'

I pulled his penis from my mouth and looked at him.

'What do you mean?'

'Well, how about getting away from all this civilisation. Find a place where we can have a simple life. Just for a few days before you have to return to your headmistress.'

'Just us. It sounds wonderful. But how, where?' I caressed his shaft restoring its stiffness.

'I will have to enquire, but first ...' He pushed me on to my back and lifted my ankles on to his shoulders. I laughed and pulled the lips of my fanny apart to aid his entry. He thrust in and we bounced merrily on the bed for several minutes before he pumped his semen into me.

He left me dozing while he pulled on some clothes and went out.

The door opening awoke me and I sat up to hear his news.

'It is arranged.'

'What, already?' I couldn't believe how quickly he had been.

'Yes, luckily the hotel manager knows of someone with a home on one of the islands just off the mainland. A telegram confirmed that he has an empty house fit for habitation. He is now booking a fishing boat or something to carry us across. We can leave tomorrow morning.'

After the hustle and bustle of the cities, the island was like a very pleasant dream. Gilbert's arrangements had indeed gone like a dream and we had been ferried across the calm, blue waters to an idyllic island straight out of the myths of Homer or Virgil. The small, lime-washed cottage nestled amongst olive trees a few yards from a small cove. Although a simple peasant's home, it had a spring supplying a constant stream of water, and the owner supplied us with bread, olives, wine and other foodstuffs. There was a bed with a mattress and blankets and a fire to boil water. But most of all it was peaceful. There was no other habitation in sight and only the sound of seabirds and the waves on the shore.

We thanked the farmer for the use of his cart and his donkey for bringing us from the island's tiny harbour and waved as they slowly disappeared from view. Gilbert hugged me and swung me round.

'What do you want to do?' he said.

'Remove my clothes, run down to the beach and make love to you,' I replied, already pulling off my heavy dress. Gilbert beat me in stripping his clothes off but in a very short time we were racing naked down the path to the sandy cove. Although the air was warm the sea was still cold so we did not spend long in the water. We spent the afternoon sprawled on the beach kissing, licking, sucking and fucking and I discovered the discomfort of getting sand in one's fanny.

That afternoon established the pattern for the next few days. We lived like wild animals, naked during the days and huddled under the blankets when the nights turned cool, eating, sleeping and engaging in sexual intercourse. Gilbert's body became as familiar to me as my own. I knew every vein and crease in his prick and balls and his fingers and tongue explored every fold of tissue in my sex. He learnt where to touch me to produce an instant orgasm and I taught him to hold his erection for hour after hour. I wondered whether I was in love with him but decided that it was too soon to decide. I certainly lusted after him, my desire insatiable for his body, for the feel of his cock in my hands, filling my mouth or sliding in and out of my fanny. His company was a pleasure but was that enough for love? I was not sure.

At last our final day arrived. Reluctantly we packed our luggage and for the first time since we arrived put our thick, restricting clothes on.

As we sat in the small fishing boat carrying us back to mainland Italy neither of us spoke at first. With our port in sight Gilbert looked into my eyes.

'Thank you, Victoria. These few days together have been the best of my life. You have taught me so much.'

'Thank you too. What will you do after we return to Venice? Will you continue your grand tour?' We had not talked of 'after' at all and had only lived for the present.

'Yes, I suppose, but very soon I must return to complete my university career. Then there is the work for father and marriage.'

'Marriage?' It had not occurred to me at all that Gilbert would be considering getting married.

'Yes, my father is arranging for me to marry the daughter of one of his competitors. He intends that the two companies should merge when we complete the ceremony.'

'And when will that be?'

'August.' There was suddenly a hole in my heart. I hadn't considered marrying him myself but the thought of him with another woman saddened and sickened me.

We didn't speak of the future again and the pleasure that his body gave me overcame the regret that I would soon lose it. We had several nights and days of fucking still as we travelled back to Venice and then I was at the door of the house waving goodbye as he sailed off in his gondola. I didn't expect to see him again. I turned and entered the villa. Natalie bounded up to me.

'Victoria, at last! Oh, do tell me, was it wonderful? Where have you been? What have you seen? Do you love him?' She grabbed my arm and we walked upstairs to my room. She was already recounting her numerous liaisons.

Chapter 11
Victoria's Nature Walk

I reached the top of the ridge and looked around. It felt as though I was on top of the world although in truth there were much higher alpine peaks on the horizon. With the sun shining out of a clear blue sky I was hot and my thighs were as sticky as if I was anticipating a large cock about to slide between them. My heart was thumping just like when I was astride one of the boys and riding his manhood. But here there was no sign of mankind and no men, just my friend Natalie, panting up the last few steps of the climb.

'*Mon dieu*, Victoria, I am done. Your legs are longer than mine; I can't keep up with you.' I took her arm and helped her onto the flat rock that I was standing on.

'I'm sorry, Natalie, but it's worth it. Look around you. Isn't it wonderful.' The look on Natalie's face told me that she wasn't so sure.

'Where is the school? I cannot see it,' she said. The Venus School for Young Ladies was indeed out of sight beyond a lower ridge we had crossed some time ago. I pointed in the general direction of our home.

'It's over there.'

'We have come a long way,' Natalie said quite correctly. 'Can we rest now?'

'Yes, let's just go down a little way and find somewhere out of the sun.' I looked down the grass-covered slope dotted with the reds, blues and yellows of many varieties of

127

mountain flowers. Down in the valley there were trees but here close to the ridge there were none. I did see a few small shrubs apparently surrounding a small dell. I pointed.

'There, come on.' I took Natalie's hand and guided her down to what indeed turned out to be a hollow carpeted with thick grass. Natalie flopped down, relieved that the shrubs provided welcome shade. I sat beside her. Natalie wriggled in her cotton dress.

'Why do we have to wear such thick clothes in the summer?' she grumbled.

'We don't,' I replied, untying the ribbon of my bonnet. I removed the hat and shook out my long hair.

'What do you mean?'

I began to undo the buttons of my bodice. 'There's no one here to see us.' I completed the unfastening and stood up to push the dress down to my feet. Natalie looked at me uncertainly but then made her mind up and began to copy my actions. I removed my laced ankle boots and slipped the stocking from my legs. Then I pulled down my petticoat. Natalie was rapidly catching me up and we assisted each other in unlacing our corsets. At last and a little nervously we sat naked side by side.

Although the direct sun had been hot, the air, high in the mountains in May, was still cool. A refreshing breeze carried the clanging of distant cowbells to us and brushed our bodies, quickly cooling us. Natalie lay back and spread her legs.

'Ooh this is wonderful,' she giggled, 'I haven't been naked outdoors since I was a young child.'

I rested on my side gazing at her white skin. Seeing her body I could not resist sliding my hand up her satin thigh. She turned towards me and my hand slipped between her legs. Her lips found my nipple. She began to suck and I could feel both my breasts swelling and my nipples hardening. My hand reached the top of her groin and my fingers slipped between her lips finding her moist crack.

'What do we have here? Two shorn lambs?' The thick, slow German words took me by surprise. I withdrew my hand and twisted to see the source of the voice. I gasped with surprise when I saw the wild face looking at us from above a shrub. Long dark hair sprang in all directions around a heavily bearded face. Natalie squealed and threw her arms around me.

He moved from behind the bush and I gasped again. The man was naked. His body and limbs were covered with fine dark hair but every bit of skin was tanned a bronze colour. Obviously he spent a lot of time exposing himself to the sun. He crouched in the entrance to our dell, grinning at us through the mask of facial hair, a leather bag hanging from his shoulder and a stick grasped in his hand. He had quite the longest flaccid penis I had ever seen. It stretched down between his legs, almost touching the ground and with it a sac of testicles dangling like those of a bull.

'Who ... who are you?' I asked.

'I am Wolfgang the herdsman,' he replied.

'But you are naked,' I said pointlessly.

'And so are you.' He smiled and I could feel his eyes examining every part of my body and that of Natalie.

'We were hot and tired,' Natalie said as way of explanation. 'We wanted to cool down.'

'Most sensible,' he agreed. 'I imagine you are thirsty after your walk.' He put down his stick, opened the satchel and took out a leather bottle. He pulled out the cork and offered it to me. I realised that I was very thirsty after our climb and gratefully gulped a mouthful of the cool clear liquid. I passed the bottle to Natalie and she too drank from it.

'Thank you, sir. We appreciate your kindness. You said you were a herdsman. Where is your herd?'

'Down in the valley, keeping cool amongst the trees. You

129

can hear their bells.' He sat down on the grass, crossing his legs.

'They are your cattle?'

'I look after them, and goats and sheep. They belong to the landowner.'

'You live here?' Natalie asked. She had unwrapped herself from me and was showing an interest in this wild character.

'I have a wooden hut down by the river where I live throughout the year.'

'On your own,' I said on a hunch.

'That's right.'

'Why do you wander the hills without clothes?'

'Why not? In paradise Adam and Eve were naked and this is as good as paradise for me. I cannot bear woven fabrics rubbing my skin and, anyway, they get dirty and wear out. When my skin is grubby I dive into the river and wash it off.'

'The mountain water must be cold.'

'It is,' he grinned. 'Parts of me shrivel but it is refreshing.'

'But what about winter?' Natalie asked, sitting up with a light beginning to burn in her eyes. 'Surely you cannot remain naked when it is cold and icy.'

'I wrap myself in the skins and furs of the sheep and goats that I have slaughtered. But as soon as spring arrives I throw them off and spend the summer months free.' He finished with an expansive wave of his arms and I admired the firm muscles of his torso.

'How do you pass your time?' Natalie went on.

'I tend to my vegetable plot, bake bread with the flour the master brings for me and carve wood into stools and handles of tools.'

'What do you do for companions?' Natalie asked again.

'I have my animals.'

'And for pleasure?' she whispered, leaning forward.

'Ah, for that I have this.' He stretched out his legs and stroked his long manhood. Immediately it stiffened, not growing in length considerably but thickening and standing erect. 'I commit the sin of Onan, but Onan lived amongst his family and I have no one so I think perhaps God forgives me. I am never without it. It goes everywhere with me so morning, noon or night, wherever I may be, I can feel the pleasure of ejaculation.' He continued to caress his member, pulling on his knob and stretching it. I wondered if it had grown so long because of his frequent attention.

'But come,' he said leaping to his feet, his balls waving from side to side, 'you should not lie here getting cold. Gambol like lambs.' He laughed and offered his hands to pull us both to our feet. He picked up his stick and waved it around catching Natalie on her thigh. She screeched and ran past him to the hillside. I followed with Wolfgang behind me flailing his stick. I tried to run but with bare feet on the rough ground and the steep slope I hobbled rather than ran. I stumbled and fell to my knees, putting my hands in front of me to prevent myself from tipping forward. Immediately his large, rough hands were on my buttocks gripping my hips and pressing forward so that I could not climb back on to my feet. My arms buckled and my shoulders went down, raising my fanny to his gaze. A knee pushed my thighs apart further, and then I felt that long snake-like penis questing between my lips. It slid up and down searching for my hole. He passed the gate, thrust open the door and rushed down the passageway. I groaned as he filled me to the hilt.

Still grasping my hips he slid in and out. The muscles of his thighs, made strong by the mountain walking, allowed him the leverage to almost exit my channel before driving in again. I greeted each thrust with a cry and a demand for more. It seemed that I encouraged him, for his reciprocations increased in frequency. His testicles banged

131

against my pubic bone and I began to think that with all the masturbation he did he would not come in me. But then he too cried out and a great gush of fluid filled me.

His penis slid out from me and he fell backwards. I crawled around to face him and lowered my head to his dripping cock. I licked it, relishing the mixed taste of his semen and my juices that made it slick. I have to admit that he was fit, for in just a few minutes of my administrations his penis began to twitch and, instead of resting his head on the grass in a stupor, he was up on his elbows watching me as my mouth moved up and down his tool.

In a very short time he was erect and I was in two minds what to do with it.

'It's my turn now.' Natalie's demand took me by surprise. In my sexual daze I had completely forgotten her. She pushed me away from Wolfgang and climbed over him. She bent her knees and lowered her fanny towards his waving cock. She trapped it in her swollen lips then descended further. I watched avidly as the long penis disappeared up inside her vagina. He watched too, a look of wide-eyed awe on his face. I wondered with whom or what he had had sexual intercourse. He seemed so surprised by Natalie's initiative that I concluded that he had never before had a woman ride him.

Now Natalie was using her own strong, if short, thighs to move up and down on his stiff rod. In my experience no man could take this for many minutes however soon after his previous orgasm. Sure enough, with Natalie crying out with pleasure, in a few moments more, Wolfgang groaned, stretched his legs, arched his back and shuddered. Natalie collapsed on top of him holding his softening penis in her fanny.

We limped back to the hollow with Wolfgang holding the two of us in his arms. We lay on the grass and hugged and caressed each other. I buried my face in his pubic hair.

132

Because he lived naked and bathed frequently there was no staleness about his odour. I detected grass with a little wood smoke and cow. It was like having sex with the mountain itself.

After dozing for a time that I failed to measure, Wolfgang opened up his satchel again. As well as sharing the water, he took out a piece of rough bread, cheese and sausage and distributed it to us.

'I must be away,' he said looking up at the sky. 'I should check my herd before nightfall.' I was suddenly aware that the shadows were lengthening and the sun was no longer high in the sky.

'Good heavens,' I cried. 'Evening is approaching and we are miles away from home.'

Natalie jumped to her feet searching for her clothes.

'We'll miss supper. Madame Thackeray will be furious.' I too leapt up and tried to sort my clothes from the jumbled pile. We fumbled with each other's corsets at last getting them fastened if not tightly laced. Wolfgang sat grinning as he watched us struggle into our dresses.

'Which way do we go?' Natalie appealed, pulling her bonnet over her head.

'Oh, up to the ridge and then down again,' I flustered, pushing my feet into my boots.

'Calm, ladies,' Wolfgang said. 'I'll guide you.' He stood up, put his satchel over his shoulder, picked up his stick and took our hands.

It felt very strange climbing the hill with a naked man between us, but without his guidance I do not think we would have got on to our correct way. At the ridge he pointed out our path across the next valley and on to the ridge above the school. We set off. I looked back once and saw his silhouette above the ridge but when I looked again he had gone.

It was difficult climbing down and impossible to hurry.

By the time we reached the track that took us back to the school, the sun had long since set behind the mountains and the sky was darkening. Eventually we walked up to the thick wooden door and hammered on it. After a few moments, Eric, one of the servant lads, opened the door.

'There you are. Madame has been demanding to know where you were.'

We stepped into the hall as the door to Madame's study opened. Madame emerged, a look of thunder on her face.

'Victoria, Natalie. Come here at once. How dare you go wandering and miss supper. Into my study now!' She shepherded us through the door and into her study bedroom. She picked up the crop which was in its accustomed position on her desk.

'Remove your clothes,' she commanded, 'you will be punished for such wanton behaviour.'

For the second time that day we undid our ties and buttons and helped each other out of our corsets. Once again we stood naked, but this time our legs trembled with anticipation of Madame's wrath.

'Both of you. Bend over the stool.' She pointed to the elephant-shaped stool which I had been bent over alone on a number of occasions, and we did as we were told. The curved shape of the padded leather back meant that Natalie and I slid together. I was able to bend over it with my toes still touching the floor but Natalie's short legs left her dangling like a sack of potatoes.

I waited for the pain that I knew would come. There was a swish through the air, and my buttocks clenched but the blow fell on Natalie, not me. She yelped and jerked. The next one was for me. A stripe of fire burned across my left buttock and I too yelled. One after another the blows came, some on Natalie's behind and some on mine. My mind was not on whether we were receiving a fair distribution of the blows. All I knew was that my buttocks were aflame and that between my sobs I could hear Natalie wailing. Madame paused, puffing slightly.

'Now where have you been?' she demanded.

'I'm sorry Madame,' I cried plaintively. 'We went for a walk in the mountains and forgot the time.'

'You silly girls. Don't you know how dangerous the mountains can be? You may have fallen and injured yourselves. There are wild animals and there is the Goat Man.'

'The Goat Man?' Natalie and I said in unison.

'Yes. They say he wanders the mountains naked and has intercourse with the goats that he herds. He's quite mad and probably dangerous. Heaven knows what he would do if he came across two stupid girls like you out for a Sunday stroll.' She brought the crop down on each of our buttocks twice more, drawing yet more cries from our sore throats.

'Now pick up your clothes and go upstairs. There is no supper for you tonight.' We apologised for our misbehaviour, thanked Madame for our punishment and hurried out with our clothes bundled in our arms.

We went together to the room I shared with Beatrice. Bea was away from school for some reason so I knew we could be alone together. I dropped my clothes on the floor and jumped on the bed sobbing. My poor maltreated buttocks were so sore. Natalie joined me and we lay together face down.

'Do you think Wolfgang is the Goat Man?' she asked.

'Of course he is; there's not going to be two naked herdsmen wandering the hills, are there?'

'No I suppose not. But do you think he fucks his goats?'

I remembered how Wolfgang had taken me from the rear like an animal when I had stumbled forward, how he had gripped my hips, preventing me from escaping his penetrating thrust. I could see him gripping a nanny goat in a similar manner, and I considered how surprised he had been

135

when Natalie had ridden him.
'I think he probably does.'

Chapter 12
Victoria's Birthday

The evening sunlight streaming in through the open window gave our skin a golden glow as the six of us sat perched on our straight-backed chairs as we had done on many evenings throughout our year at the Venus School for Young Ladies. Each of us wore a scarlet basque and stockings signifying that we had had the experience of a penis slipping into our vaginas on at least one occasion. For I think all of us, it was in fact many bouts of intercourse and at least six different cocks. I was trying to concentrate on what Madame Thackeray was saying although in truth I was too excited to sit still as it was my birthday.

'I know you have learnt a great deal here,' Madame continued. 'You have begun to learn the skills required by a wife, a hostess, a housekeeper, a woman of finance. You know and understand a little of culture and art, of couture and gastronomy, of business and politics. You have also commenced your training in the arts of pleasure. I believe you have come to understand your own bodies, the source of your desires, the means of your arousal and you have begun to discover what motivates others to seek satisfaction in relationships with other men or women. You have all developed skills, some more than others.' Here, for some reason, Madame glanced to the end of our row. For a moment her gaze fell on me and I blushed and wondered what she could mean.

'But do not think that your education is complete. Very soon you will be returning to your homes for the summer vacation. It is wise to practise the techniques you have learned but do not for one moment consider that you have acquired all the wisdom necessary to understand the nature of love. You are but a part of the way on your journey. In September you will return to continue your studies and I can promise you that Madame Hulot and I will work you hard to complete your education.'

The events of the past nine months flashed through my mind. I recalled the effort and embarrassment in our initial fumblings but principally I remembered the pleasure I had discovered in using my body and the skills I had learned to bring satisfaction to myself and my partners. I also revelled in the glow of friendship that my seventeenth birthday had highlighted. My close friend Natalie had made me laugh early this morning when she gave me her present, a handkerchief embroidered with scenes from the Kama Sutra. Later Beatrice had presented me with a very strange object: a soft rubber cup with a metal spring in its rim. She called it a Mensinga diaphragm which meant absolutely nothing at all to me. She said it was a device to prevent the risk of pregnancy during intercourse. Of course she had to show me how to use it. While I lay on the bed, she knelt between my legs and parted my labia. Then she squeezed the rim of the cup and inserted it into my quim. She pushed it up inside me and released it. I could barely feel it but she said it would sit over the opening into my womb and prevent the seed from entering. Naturally, Bea didn't finish there. Having removed her fingers from my hole she lowered her head and began kissing and licking my crack. Accustomed as she was with my likes and dislikes she soon had me writhing and begging her to stop, no, to continue. She gripped my buttocks in her hands and held on, her tongue lapping at my juices and teasing my clitoris. My orgasm went on and on until I sank back breathless and Bea released me.

'There,' she said, 'that was another part of your birthday present.'

I awoke from my reverie to find Madame still talking and once again looking straight at me.

'But, of course, this evening is a special occasion as it is Victoria's birthday.' The other girls clapped politely. 'Stand up, Victoria, and come here.'

I did as I was told and took the few steps necessary to stand alongside Madame with my back to the fur-covered divan. I faced my five fellows who were tittering in anticipation, of what I had no idea.

'Now, Victoria,' Madame continued, 'as we have few evenings left, we have a treat for you and the rest of the girls.' She clapped her hands sharply, just once, and immediately the door opened. The six young men entered, led by Eric. Each was barefooted and barelegged but wore a black silk gown which reached to mid-thigh. They formed up into a line facing me and Madame but at right angles to the line of chairs occupied by my classmates. Madame clapped her hands again and, as one, the six men removed the gowns to reveal their naked bodies, each of which shone with a bronze light in the evening sunshine. All six cocks rose to attention like the instruments of a row of trumpeters preparing to blow a fanfare.

Eric, fair and tall, stood proudly to attention with his marvellously proportioned cock. Next to him was Hermann, dark, not as tall but more thickset, with a penis of matching girth. Then there was Johann, with his straw-coloured hair and his massive circumcised purple knob. Alongside stood Mario, the dark Latin lover of the group with his strangely curved tool bending upwards like the prow of a ship. The penultimate was Wilhelm, the oldest by a few years but who nevertheless displayed magnificent musculature beneath thick dark hair and an eager manhood. Last was Albert, the smallest and youngest who yet had the largest, thickest, most intimidating penis of the lot.

There was no sound. Every one of us held our breath and awaited some signal for whatever was to begin. I was stupefied. Yes, of course I had seen each one of those fine tools before. Every last one had entered me on numerous occasions. I had seen two or even three of the boys in action at once as we practised some technique or other. But never had all six paraded their masculinity in such a fashion before us.

'Commence,' Madame commanded and stepped aside. The six men moved towards me. I felt a sudden fear. What was expected of me? What was going to happen? I stood still waiting for some signal.

Eric stood in front of me, while the others formed a circle around me.

'Happy birthday, Victoria,' he said in his strong German accent. Then he leant forward, took my face in his hands and kissed me on the lips. His tongue pushed between them and I opened my mouth to accept him. At the same I felt fingers working to undo the lace ties of my basque, pulling on the ribbon of my knickers and unfastening my silk stockings from the suspenders. While Eric continued to explore the interior of my mouth and I rubbed my tongue against his, the few clothes I was wearing were removed. In moments I was naked.

Eric released my mouth, his tongue flicking my lips as he parted. Firm hands grasped my thighs and my shoulders. An arm or two encircled my waist. I was lifted up and carried a step to the divan where they laid me gently on my back. My legs were parted and my hands held. For a moment I felt vulnerable, and then the sensations started. Gentle hands caressed my thighs from knee to crotch. Fingers played my arms as if finding notes on a flute. More fingers smoothed my brow. Still more hands palpitated my abdomen, circled my breasts and at last reached my nipples, which were already as hard as acorns. My mind was overwhelmed with the sense of touch. Every square inch of my skin seemed to be in contact with the sixty fingers and thumbs that were presumably active. Eventually a hand found my sex and for a moment the burst of electricity drove away all other sensations as the fingertips parted my lips and found my little knob. Then all the nerve endings fired in unison and my brain seemed to explode.

One by one the hands were replaced by mouths. A tongue, it may have been Eric's again, slipped inside my gaping, panting mouth. Moist, warm lips and tongues sucked on my fingers then ran up my arms to find my nipples. Others sucked my toes, and another quested deep within my channel. I had been immobile, frozen by the variety of feelings, but now I waved my hands in an almost random fashion. The fingers of my left and right hand simultaneously found two dangling sacs each containing two hard but mobile nuts. I held them while their owners continued to suck on my breasts. The sacs were connected to two hard shafts. I gripped them, squeezing almost involuntarily as the tongue and mouth drew hard on my clitoris. I was vaguely aware of sounds – clapping, laughter, raised voices urging the men on.

The tongue retreated from my mouth and I was conscious of its owner shifting his position to squat over me. His cock touched my lips and I opened my mouth to accept him greedily. The head slipped inside and I sucked on the swollen knob. The other tongues moved away too and my feet were lifted, parted and held against the crotches. I felt pubic hair under my toes and my heels pressed against their erections forced from their horizontal positions.

With my vision obscured by the root of the shaft that was thrust in my mouth, the swinging balls and the lean buttocks either side of the puckered arsehole, I could not see which man kneeling between my legs was in possession of the ramrod that then thrust into my cunt. My legs stiffened but were held firmly in their embrace. My grip on the two cocks tightened and I clamped my lips around the shaft that was pushing towards the back of my throat. The long, thick penis penetrated me as far as it could. I could almost feel it bashing at the rubber diaphragm that protected my womb.

Then all the men began to move in rhythm as if taking part in some strange dance. The two that had penetrated my mouth and sex moved their members in and out, the two in my hands strained to push and pull and the two that held my feet pressed them against their crushed balls. The reciprocating movement was hypnotic and I almost swooned before reaching a shuddering climax and was filled from two ends with gobbets of semen.

While still gulping down the creamy fluid and before I was aware of what had happened the penises withdrew from my mouth and sex, my feet were released and the cocks slipped out of my hands. I was turned on to my stomach and lifted to my knees. Then hands gripped the side of my head and pulled me down onto another erect manhood. Without thinking I opened my mouth to accept it. My lips slid down the shaft and the knob rubbed against the back of my throat. Once upon a time I may have gagged but I was proud of my skill to ignore the feeling and take the cock as deep as its owner wished.

My buttocks were parted and I felt a fresh, hard cock rub against the crack between them before finding and entering my fanny. It was thrust in to the hilt. It felt as if the two cocks would meet somewhere in my abdomen. I loved it. I slid up and down the two shafts as if they were connected and formed a single thick rod on which I was skewered. My movement drew a response. The two men groaned and moaned as they made their thrusts until almost simultaneously they spewed their loads of sperm into my two orifices.

Once again there was no pause as the two withdrew. I sucked the last drop of semen as the penis reversed out of my gullet. Hands grasped my armpits and hoisted me up. A man slid between my legs. I glanced down to see Hermann lying on his back, his cock towering up towards me. I was lowered gently and guided on to his organ as if impaled on a spike. With my crack and thighs slick with fluid he slid in with no resistance whatsoever despite his girth. The arms released me and I squatted with my buttocks pressing on his testicles. I straightened my back. For the first time I looked around and took in what was happening. My four spent lovers were reclining on the floor being ministered to by my classmates. They too were now naked and were licking the juices from the cocks and balls of the young men. I looked down at Hermann lying beneath me, his penis throbbing deep in my channel and his arms reaching up to grasp my pendulous breasts.

Little Albert climbed onto the divan and stood over Hermann. His immensely long cock waved in front of my face. Once again I opened my mouth, this time as wide as possible in order to accommodate Albert's girth. I raised my bottom and Hermann began to thrust his hips upwards. Despite having had four men already I was now unstoppable. I was desperate to bring these two proud tools to a spurting climax.

When I first met Albert he would come in seconds but now he was as experienced as I and we worked together for minutes on end while Hermann utilised his own youthful muscles. Eventually, with both men grunting like pigs, they both filled me and I too shuddered to an orgasm.

Now fatigue hit me and I sank onto the bed, rolling off Hermann to lie on my back. I thought that would be it. I had satisfied the six boys. Each had shot their loads inside me. With them finished I would slide into a well-deserved and satisfied sleep. But this was not what they had planned for me. As my eyes closed and my breathing stilled, I was aware of a softer, smoother face between my thighs and a hot tongue lapping at my sopping cunt. I raised my head just sufficiently to see that it was my friend Natalie who was cleaning the love juices from my fanny. She worked eagerly, removing the slick fluids and soothing my swollen parts. I watched as Eric moved behind her, knelt and presented his rejuvenated cock to her raised behind. His entry took Natalie by surprise. She paused in her sucking, looked up and caught my eye. A huge smile spread across her face as Eric's cock slid into her; then she resumed her ministrations. Eric began to rock back and forth and the vibrations passed through Natalie to me. Each thrust of his penis pushed Natalie's face deeper into my sex. The pace quickened and Natalie licked and sucked feverishly with each oscillation. I could feel her starting to quiver as her climax approached and I felt a similar sensation in my abdomen. Eric was crying out on each drive forwards and now as my own orgasm took over I clamped my thighs around Natalie's head. I think the three of us came together. I can only guess at the moment that Eric's cock propelled its cargo into Natalie's vagina but she ceased to chew on my knob at the moment that I succumbed.

I thought that now I would be allowed to relax but as Natalie sank back onto the floor, another girl, Freya, I think, from the colour of her pubic hair, clambered over me to take her turn lapping at my mount. Her knees were planted on either side of my head and I looked up her thighs into her gaping hole. It occurred to me then, in that moment of tranquillity, that we are all different. The sparse, fair curls of hair and the pink engorged folds of skin that guarded the entry to her canal varied in colour and shape to mine or indeed any other woman's that I had examined. They were as different as the features on a face. I wondered if it would be possible to recognise a person from the convolutions of her vulva or the form of his penis. Freya was licking at me enthusiastically and her excitement showed in the moisture glistening in her quim. A tiny drip rolled out of the crack, hung on a wisp of hair then fell onto my lower lip. I licked it and my mouth filled with the flavour of girl and sex. I was about to reach up and pull her down to my mouth to suck more of her honey but before I could do so a long, erect cock appeared and speared her hole. The owner of this magnificent organ knelt just behind my head and while his sac swung from side to side above my forehead I had the closest view possible of a penis fucking a cunt. I could see every swollen vein, every crease in the skin, and with each retreat the purple head appeared only to disappear again straight after.

Despite the distraction of the shaft sliding in and out of her crack, Freya devoted herself to keeping me on the crest of a continuous orgasm. My nether region felt as if every nerve fibre was burning with excess electricity, an electric light with too high a voltage about to burn out and explode in a brilliant, if short-lived, flash. I watched the pistoning penis appear and disappear inside Freya's hole faster and faster until ... he withdrew. The glistening, dripping rod dipped and pulsed and a flood of white salty fluid sprayed over my face. I licked my lips, catching the drops of fluid as if they were the nectar of the gods.

Then Freya crawled away and my memory becomes clouded because it seems that I just lay on the bed as penis after penis filled my channel one after another, each taking its turn, each thrusting, banging into me, minute after minute, hour after hour, until each, exhausted and relieved of its cream, shrivelled and withdrew.

At some point I fell into a stupor. When I regained consciousness it was to find someone wiping my face with a cool, damp cloth. I opened my eyes to see Madame

145

Thackeray sitting by my side wielding the flannel.

'Magnificent, my dear,' she said softly, 'you have drained them all.' I attempted to sit up but found that every part of my body was as heavy as lead. I succeeded in raising my head and saw that scattered around the divan were naked bodies, male and female, prostrate, dissolute and fast asleep. I realised that it was now dark and two or three oil lamps provided the light for me to survey the scene.

'Rest, Victoria. Recover your strength. It may be a while before you feel like having a man, or a woman, between your legs again.' She covered me with a cotton sheet, kissed me on the cheek and left me. After a few moments I drifted into a deep and refreshing sleep.

I awoke to find the morning sun lighting the sky and filling the room. For a moment I was unsure where I was and then I realised I was still on the divan in the drawing room and the memory of the previous evening's activities returned. I confess to feeling proud of myself. I had taken on six lusty lads and drained the spunk from them. The memories were making me smile with satisfaction when the door opened and Natalie entered.

'Ah, Victoria, you are awake,' she whispered. She was dressed in a simple slip which barely covered her bottom. She came to me and sat on the side of the couch. 'How do you feel after your adventure? You were incredible.' I confessed to being a little stiff and sore in my nether regions and that my memory of the proceedings was a little confused, particularly after the first round of intercourse with the boys.

'But, Victoria, you were insatiable. You lay back with your knees up and your thighs wide apart and goaded them into filling you up one after the other. You bounced and thrust on the couch until each spilled his load and then you urged the next to take his place.' I expressed some surprise since my part in this activity was like something in a dream. 'Each of the men came at least four times during the evening and you had most of them. We just helped them to recover between bouts.' She giggled, lifted the sheet that covered me and placed a hand on my poor overused fanny. 'I can still feel the heat,' she said.

'It is indeed burning,' I admitted.

'Then come with me. We have a bath prepared and soothing lotions to hasten your recovery.' She pulled the sheet from me, took my arm and gently helped me to my feet. My legs felt as wobbly as if I had undergone a strenuous activity, which I suppose I had. I climbed the stairs like an old lady, one step at a time in the arms of my dear friend.

The bath was indeed a pleasure and the administration of the cooling creams by Natalie's gentle fingers brought considerable ease to my discomfort. Later I lay in my bed and entertained guests. Madame Thackeray called to congratulate me on my display of uninhibited sexual pleasure. The other girls came to giggle and gossip about what they had seen and done and one by one the boys visited, bowed, kissed my hand and thanked me for giving them such satisfaction. I asked coyly about the state of their members after such activity and they confessed to being a little sore themselves. After the last one left I rested my head on my pillow and reflected on the most enjoyable and memorable birthday I had had so far in my short life.

Chapter 13
Victoria's Vacation Occupation

I was bored. Just a week spent in my father's town house had left me frustrated and wishing that I was back at the Venus School for Young Ladies. My father left home early in the morning and did not return until late evening so we had little time to talk or entertain guests. He had also dismissed most of the servants for some reason, just leaving me with a single maid and the cook-cum-housekeeper. With no governess I had no chaperone to accompany me to the shops or the parks, although in the hot summer weather that we were having, the odour of the city made a walk outside somewhat unpleasant. When I did see my father I pleaded to be allowed to go to our Berkshire home but he said he didn't want me dilly-dallying with the country folk. I think he was referring to Bill, the stable-lad I once fancied. So I remained shut inside the stuffy house with no one to converse with or to entertain me.

In the mornings, before I had my maid fit me into my corset, I lay in my bed fingering my nipples and rubbing a hand against my clitoris. Just thinking of Eric's or Albert's thick cock was enough to give me a brief orgasm but it was nothing to the sensations they and the other boys had engendered. I missed their company as much as their attributes and I also missed the chatter and the touch of my friend Natalie. During the day, dressed in my petticoats and high-necked dresses I could do little other than sit in the library and read improving literature. I was bored.

Thus it was that I received a letter from Beatrice with great excitement. Though I had shared a room with Bea at school, I had not seen much of her in the last months of the term. She was mysteriously absent; marrying a gentleman was, I thought, the most likely explanation. Her letter reported that she was now established in a south coast resort and invited me to join her for a few weeks over the summer. I was so excited, I could not even wait for my father to return to ask his permission so I started packing straight away, and I think my maid was surprised by my efforts. When Father returned late that evening I was waiting with my request. In fact I think he was pleased to pass me into someone else's charge even though Bea was only a year or so older than me. He approved my vacation as long as suitable travelling arrangements could be made. Hence a couple of days later I was put on the train to Brighton.

The cab delivered me in late afternoon to an elegant Regency town house. A smartly dressed maid opened the door and guided me to the drawing room. Bea rose from her chair as I entered and I marvelled at the colours in her silk tea dress.

'Oh, Victoria, it is so wonderful to see you. I am so pleased that you could come to stay.' She kissed me on the cheek and gestured for me to sit beside her on a settee. I looked around at the newly decorated room filled with rich furnishings and exquisite ornaments.

'Is this your husband's?' I enquired, worried that I may be a little presumptuous.

Bea giggled, 'I am not yet married, Victoria, and have no intention of being.'

'But this wonderful house. Is it yours?' I knew of no

single woman, certainly of Beatrice's age, who owned such property.

She laughed, 'Well, yes and no. It belongs to a trust of which I am the sole beneficiary. I have patrons who have contributed to it and continue to support me.'

'Patrons?' I asked innocently.

'Gentlemen. Come, let me show you around. I'm afraid the decoration work has not yet been finished but your room is ready.'

Bea led me from the drawing room and back into the wide hallway. She showed me the dining room set for dinner in the evening and then guided me up to the first floor to her bedroom and then to mine. Both rooms had a wonderful view over the promenade and the sea and both had the unheard-of luxury of their own bathrooms. I also noticed that both rooms were thickly carpeted and equipped with large comfortable beds, ample wardrobes and chests of drawers, more than adequate gas lighting and plenty of mirrors. Back on the landing Bea pointed to the stairs leading to the second floor.

'There will be two more bedrooms on the next floor and the maids' quarters are in the attic.'

'Do you intend to take guests?' I asked. Bea looked at me as if I had missed something.

'I will be employing a couple of suitably qualified young ladies to occupy the rooms.'

I realised at last the venture that Bea had undertaken.

'Oh, I see. And these ladies will entertain your patrons.'

'No, that will be my pleasure, but there will be friends and acquaintances that will require, ah, entertainment. For example, this evening we will be welcoming one of my patrons, Sir Stephen, who will be bringing a guest. I do hope that you will be able to satisfy the guest while I attend to Sir Stephen's desires.'

I grasped what Bea was intending and nodded my

agreement. Bea took my arm and escorted me back downstairs.

'Now tell me about the end of the term at the Venus School. I hear that you had an exciting party.' We giggled together as I described what had happened on my seventeenth birthday.

Dinner was a pleasant affair. Sir Stephen was a healthy forty-year-old banker who was evidently much enamoured with Bea. They gossiped and giggled throughout the meal and Sir Stephen's hand spent a lot of time resting on Bea's thigh. The other guest was a business colleague of Sir Stephen who told me in a soft voice that his name was Theophilus. Older than Sir Stephen, rather more portly and a little shy, he was nevertheless pleasant company. He chatted to me about the banking profession while Bea and Sir Stephen laughed at each other's jokes. When the fine meal was over, Bea and Sir Stephen stood.

'We'll, hmm, retire now,' Sir Stephen said.

'Look after Theophilus, Victoria,' Bea instructed.

'I will,' I replied and looked at the banker who had turned a shade of pink. I held out a hand to him. 'Shall we withdraw, too?' I asked. He swallowed and nodded.

I led him up the stairs. There were already muffled shrieks and laughter coming from Bea's room. I opened the door to my bedroom and stood aside to let Theophilus enter. He looked at the bed rather uncertainly and turned to look at me. I realised that if anything was to come of this union then I would have to take the lead. I closed the door behind me and stepped onto the carpet.

'Can you help me unbutton this dress, please, Theophilus, it is so tight and I would like to get out of it.' His fingers, used to counting out sovereigns and guineas no doubt, also proved adept at unfastening the tiny buttons. Soon I was able to step out of the full dress and then push

151

down one, two, three, four petticoats. That left me standing before him in my tightly laced corset that squeezed my waist and stretched from my bosom to my thighs.

'Please, Theophilus, can you release me from this constraint?' This time his hands shook as he took hold of the cords and undid the garment.

When the corset fell to the floor, Theophilus let out a small gasp. I allowed him to gaze at my body; after all, I was proud of my figure. I watched his eyes taking in my bosom, my flat stomach, the V of hair at my crotch.

'You are most attractive, Victoria,' he whispered.

'Come, let us see your attractions,' I said in an attempt to lighten the atmosphere and move the proceedings along. Theophilus stood still, not knowing what to do next. I knelt at his feet and began to unbutton his trousers. He took the hint and took off his jacket, undid his bow tie and began to undo his shirt. Soon he was standing before me in his combinations. I confess I tittered a little behind my hand as he did look a little like a penguin standing there in the evening light.

I eventually got him out of his undergarment and looked at his rather unprepossessing body with a little disappointment. A small, sad penis and crumpled sac dangled between his two scrawny thighs. I was not sure that I relished engaging in the arts of love with this middle-aged, somewhat overweight gentleman however pleasant he was as a dinner companion. Nevertheless I had promised Bea that I would look after him so I would do so. I was still considering how to start when Theophilus signalled to me to lie on the bed. I did as I was told, wondering what he intended.

He began with my toes. He caressed each between his soft fingers then sucked on each in turn. Then he kissed my feet, one after the other, and on to my ankles. His moist, warm tongue touched my calves and my knees and then

152

stopped. He moved to my side and repeated his actions on the fingers of my left hand, caressing my hand and arm right up to my armpit. Then he did the same to my right arm. He rolled me over on my stomach and returned to my legs, licking the back of my thighs right up to my buttocks, then starting at my neck and shoulders working down my back making sure that every square inch of skin received attention from his lips and tongue.

By this time I was in delight. Every touch was an electric shock and a telegraph signal that my fanny responded to with an itch that became a fire of longing. I wanted something to enter me, to fill me up, to rub my knob and make me come. But he wouldn't. He went on with his patient licking. He circled my buttocks then ran his tongue up the crack pausing to repeatedly orbit my arsehole.

Then he turned me over and began again at my neck and worked down to my bosom. He spent a lot of time on my breasts and nipples and every minute that passed made me more desperate for a climax. Finally he moved down to my stomach, lingered around my navel and then buried his face in my curls. At his urging I opened my thighs and at last I felt his lips on mine and his tongue delving deep into my crack. I know that my juices were flowing and he drank deeply, slurping up the liquid. He found my knob and began sucking. Now at last I found release. I bucked as my orgasm ripped through me but he held on, clasping my hips in his hands and keeping his mouth locked to my quim.

As my climax passed I peered down to look at him kneeling between my legs. His little penis had grown a little but even erect was still no bigger than a chipolata. He raised his head and came forward to plant a kiss on my lips. I tasted my sex on him. I was barely aware of him entering me and a few moments and grunts later he came and subsided by my side. I marvelled at how one so considerate with his foreplay, who had brought me to a peak of excitement with his lips, could be so ineffective at intercourse.

Theophilus was asleep and snoring softly. I pulled the sheets over us and I too fell into a slumber.

I awoke with the morning sunshine streaming into the room. I was alone and there was no sign of Theophilus or that he had spent the night with me except that when I looked at the table alongside the bed I noticed a gold coin. I picked it up and looked at it. It was a whole sovereign. I had never held so much money in my own hands although I knew that my father dealt with hundreds every day. I pulled on a gown and went downstairs. Bea was in the dining room eating breakfast, alone.

'Good morning, Victoria. How are you?'

'Very well, Bea. Where are Sir Stephen and Theophilus?'

'Oh, they left this hour since. Business. Theophilus asked me to thank you for a most enjoyable night.'

'That was very kind. I think he left this behind.' I held up the coin.

'That is for you, Victoria. It is the sum agreed for your service and expertise.'

'You mean that Theophilus has paid one pound to spend a night in my bed?' I knew that many families lived for a week on just one pound.

'That's right. Do you think it is enough? Should I charge more?'

'Good heavens, I don't know, Bea, it is a lot of money. It is just that I haven't been given money before, for any reason.'

'Well, you wouldn't service someone like Theophilus for nothing, would you? I haven't seen him without his clothes but I can't imagine he was a pretty picture.'

'Well, no, but he did do lovely things to me.' I described Theophilus' lovemaking.

Beatrice looked surprised, 'He did that? There's a surprise. Well, that was a bonus for you. He was very happy to pay.'

'So the money is mine.'

'That's right.'

'Don't you want a share to pay for your expenses?'

'Not from you, Victoria. You are my friend. But when the girls occupy the other bedrooms I will be taking a percentage.'

'Ah, now I see, Bea. This is a commercial venture is it not? A house of delights.'

'Yes, Victoria. My patrons have put up the capital and of course get preferential treatment but we will be welcoming paying customers. This way I get as much pleasure as I want and control my own affairs. And you are welcome to join me until it is time for you to return to your home or school.'

I considered what Bea was offering. It promised to be a lot more fun than staying shut up in my father's stuffy house, and lucrative too. I resolved to remain and join in with Bea's endeavour.

In reality my stay was very relaxed. We spent the days reading in the drawing room or taking a stroll along the seafront. Most evenings we entertained one or other of Bea's patrons and their friends or guests. Although none of the men was as virile as the boys at the school, I nevertheless found the exercise quite satisfying and I was content to stuff the growing number of gold coins into my luggage.

One morning at breakfast Bea looked up from buttering her crumpet.

'Today we are having a different sort of guest, Victoria.'

'Oh,' I replied.

'His name is Neville and he will be arriving shortly to spend the day with us.'

I grinned, 'All day. He must have some stamina.'

Bea shook her head. 'No, it won't be like that. He wants our company and our assistance. Come with me.' She took my hand and led me up to her bedroom. There was a large trunk in the centre of the room. It was open and I could see that it was filled with petticoats, corsets, dresses and other items of ladies' attire.

'Neville had this delivered early this morning.' I was nonplussed but before I could question Bea further the front door bell rang.

'That will be him now. Come, let's greet him.' I followed Bea back down to the hallway where the maid was showing a man through the door. He removed his hat and looked up at us as we approached. He was in his twenties with a smooth white face and short light brown hair, slightly built and no more than a couple of inches taller than me.

Bea welcomed him with a kiss on his cheek and he blushed.

'Welcome, Neville. This is Victoria. She is going to help us out today.' He took my hand and kissed it graciously. We exchanged greetings and I began to anticipate the feel of his soft hands and lips on my skin.

'Let's go upstairs and make a start.' Bea turned and mounted the stairs with Neville and me following. All three of us entered Bea's bedroom and she closed the door behind us.

'Now, Neville, let us get you undressed.' There was something about Bea's tone that surprised me; she wasn't acting as if she was getting ready to pleasure this young man. She helped him out of his jacket and shirt and let him remove his shoes and undo and pull down his trousers. He stood in front of us in a pair of drawers and nothing else, while neither Bea nor I had made any move to remove any clothing whatsoever.

'Let's get rid of those too, shall we?' Bea pointed to his underwear. Self-consciously he pulled the garment down and stood naked in front of us. He had a neat cock which nestled against his balls but showed no sign of interest in any action.

'Now, before we make a start we will have to hide that, won't we, Neville,' Bea continued but I was at a loss to understand what she was talking about. Neville nodded, however, and Bea reached into the trunk and pulled out a roll of bandage. She wound it around Neville's waist and then passed it down between his legs and up between his buttocks. She pulled tight and his penis and scrotum were pulled up and back. She wound the bandages around and between his legs a few times and then tied off the ends. Now Neville stood before us with no sign that he possessed a manhood.

'That's better, isn't it, Neville? No dangly bits to spoil the appearance.' Neville smiled thinly. Bea reached into the trunk and pulled out a white satin corset, 'Would you like to wear this one today?' Neville nodded and at last I realised what we were about.

'Oh, I see. Neville wants to dress up as a lady,' I said aloud, laughing. A cloud descended over Neville's face, and Bea glowered at me.

'It's not funny, Victoria. And Neville doesn't want to just dress as a lady, he wants to be a lady, don't you, Neville?' Neville nodded.

'I'm sorry I laughed,' I said, rather taken aback by Bea's fierce support for the strange young man. Then I remembered that Neville was probably paying us handsomely for the day's activities.

Bea held the corset around Neville's torso and began to do up the laces.

'Help me, Victoria. Let's see how tight we can get it.' Together we pulled on the laces, cinching Neville's waist. I was sure it must be hurting a great deal but apart from one or two grunts he did not complain at all. It was obvious that he had worn a corset before. At last, when he was fastened from buttocks to shoulder blades, we had reduced his waist to about twenty-four inches and I wondered whether he could breathe. Bea stuffed some cloth into the bosom completing his S-figure. The rest was straightforward, stockings, a number of full petticoats and an elegant white high-necked dress. Neville was beginning to look feminine. As we added layer after layer he looked in the mirror and gradually began to smile with approval. We placed dainty silk slippers on his feet.

Bea asked him to sit at her dressing table and she got to work with powders and creams, turning his male features into a passable imitation of a woman. The final transformation was a wig of long blonde curls that cascaded over his shoulders. At last he took one final look in the mirror then stood up and faced us. He spoke in a soft, higher-pitched voice.

'Thank you, Beatrice and Victoria. You have done a marvellous job. Now you may call me Amelia.'

We went downstairs and sat in the drawing room while Bea's maid brought us tea. I noticed that Neville, or rather Amelia, took only a few sips of hers. Amelia explained that he or she, I was not sure how to think, had from a young age desired to be female. Now that he had inherited from his deceased parents he was learning what it meant to be a woman in our age.

'Perhaps one day I will dress as a woman all the time,' she ended. 'Shall we go out now?'

'Out,' I said, 'you want us to go out with you dressed like a woman.'

'Of course,' Bea said calmly, 'that was always part of the day's plan.'

'But what if someone sees us?' I asked.

'What will they see?' Bea shrugged.

'Three women,' Amelia said, 'or to be more precise two

beautiful young ladies and an older woman acting as chaperone.' I looked at Amelia closely and realised that she was correct. In her costume with the wig and Bea's expert make-up she did indeed look like a smart, mature woman.

With Amelia carrying a parasol to provide some shade from the midday sun, we walked arm in arm along the promenade. Passing ladies nodded a greeting and men doffed their hats but it was quite apparent that no one took us for other than three ladies out for a walk.

We entered a tearoom and were shown to a table by a polite waiter. As we ate a light lunch of cucumber sandwiches and fairy cakes we chatted about the things that ladies chat about – the fine summer weather, the latest fashions, the comings and goings of famous names.

Afterwards we continued our walk out onto the pier. We looked at the crowds on the beach taking their annual holidays. In the pavilion at the end of the pier a small orchestra was playing music for dancing. We entered and took seats around the edge of the dance floor. It was not long before some young gentlemen came up to us and asked Amelia to give her permission for us to dance. As I waltzed around the hall with my partner I tittered to myself wondering what he would say if he knew that our chaperone was a man in disguise. When we returned to our seat we found that Amelia herself had been invited to dance. Bea and I watched in admiration as she performed the female steps with skill.

It was around teatime that we at last returned to Bea's home and rested our weary legs and feet. Amelia announced that reluctantly she would have to depart soon as she was expected to attend a function that evening as Neville. We returned to Bea's bedroom and helped Amelia undress. I found that during the day I had come to accept her as another woman and at times had almost forgotten that she had a penis and testicles confined between her legs.

Now that Amelia's dress and petticoats had been removed and her torso released from the confining pressure of her corset she stood before us again clad only in the bandage that hid his manhood. Bea untied the knot that held it and unwound the cloth. As his genitals fell free from their bondage Neville's penis swelled. It pleased me to see that it was an admirable size. I reached out a hand to caress it.

'No thank you, Victoria. This swollen thing appals me.' I withdrew my hand hurriedly.

'But would you not like relief?' I asked.

'Only if I could experience intercourse as a woman,' Neville replied.

'I know what he would like,' Bea said moving to her dressing table. She took out a leather-covered box and opened it to reveal a glass dildo. She removed it and covered it with cold cream. 'Bend over the bed, please, Neville,' she commanded and he obeyed.

She stood between his splayed-out legs and parted his buttocks with one hand. Then wielding the dildo in her other hand she pressed it against his puckered hole. The glass rod slid into his arse and he gasped.

'Oh, yes. More!'

Bea pushed harder until it was in up to its flared end. She moved it in and out and from side to side and in just a few moments Neville groaned and shook. Bea withdrew the implement and stepped back. Neville stood up and turned to reveal a slack but dripping cock.

'Thank you, Bea. That was most satisfying.' He began to dress in his male attire. I must confess to being somewhat unsatisfied. The sight of his sex and the violation of his anus had made me considerably excited. When we had shown Neville out of the front door I confessed as much to Bea. She too admitted to having similar feelings and dragged me back to bed where we flung off our own clothes and had a great deal of fun exploring each other's bodies.

160

We entertained Neville/Amelia on more occasions during my stay with Bea, but promenading with a man dressed as a lady was not my most unusual experience. One morning at breakfast, Bea made another announcement.

'I have a client for you this morning, Victoria.'

'Oh, is Amelia joining us today?' I replied misunderstanding her news.

'No, it is not Amelia. It is Colonel Baxter, a friend of one of my patrons. He will be arriving at eleven to spend the day with you and he wants you dressed.'

'Dressed?' I asked mystified.

'Yes, as a boy.' I couldn't understand for a moment why a man should want me to dress as a boy but Bea confirmed that the Colonel was prepared to pay handsomely for the service. I followed Bea to her bedroom where she had laid out on the bed a set of clothes for me to wear. She told me to undress.

When I was standing naked in front of her, she looked at my bosom.

'We're going to have to flatten you, Victoria.' She picked up a role of bandage, possibly the same as Neville used, and wound it tightly around my chest. It was quite uncomfortable squeezing my breasts so, but Bea was determined that my figure should resemble a man's. With my bosom as flat as a pancake I pulled on a pair of men's drawers and tied the cord around my waist. Bea handed me a rolled-up pair of stockings.

'Stuff these down the front of your drawers,' she said. I did as she suggested and looked down at the bulge at my crotch wondering what it would feel like to have a penis and testicles. Then I donned a white shirt, brown tweed breeches, woollen knee-length socks, a pair of Oxford brogues on my feet, a cravat around my neck and a tweed jacket to match my trousers. I was conscious of how thick and heavy the clothes were – I was already perspiring in the summer heat– but the freedom of movement that I had without the encumbrance of a tight-laced corset was quite liberating. Bea had me sit while she plaited and tied up my hair. A touch of make-up darkened my complexion a little and I was ready. Bea placed a tweed cap on my head as I gazed into the mirror scarcely recognising the handsome young man that I saw reflected.

'Don't forget to take the cap off indoors,' Bea reminded me. 'You had better sit in the drawing room to await the Colonel's arrival.'

We were only just in time as shortly after I had seated myself and experimented with crossing my legs, the bell rang and the maid showed the Colonel in. He was obviously well into middle age because the hair on his head and the full moustache on his upper lip were more grey than brown, but he still retained a military bearing. Bea rose to greet him.

'Ah, Colonel. So pleasant to see you again. May I introduce, um, Victor.'

'Good morning, madam,' the Colonel replied, in a gruff but cheerful voice, 'and hello young man.'

'Good morning, sir,' I said lowering my voice as much as possible. I could feel the Colonel's eyes inspecting me.

'Is all to your satisfaction?' Bea enquired.

'Hrrumph. Yes, indeed, madam. Victor, you will be my nephew for today. You are the youngest son of my dear sister, down from London for a day's visit. Understand?'

'Yes, sir.'

'Right, well we'll take our leave then. I'll return the lad to you this evening, madam.' I giggled a little at this and Bea gave me a dark look.

'Very well, Colonel. Enjoy your day.'

I followed the Colonel out on to the street and as the door closed behind us I suddenly realised that I had no inkling of what my purpose was to be. The Colonel set off at a quick march along the promenade and I ran to catch him up. He immediately began telling stories of his exploits overseas with his regiment. I tagged along, occasionally asking a brief question, while looking around at the passers-by. As with Neville/Amelia, the numerous holidaymakers did not give us a second glance. We were obviously a boy out with his uncle.

We had walked about a mile along the seafront and I was feeling very hot in my tweeds. The Colonel stopped, swung about and crossed the road to the entrance to a public house.

'I think we need some refreshment, lad,' he said. He pushed the door open and I followed him in, and for the first time in my life entered the male-only preserve of a saloon bar. It was filled with tobacco smoke and men of all ages and states of drunkenness, obviously enjoying their vacation. Some were playing cards, dominoes and shove-ha'penny. Others were standing talking loudly. The Colonel drew the attention of the landlord and acquired two half-pint jugs of brown liquid. We found a couple of chairs by a table next to a window and sat down. The Colonel placed one of the jugs in front of me.

'There, lad, get that down you.' I had sampled wine and sherry, and at school we sometimes had a small glass of pils but this was my first experience of English dark bitter beer. I sipped it experimentally. It was indeed bitter, and warm, but I found it quite refreshing. The Colonel downed his in one gulp and called for more. He took a large cigar from his top pocket and lit it expertly. He took a few satisfied puffs. The smell was a lot more pleasant than the harsh smell of the cigarette and pipe tobacco being smoked by most of the other men in the public house. The Colonel offered the cigar to me.

'Go on, my boy. Take a puff. Clean out your lungs.' I placed the cigar to my lips, sucked and immediately began coughing uncontrollably. The Colonel took back his cigar and chuckled while I recovered my composure.

After the second glass of beer I was feeling quite relaxed and beginning to find the Colonel's stories quite amusing. He ordered a plate of bread and cheese for us and more beer. The food was welcome even though the bread was more gritty and heavy than I was used to. But after the third half pint I realised that my bladder was in need of some relief. I indicated my need to the Colonel.

'Ah yes, boy, I think I could do with a piss too, you know. Come, I know where we can go.'

We left the drinking house and walked a hundred yards or so back along the promenade.

There on the sea wall was a small cottage-like building built, so a plaque recorded, to commemorate the Queen's jubilee. It was a public convenience. We entered the gentlemen's section. There were a couple of men standing at the urinal pissing into the drain. The Colonel went to join them.

'Uncle,' I whispered, 'I can't.' He looked at me for a moment as if he did not understand.

'Use a cubicle.' He pointed to the row of four doors. Two doors were open revealing water closets. I took his hint and entered one of the compartments taking care to close the latch on the door. I unbuttoned my breeches and pulled them down and untied my drawers and tugged them down too. Then I sat and did my business. In the moments that it took I looked at the thin wooden board that partitioned off my private lavatory. There were drawings carved into the wood showing male and female parts and various conjunctions of the same. As I stood to replace my clothing I stooped to examine some of the lurid diagrams more closely and then I noticed that at about waist height a hole about two inches in diameter had been cut right through the partition. While I wondered what purpose the opening had, I heard someone enter the adjoining closet. There was the rustle of clothing being unfastened and then I was astonished when the knob of a penis was thrust through the hole. The cock was hard and at least six inches protruded through the hole in the wall. The foreskin was pulled back and the purple knob glistened. It quivered as if beckoning to me. I needed no more invitation and, kneeling, placed my lips around the glowing head. The cock flinched slightly but then it remained throbbing in my mouth. I moistened it with my tongue and then opened my mouth wider to take in more of the shaft. I engulfed it until my nose touched the wooden board and the knob tickled the back of my throat. I backed off a little and began to suck. The cock pulsed and I was sure I could hear groans from the other side of the partition. In moments a stream of semen filled my mouth. I swallowed and released the softening prick. It withdrew through the wall like a mole into its hole. I licked my lips, stood up and straightened my attire, and left the public convenience hurriedly, taking care not to stare at the other men that were lined up at the urinal. The Colonel wasn't outside but he emerged a few seconds later.

'That's better, isn't it, Victor?'

'Yes, Uncle,' I replied.

'Let us continue our walk and I shall tell you of my adventures in India.'

We spent the rest of the afternoon meandering along the sea front. We stopped to watch a Punch and Judy show and the donkeys giving rides to children. But mainly the Colonel talked and I listened.

Eventually we arrived at his hotel, one of the grand sea front establishments. The Colonel showed me into his suite and I noticed that he took care to lock the door behind him. He lit up another cigar, then took off his jacket and folded it carefully before laying it on the back of a chair.

'You can take your jacket off too, Victor.' I must say I

165

was relieved because the heavy cloth was stifling me. I took off the jacket and the Colonel took it from me and laid it on his own.

'You may unfasten your trousers now.' I didn't move as I was not sure what he meant.

'Do as I say, boy. I will not tolerate disobedience.' His raised voice carried menace and I realised that I must do as he commanded. I fumbled to undo the stiff, unfamiliar buttons of the breeches.

'Face the bed and drop the trousers.' I shuffled to the side of the bed and did as he asked. The breeches fell to my ankles.

'And your drawers.' My underwear joined the trousers. Now I was naked from the waist down and from the cigar smoke and beery breath I knew the Colonel was standing right behind me.

'Hold your shirt up. Let's have a look at you.' I pulled the shirt-tails around my waist.

'Yes, yes, a fine arse. Bend over.' I leaned forward.

'Lower!' I bent further until I was resting on the bed. My bottom was stuck up in the air. I could hear him fumbling with his attire.

'All boys need discipline if they are to become men,' he said. There was a swish through the air and my right buttock burst into flame. Through the pain I realised that he had struck me with his wide leather belt. I cried out and tried to lift myself up. He thrust me back down onto the bed with a palm in the small of my back.

'Don't move or make a sound,' he commanded and another blow struck my bare cheeks. I cried again and made to push myself up.

'I said silence,' he said as he pulled my arms behind my back and bound my wrists with a thick cord. Trussed like a pheasant I couldn't move. He stuffed a handkerchief in my mouth and tied another around my head. I struggled to breathe. Now I was scared.

'Perhaps that will keep you still and quiet,' he mused as he began to lay into me with his belt. Blow after blow fell across my naked bottom. I squirmed and choked on the cloth filling my mouth. Tears filled my eyes as the fire in my rear grew with each lash.

'Boys have to learn to take their punishment,' he gasped between blows, breathing heavily. 'They learn respect and obedience.' Another fiery stripe crossed the top of my thighs.

The belt made a thud when he dropped it on the floor. The rough tweed of his trousers pressed against my bare thighs and I felt his hard knob questing between by buttocks. For a moment I thought he would force his way into my arse but an instinct made me lift my burning buttocks. The tip of his cock slipped down my moist crack and into my hole. I heard him gasp with pleasure as he felt his manhood slide into my slot. His hips thrust forward and his tool filled me. His hands pressed against my shoulders and his weight pressed down on me as he pulled his penis out and drove in again. I grunted as the air was pushed out of me, the gag still preventing me from breathing easily. With my legs trapped by my trousers and my arms tied behind my back I could play no part in the intercourse. He used my body to achieve his own satisfaction. A couple of minutes of thrusting brought him to orgasm and I felt his semen flood my fanny.

He withdrew, panting hard, and left me trussed up on the bed. I wriggled until I slid off the bed and onto my knees.

'Who told you to move,' he said picking me up by my shoulders and throwing me back onto the bed. Then he resumed the beating. Stroke after stroke lashed across my buttocks. Each one burned into me but I couldn't scream, couldn't make any noise and couldn't even breathe. At last he stopped and pulled me from the bed so that I crumpled in a heap at his feet.

'Get up on your knees, you whelp,' he commanded. I struggled to push myself onto my knees with my arms bound, struggling to get air through my nose which was filled with tears and mucous. At last I made it into a kneeling position. He held my head, undid the gag and pulled the sodden handkerchief from my mouth.

'Now, boy, thank me for showing you what discipline is all about.' I said nothing as I was taking deep breaths. 'Come on, lad. Every boy needs to learn who his master is and how he can satisfy him. Show your appreciation or I'll give you another tanning.'

'Thank you, Uncle,' I said in a quiet shaking voice.

'Good. Now see to your dress. It is time for dinner.'

I pulled my drawers and breeches over my sore and throbbing buttocks. Then I followed the Colonel down to the dining room. We sat at a dining table covered with thick white cloth and the Colonel ate heartily while continuing to tell of his heroic exploits. I barely touched the food, appetizing though it was. Sitting on the upholstered but hard seat was painful and I was filled with resentment at how the Colonel had used me. Was this how men, military or otherwise, treated young boys? I think I was most disgruntled that I had not been called on to use my expertise in the arts of pleasure. My body had simply been used, or rather abused, as a receptacle for his cock, and as a target for his swinging arm. The Colonel made no mention of what had happened in his bedroom. After the meal he took me out of the hotel and put me in a cab. He thrust a sealed envelope addressed to Bea into my hand and instructed the driver to take me back to Bea's house.

The maid opened the front door and Bea ran out of the drawing room to greet me. She saw me limp into the hall and her face darkened.

'What in heavens has happened to you, Victoria?' she

asked.

'My bottom is somewhat sore from the beating the Colonel gave me,' I replied.

Bea turned to the maid.

'Quickly. Run a bath in my bedroom.' Then to me she continued, 'Come on, my dear, let's look after you and soothe those poor buttocks. Tell me all about it.' I handed Bea the envelope as she took my arm and helped me up the stairs.

Later, after a soothing hot bath, I lay naked on Bea's bed. Gently she rubbed cooling cream onto my poor backside.

'Did the Colonel know I was a female?' I asked.

'Of course,' Bea replied, 'why?'

'Well not once throughout the whole day did he acknowledge that I was anything other than a boy. I think he even wanted to fuck me as a man would another man.'

'He may be the type of man who likes to fuck young boys but, in his position, being caught with a young woman would be less of a scandal.'

'I am not sure what he wanted from me.'

'Oh, I think he got what he wanted. His note is full of appreciation for your company and look, he has included his payment with a generous tip.' I turned my head to see Bea waving a banknote which I could see had the value of five pounds. It was a huge amount of money.

'There, does that make the beating worthwhile?' Bea asked. I wasn't sure about that and hoped I wouldn't be called upon to entertain the Colonel again, but I was happy to add the note to the others that I was storing in my trunk.

Chapter 14
Victoria, Head Girl

The fresh mountain air felt lighter in my lungs and my pulse quickened at my first sight of the Venus School for Young Ladies further up the rough track. When at last my cart drew up to the main entrance the doors were flung open and Eric, Hermann and Albert ran out to greet me. I flung my arms around each in turn and planted huge kisses on their cheeks. With the help of the carter they lifted my trunk down and carried it into the vestibule of my school. Although I had had an enjoyable summer vacation it felt good to be back. A year ago I had approached the school apprehensively and angry at my father for sending me away from home. Now I was back among friends – and lovers.

Madame Thackeray had asked me to return a few days early so there were no other girls to greet me, but Madame herself emerged from her study, obviously having heard the noise of my arrival.

'Ah, Victoria, you have arrived. I am pleased to see you. Come in to my study; the boys will take your luggage to your room.'

I followed her into the room that doubled as her study and bedroom. The furnishings were familiar as were the objects on her desk – a massive ebony dildo and a black leather crop. Having experience of both I was always a little nervous standing at Madame's desk. She sat down and looked up at me.

'I was very pleased with your progress last year, Victoria. You tried your hardest in all the subjects you studied. In particular, despite an occasional lapse in concentration, you excelled in the arts of love.'

'Thank you, Madame,' I said feeling pleased with myself.

'It is for that reason,' Madame continued, 'that I have asked you to return before the normal start of term. I would like you to present this year's demonstration to the new pupils and help the new girls settle in to school life.'

'Oh,' I said, suddenly overwhelmed. I recalled Beatrice's display on my first night at the school, and had had no idea that I would be called upon to follow her example. To be selected by Madame to represent all that she had taught us during our first year was the most sought-after honour.

'Well, Victoria. What do you say?' Madame asked. I recovered my composure.

'I am honoured and delighted to do as you say.'

'Very good. We shall commence rehearsals this evening. Eric and Hermann are familiar with the usual programme, of course, and they will help you through it. Now you can go and settle in and prepare yourself.' I left Madame's room feeling light-headed and made my way up to the room that I had shared with Bea for the last year. I felt proud to be following in my friend's footsteps.

A few hours later, Madame and I entered the large drawing room, brightly lit by the evening sun. Madame had laced me into my scarlet corset and helped pull up the matching silk stockings. Her fingers had lingered at the top of my thighs and if we had not been expected downstairs I believe that she would have pleasured me there and then. Eric and Hermann leapt to their feet as we entered looking resplendent in their traditional Tyrolean dress. Madame addressed us.

'Now, Victoria, remember this, and you boys also. This demonstration is to show the new class what they have to learn over the next year. Giving and receiving pleasure is on this occasion not your first priority but of course to give a genuine show you have to put everything you have into your performance. Just remain aware of what you are doing and do not give yourself up entirely to the ecstasy of orgasm.'

'Yes, Madame,' the three of us chorused. Madame sat in the middle of the row of high-backed chairs facing the fur-covered divan-style couch.

'Now, we will start when Eric enters and the action begins. To your places please. Victoria, you lie on the couch.'

I lay down on the furs, carefully draping my red lace gown. Eric came to me from the doorway, took my hand and drew me slowly and gracefully to my feet. When I was standing he took my head in his hand and kissed me hard on the lips, his tongue pushing between them and exploring my mouth.

'Start to undress her, Eric. You do not need to spend too long on the first kiss.'

With practised skill, Eric divested me of my gown, knelt to roll my stockings down my legs and then with a flicker of his fingers released me from the constraining corset. In moments I was naked before him.

'Very good, Eric. You haven't lost any of your skills. Now, Victoria, undress Eric. Concentrate on his lederhosen; he will remove his own shirt.'

I did as I was told. Kneeling in front of him I unbuttoned his leather shorts and pulled them down over his buttocks. He was not wearing drawers so his long erect penis leapt out at me.

'Don't be surprised, Victoria, look impressed,' Madame admonished, 'and turn slightly so that we can all see Eric's whole length. That's it. Now caress it.'

Using the techniques I had learned over the last year I cupped his testicles in one hand and slid a finger down the shaft from the hair in his crotch to the swollen purple knob. Eric sighed and I do not believe he was acting.

'Lift Victoria onto the couch,' Madame instructed. Eric took me in his arms and lifted me as if I was as light as a feather. He laid me gently on the bed.

'Now, Victoria, spread your legs. Let us see your fanny. We need to see your swollen, glistening lips. Eric, get down there and open her up.'

With my feminine parts completely open and exposed to the watchers I felt particularly wanton. Eric's gentle fingers caressing my labia sent shivers of excitement up and down my back.

'Right, Eric, go down on her now – just for a few moments. Find her clit and make her shake. Open your legs wider, Victoria; we want to see what Eric is doing.'

I was struggling to remain in control of my senses now. As Eric nibbled my knob and licked up the juices flowing from my cunt, the first waves of orgasm rippled through my abdomen. A moan escaped my lips.

'That's it, Victoria. If you're acting then keep it up. If it's a real orgasm then hold on to it.' Eric continued to gobble me and my climax built before slowly fading.

'Don't relax, Victoria. This is no time to fall asleep. You've got to go down on Eric now.'

We changed positions as elegantly as possible. I knelt in front of him, his penis wobbling in front of my face. I opened my mouth.

'No, stop,' Madame commanded, 'you are in the wrong position. We need to see the cock entering your mouth.' We shuffled into the new position and I began again to engulf his engorged knob with my lips.

'Slowly, Victoria. Let us watch as you swallow it inch by

173

inch.'

I did as instructed, bending my head back so that I could take every last bit of Eric's magnificent manhood into my mouth. When I felt his balls on my chin I knew I had gone far enough. I allowed him to withdraw and his penis reappeared dripping with my saliva.

'Now make him ejaculate, Victoria. But make sure it does not happen inside your mouth. We want to see him coming.'

I got to work sucking and bobbing my head on the end of his cock. At other times I would love him to come in my mouth so that I could taste and swallow every drop of his semen. As I worked I could feel that Eric's legs were weakening. He grabbed my head to steady himself.

'Take your hands away, Eric; we can't see what's happening.' He lifted his arms and at that moment he began to come. I pulled my head back and a torrent of semen hit my face like water from a fireman's hose. I licked off all that I could reach with my tongue but could feel drips of it on my chin.

'Very good. Now Hermann, don't stand back. Take over the action.'

I stood and turned as Hermann approached, stepping out of his shorts and pulling off his shirt. By the time he reached me he too was naked. He scooped me up, lay me on the couch and set to work kissing and caressing my breasts. My nipples that had been erect before now threatened to burst out of my bosom. He was astride me and I watched his thick cock sway from side to side while his balls dangled between his thighs.

'Now, Hermann,' Madame ordered. Like tossing a wet salmon, Hermann spun me onto my stomach and hauled me on my knees. He positioned himself behind me, his cock pressing against my left buttock.

'Easy now, Hermann. The angle is important here. We

need to see your penis entering her. Make sure her thighs are as wide as possible and part her cheeks so we can see the full length of her crack.' Hermann did as instructed and I felt that he was going to tear me into two halves. He positioned his manhood at my doorway and rammed it in. I let out an involuntary shriek.

'That's good, Hermann. A little less of the surprise in your scream please, Victoria. Make it more of an acceptance. Now, Hermann, finish your task.' Hermann gripped my buttocks and with his knees firmly wedged between my own, began to thrust in and out of my cunt. If I had any control before, I lost it now, gasping and groaning with each stroke and, as my orgasm began to build, appealing for him to fuck me even harder. Being the young, fit man that he was he was able to keep up his exertions for some time so that with a cry from both of our throats we came together. He pumped his sperm deep into my womb and I sank onto the couch thoroughly spent.

'Very good, very good,' Madame clapped her hands. 'Excellent for a first rehearsal. There are some points we can improve and perhaps develop further, but a most acceptable start.'

Over the next two days we repeated the performance with Madame making adjustments and suggestions. I found that I was able to detach myself to observe and evaluate my part in the proceedings while still being excited by the actions of the two boys.

A few hours before the demonstration was due to take place I was relaxing in my bedroom dressed just in the lace gown. I had heard other girls arriving and being shown into other rooms but now there was a knock on my door.

'Come in,' I said. The door opened and a small mousy girl was ushered in by Madame Thackeray.

'Ah, Victoria, I'm glad you are here. This is Lydia. She

will be sharing your room this year.' I jumped off the bed to greet the timid-looking girl. Two of the men entered carrying the girl's luggage and left without a word.

'I'll leave you two to get to know each other.' Madame withdrew closing the door behind her.

Lydia was staring at me. I looked down at my body wondering what it was that had attracted her attention but I could see nothing obvious.

'Is there something wrong with my appearance?' I asked. She blushed.

'I am sorry, but I was surprised by your state of dress. Your gown is almost transparent.' I looked down again and realised that she could see my breasts, stomach and the dark V of hair at my crotch through the thin red lace.

'You are correct, Lydia, but this is not unusual here at the Venus School for Young Ladies. We wear what we are comfortable in. Sometimes that may be nothing at all.' I looked at Lydia's clothes. She was wearing a dusty travelling coat over a long high-necked linen dress with any number of petticoats.

'You must be feeling hot and dirty after your journey,' I suggested.

'Yes, I am.'

'Well, let me help you get it off. Would you like a bath? There is plenty of hot water.' Lydia agreed and I helped her remove her outer clothing. I went into the adjoining bathroom to fill the bath while she removed her underclothes. When she came into the bathroom it was my turn to stare. She was a small girl with the merest pimples for breasts but while she may have turned sixteen what struck me most was that her mound was completely hairless.

She saw me looking at her crotch and covered herself with a hand.

'Is there something wrong?' she enquired.

'No, not at all. It's just that I've never seen a girl without

176

any pubic hair. I trim my own but I haven't thought to remove it all.'

'I didn't like it,' she said determinedly, 'when hairs started to grow down there so I pulled them out. Every one.'

'So you have looked at yourself.'

'Of course. Don't you?' I was surprised by her defiant tone.

'Well I do now, but I confess that before I came here I had not paid much attention to my private parts.'

I helped her get into the hot bath and began to soap her slim white body.

'I think I've always been interested in my fanny, especially as I am different to my cousin Edward. His birthday is the same as mine and we look quite alike in most ways.'

'Oh, you know that boys and girls are different.'

'Of course. He has a willy. He often came to stay with us and our parents let us sleep in the same bed. We spent many nights comparing our bodies and we found that when we tickle each other down there, it gives us both a nice feeling.'
I was becoming intrigued by Lydia's story.

'Your cousin used to touch you between your legs.'

'Oh yes. There's a little button, hidden under the folds of skin that I play with and he does too. Do you have one?' I was surprised at her naïveté. I rubbed her back with a sponge.

'All girls do. Did you say that your cousin still plays with you?'

'Oh yes. Of course he was away at school a lot of the time but during holidays we play in each other's rooms.'

'And what else do you do when you're at play?'

'He likes me to touch his thing. When I hold it, it grows long and hard.'

'I imagine it would.'

'He tells me to hold it firmly and rub it and then he jerks

and a white fluid comes out of it.'

I held a towel up for her as she stood to get out of the bath.

'You have an amazing story to tell. Perhaps you will tell me more later. But now we have to get ready for supper and the evening's entertainment.'

I helped Lydia dress in the white corset, stockings and gown of the novice although I confess I wondered from her story whether white was the most appropriate colour for her. She helped lace up my corset and together we went down to the dining room to meet the other girls.

Later Eric, Hermann and I performed our demonstration to much amazement. The girls squealed with delight when I swallowed Eric's cock and gasped when Hermann buried his prick in my fanny. Madame congratulated us on our performance and I mounted the stairs to my bed feeling quite exhausted. Lydia followed me into the room and I assisted her in removing her attire. We climbed under the sheets together. Lydia was full of questions about the tableau I had taken part in.

'Did you find it easy to get Eric's thing in your mouth?' she asked.

'Well he has got a big penis, but I suppose I've got a big mouth,' I chuckled.

'I tried putting Edward's in my mouth a few weeks ago, but I couldn't get it in.'

'Oh, your cousin must be quite big, then,' I said.

'Oh yes it's at least as big as Eric's.' I tried to imagine a boy similar in appearance to Lydia but with a massive cock. The image was quite troubling.

'What did you do?'

'Well I sort of licked it and just sucked the tip. Edward liked that.'

'I'm sure he did.'

'He spurted over me like Eric did over you. It tasted

salty.'

'Hmm, yes. Does Edward do anything else?'

'Well, I like it when he puts his fingers inside me.' I rested my hand on her smooth, hairless mount and slid my fingers down her crack parting her lips.

'Like that?'

'Oh much deeper than that.' She spread her thin thighs for me and I dug deeper. My fingers slipped into her hole. Her crack was slick with her juices. Two, three, four of my fingers entered her. She was hot. I rubbed my thumb against her tiny erect knob. She began to pant and move against my hand buried up to my wrist inside her.

'Is that it?'

'Yes, that's nice.' I rubbed harder and her breaths came faster. Leaning against her I could feel her heart beating more quickly. Her thighs began to tremble and I felt her come with a gasp. She subsided and I withdrew my hand. She put her arms around me and rested her head on my left breast.

'Is that what your cousin did; just used his hands?' I was beginning to worry about what she would say next.

'Well, sometimes he would put his head between my legs and lick me like Eric did to you.'

'And did you like that?'

'Oh yes, very much.' I confess that Lydia's tale had made me wish for a tongue on my clitoris. 'And once he put his thing in my hole.'

I gasped.

'You mean Edward fucked you.'

'What do you mean?' I realised that Lydia was a complete innocent regarding the arts of love and had no understanding of the acts she engaged in. For her it was all just play.

'I mean, your cousin placed his penis inside your fanny.'

'That's right.'

'And what happened then?'

'Oh, he pulled it in and out for a while and he got excited. And afterward it went small again.' Lydia really did deserve a red corset for having engaged in intercourse! What could I say?

'Did you like it?' was all I could think of.

'Well, it hurt a bit and I was a bit sore afterwards, but he said he enjoyed it a lot, so I would have done it again.'

'Here you'll learn a lot more about what men and women like to do with each other, but I don't think you should tell anyone else your story, Lydia. And perhaps you shouldn't let him put his penis inside you the next time you are home.'

'Oh, he won't be doing anything any more.'

'Why?'

'My uncle has sent him to Australia. I won't see him ever again.' She sobbed and flung her arms around me. I wondered if her cousin's departure was anything to do with his relationship with his sister. Would the parents know? Perhaps they thought their children were very close but would they really suspect what they got up to together? Did the parents know what Lydia would learn at the Venus School for Young Ladies? I suspected not. Lydia was still sobbing gently and making my chest damp. Our bodies were entwined.

'Don't be upset, Lydia,' I soothed, 'you will soon make a lot of friends here and you'll get those nice feelings you had with Edward from the other boys and girls.' I took her hand and placed it between my legs. 'Perhaps you'd like to touch me ...'

Chapter 15
Victoria Discovers the Dark Arts of Pleasure

The six of us, each dressed in our red ensemble of corset, stockings, slippers and gown, mingled in the hallway. It was our second day back at the Venus School for Young Ladies and we had already commenced lessons in bookkeeping and poetry reading, but this was our first evening session and we did not know where to go. The white-clad new girls were in the drawing room awaiting instruction by Madame Thackeray. We were expecting Madame Hulot, the deputy, but there was no sign of her. Instead we meandered around chatting to each other.

Madame Thackeray emerged from her study and looked in surprise at the mêlée.

'What are you doing here, girls? Madame Hulot is expecting you.' As the newly appointed head girl, I decided that I should be our spokesperson.

'We don't want keep Madame Hulot waiting, Madame, but we don't know where to meet her.'

'Downstairs of course, in the cellar. Get down there now.' Madame Thackeray pointed to a low, narrow door under the stairs which, if I had noticed it at all previously, I had assumed was merely a cupboard. Freya was closest to it and, turning the handle, tugged it open. A flight of stone steps descending into the dark was revealed. Taking the lead again, I lowered my head to pass through the doorway and carefully negotiated the steep and uneven steps. The other girls followed close behind. At the bottom of the stairs I stepped into an open area interspersed with stone pillars and with an arched ceiling of stone that supported the floor of the main house. The floor was dusty, hard earth. Flickering candle flames partly illuminated one end of the crypt.

'Ah, there you are. Bon.' Madame Hulot appeared out of the shadows in front of me. My eyes opened wide in surprise. Madame Hulot was a short, stout lady who normally, in our daytime lessons at least, wore dull grey linen dresses that covered her from neck to foot. She was not wearing a grey dress this evening. The trunk of her body was encased in a black leather corset that reflected the candlelight. The top of the corset was shaped so as to support, but not cover, her ample bosom. She wore black leather boots with a narrow heel that added at least four inches to her height. Above the knee-high boots were the tops of black silk stockings fastened to straps at the bottom of her corset. She wore no drawers. Her fleshy buttocks and her black curl-covered mound were exposed for all to examine. A long whip was coiled in her right hand. She frowned at us.

'Those gowns will get in the way, girls. Take them off.' Each of us slipped the light garments from our shoulders and looked for somewhere to hang them.

'Just drop them on the floor, don't waste time.' We did as we were told.

'Come this way.'

She led us into the illuminated part of the cellar and for the first time I was able to see clearly. What I saw took my breath away. A man was bound between two of the pillars. His arms were outstretched and his wrists were held by steel rings fixed by chains to the top of the pillars. His ankles were similarly confined and his legs pulled apart so that he apparently balanced on his toes. He was naked. We saw first his rear. He was not one of the young men who worked in the school. This man was in his forties, his waist thickening and his buttocks sagging. His body was hairy but through the hair his skin was pink wherever one would expect it to be clothed and covered with tiny white curlicues that formed a lace-like pattern. As a group we walked around the pillars to survey the front of the suspended man. His chest, abdomen and legs showed a similar pattern of white threads. His testicles dangled between the outstretched thighs but there was almost no sign of his penis, shrunken and shrivelled as it was. The man's head was covered with a hemp bag.

'You may not know our guest,' Madame Hulot said, 'but if I remove his headdress you may recognise him.' She pulled the bag from his head and I gasped for I did indeed know the man. He was the carter who brought goods to the school and sometimes carried us to and from the village. His head hung down and he made no attempt to look at us.

'Ludwig visits us about once a month to satisfy his lusts and this evening he is going to provide you with your first lesson in the dark arts of pleasure.' She looped the whip around his scrotum and tugged, setting his balls swinging. There was the merest twitch from his cock. She turned to face the six of us who had clustered together like frightened wildebeest.

'Over the last year you each learned how to give and receive pleasure. It was all very comfortable, jolly good fun and I am sure you took much enjoyment from it.' We nodded in agreement.

'Well, this year,' she continued looking at each one of us in turn, 'you will learn that there are other aspects to pleasing a lover. Some of you may already have discovered that a little pain prior to lovemaking can accentuate the pleasure one feels.' I felt that her eyes had coincidentally fallen on me. I reflected on the beatings Madame Thackeray had given me. They were certainly painful but they had been followed by exquisite ecstasy as she caressed and manipulated my sexual parts. There was truth in what Madame Hulot said.

'In our lessons we will explore the principle further. Similarly, restraint and humiliation can heighten sexual pleasure. You will discover that some of your lovers will desire the role of victim which implies that you have to be the mistresses of their excitement, while others will wish to impose their domination on you in order to achieve satisfaction. We will explore all the variations of relationships to prepare you for those that you will make when you leave this establishment.'

I was bemused by what Madame Hulot had to say. Pain, restraint, humiliation, what did she mean?

'This may sound confusing at the moment, but I promise it will become clear over the coming months. But let us take the example of Ludwig here.' Madame Hulot turned to look at the naked, bound man. 'As you can see from his manhood, he is in no way excited by having seven partially clad women before him. Ludwig requires stimulation before his member shows any interest.' She turned to face us again and held up the whip. 'Stimulation with this or another instrument.'

She walked to the wall at the side of the cellar. There hanging from the wall were numerous implements for inflicting pain on a victim. I recognised a number of riding crops of differing lengths and thickness, whips, some with knots along their length, canes, straps, paddles, a cat o' nine tails and a brush of birch twigs. She picked up each in turn, named it, gave it an experimental swish through the air and returned it to its storage position.

'All of these may be used to good effect but I favour the lash,' she said stroking the long leather tail of her whip. 'Let me show you how to use it.'

184

She led us to Ludwig's rear. We stood in a row behind Madame Hulot while she was about six feet from his bare buttocks. She dropped the coils of leather and took a firm grip of the handle. In a blur of movement she raised her arm and cast the lash. There was a crack as the end of the whip travelled through the air. Each of us jumped and Ludwig cried out. A curling red weal appeared across his right buttock. He flexed his legs and pulled on the chains that held his wrists but he could not move from his position. Again she raised her arm and another crack and cry announced the manifestation of another stripe on his back. Time after time she repeated the action until the marks criss-crossed his shoulders, back, buttocks and thighs.

'Now, girls, it is your turn to wield the whip. Here, Victoria, you have a go.' I took the handle of the whip from Madame Hulot and made a number of quite ineffectual strokes. The other girls also each had a turn. Bertha, a large, plain girl from Prussia, seemed to have some experience with the lash. She quickly raised fresh weals on Ludwig's poor buttocks. Madame retrieved the whip and gave the man a few more strokes for good measure.

'Let's look at his other side, girls.' We followed her in a line to gaze at the poor man's front. What a change had taken place. Now his penis stood to attention, the purple knob glowing like a beacon. Madame Hulot flicked her wrist and the end of the whip coiled around his cock. She tugged on it causing him to pull at his wrist and ankle chains. He groaned.

'Do you see, girls? The pain itself has excited him. A little more and he will be completely satisfied.' She relaxed her grip and the coils fell from his cock. She raised her arm and again cracked the whip over his chest and abdomen. He cried out again but his penis grew noticeably and pulsed.

'Now, Victoria. Finish him off.' I did not understand what she wanted me to do, 'Come on, you silly girl, use your hand or mouth to give him release or else I'll have to beat him some more.'

I realised what she wanted me to do. I stepped forward and knelt in front of him then reached up and took his penis in my hand. It was rock hard and throbbing. I looked up at his bowed head. His cheeks were flushed and wet with sweat and tears and he panted. His lips formed into a word although no sound came. They said 'please'. I pushed out my tongue and touched the end of the cock. It quivered in my hand. I licked around the small gaping hole. I had no chance to do anything else because a torrent of white fluid poured out, spraying my face and spattering my shoulders and breasts. I released the shrinking penis and Ludwig sagged in his chains.

'There,' Madame Hulot indicated, 'you can see what little it took to bring him to a climax. That burst of pleasure makes up for the pain of the whipping but in fact Ludwig can only achieve orgasm after such a beating. So that is your first lesson. Tomorrow you will begin to gain some experience yourselves and you will be dressed more appropriately. Off you go now.' We almost fell over each other in our haste to leave the cellar and I am sure each of us was terrified of what would happen in subsequent lessons.

The following evening we assembled at the bottom of the cellar steps. We looked at each other in wonder at our transformation. Each of us was now wearing a black silk basque that fastened with numerous hooks and eyes from our crotch to our breasts. Our bosoms nestled on the shaped wired top of the garment that did nothing to cover our nipples. We each wore leather ankle boots with a narrow high heel and sheer silk stockings that clipped to the straps at the bottom of the basques.

'Ah, you are here, girls,' Madame Hulot welcomed us into her lair. I had come to think of her as a dark, malevolent spider drawing victims into her web. She was dressed in the same way as the previous evening but was not carrying her whip. She guided us to a pillar that had chains hanging from it. There was no sign of Ludwig or any other victim this evening.

'This evening it is your turn to learn how to wield the instruments of chastisement. Who shall be first?' She looked along our row. Not one of us made a move to volunteer. Madame Hulot's gaze returned to me.

'Victoria. You have been chosen to be the head girl of your group. You shall take the lead.'

'Yes, Madame,' I stepped forward reluctantly.

'We need a victim. Who shall it be?' Again Madame Hulot appeared to be contemplating each of the girls in turn. 'I know. Natalie is your special friend, isn't she?' She placed an emphasis on 'friend' indicating that she knew that Natalie and I often shared each other's bed.

'Let Natalie be your first victim. Natalie, step forward.'

My dear friend Natalie edged forward, a look of terror in her face.

'Remove her clothes, girls.' The other girls, now that they seemed to have escaped the intended punishment, eagerly stripped Natalie and helped Madame chain her to the pillar. She hung from her wrists ,her toes barely touching the floor.

'Now, Victoria. Which instrument are you going to choose?' I looked at the various weapons hanging on the wall. I did not want to hurt my darling Natalie. Which would be least painful? I reached for a paddle. It was a flat piece of wood with a short handle.

'I understand your reasoning, Victoria. You think that a slap from a paddle will produce little pain. You are correct. To use a paddle is to make a gesture towards inflicting discipline. It has very little effect. Choose again.' I placed the paddle back on its hook and took down a riding crop.

'That's better. Now get in position.'

I stood behind Natalie's naked form. She was trembling with fear. Her beautiful small buttocks wobbled as she strained at her chains.

'Begin,' Madame commanded. I raised the hand holding the crop and swung. There was no swish through the air and no noise when leather met flesh. Natalie didn't even cry out.

'That was no good at all,' Madame admonished. 'Again, harder.' I swung my arm faster and the crop landed across Natalie's buttocks. She yelped. Madame did not look satisfied.

'If you think that was adequate, Victoria, you can think again. If you want to protect your friend then you are going to have to give her a good beating, because for every stroke that I think is weak I will give two of my own. Now get on with it.' Tears filled my eyes.

'I am sorry, Natalie,' I cried.

Natalie tried to look at me over her shoulder. 'Do what you must, Victoria. Please don't give Madame the excuse to whip me.'

I raised my arm again and swung as fast as I could. The crop sang through the air and fell on Natalie's rump with a loud crack. She yelled and a red strip appeared on her skin.

'Better, Victoria. Again!' Madame commanded.

I swung again and again. After a while I did not hear Natalie's screams. I got into a rhythm of deep breath, raise arm, strike, and found myself selecting my target and making patterns of the stripes on her rear. She cried and swung on her chains trying to avoid my blows but all she succeeded in doing was to present fresh flesh for me to assault.

'That's all, Victoria. You can stop now.' I stood still looking at the livid weals on Natalie's back, all caused by me. The crop fell from my hand.

'Help me get her down.' Madame and the girls

unfastened Natalie's ankles and wrists and she collapsed into Madame's arms.

'She is your victim, Victoria. Take her back to her room and look after her.' Madame passed Natalie's limp body to me, and turned away from us. 'Right, girls, who will be next?'

Trying hard not to touch Natalie's abused rear, I half carried, half supported her up the stairs to her bedroom. I laid her on the bed and hurried to the bathroom to get cool wet cloths to sooth her wounds.

'I'm sorry, my love,' I sobbed as I dabbed at each red mark, vainly trying to cool the heat.

'Do not worry, *ma chérie*. Just make love to me.'

'What?'

'You heard what Madame said. Pleasure should follow the pain.'

I realised what I should do. Natalie was lying face down on the bed. I pushed pillows under her stomach to raise her bottom and gently parted her legs. Her sex was already swollen and a vivid red. I lay down between her thighs and reached out with my tongue. I touched her lips and she shivered. I wriggled forward a few inches so that my hair was brushing the skin of her inner thighs and pushed my tongue between her lips. Honey was oozing from her crack. A bit further and my tongue found her hole. I licked her out, savouring her special taste, then ran my tongue up to her arsehole. I licked around the puckered orifice and then ran my tongue down until I found her little hard knob. My nose rubbed her crack while I nipped and chewed at her clit with my tongue and lips. She shuddered and moaned, 'That's nice.'

I repeated the motion – up to and around her arsehole, down and deep into her cunt then rub her clitoris. She started to buck so I put my arms around the knees and held her firmly. I continued to stimulate her and found myself becoming excited too. At last she gave a huge groan and a great convulsion passed through her body after which she appeared to sag into the bed. I released her legs and moved to lie by her side. She lay across me and kissed me on the cheek.

'Thank you, Victoria,' she whispered, 'that really was the best remedy for the pain.' She dozed off to sleep with her head on my breast.

Over the next few days the marks of Natalie's beating slowly faded and the rest of us acquired our own trophies which we compared with each other. I had drawn Bertha to administer my beating. During the previous year Bertha had been quiet and a somewhat reluctant lover. She did not seem to care much for oral and manual stimulation of the males nor for intercourse. It became clear that discipline was to be her forte. She showed skill in wielding each of the instruments of punishment and laid into me with gusto. Madame Hulot showed her satisfaction by clapping and shouting 'bravo' with every well-placed blow on my behind. When my ordeal was over, Natalie helped me return to my bedroom and did for me as I had done for her. As we lay together, my backside still tingling and my fanny throbbing, Natalie looked into my eyes and said, 'Do you think Madame is correct and that men and women like to be beaten before making love?'

'I am sure she is correct,' I replied, 'look at Ludwig. Swinging a whip also seems to get Bertha more excited than anything else we have done.'

'I don't think it is for me, although I will admit that the pain of the lash does increase my desire for pleasurable stimulation.'

'It is the same for me, my dear. I have no wish to inflict pain on my lover, but if it is what they wish or if it is their desire to beat me then who knows. Love and lust can change one's deepest convictions.'

'You are correct as always, Victoria. No doubt Madame Hulot has more revelations for us.' We reflected that discipline was just the first of her dark arts. We trembled as we held each other tight and wondered what future lessons in the crypt she would have in store for us.

Chapter 16
Victoria Learns Restraint

I was doing up the hooks and eyes of my black silk basque when my room-mate Lydia ran in.

'Oh dear, what's the time?' she asked pulling her dress over her head.

'I'm not sure,' I replied, 'but I imagine you are late for your evening lesson with Madame Thackeray. She won't like it if you are not punctual.' She shrugged, took her slip off and stood there in front of me naked. I was still surprised by her hairless body. She meticulously plucked out every hair that appeared in her mound and elsewhere. With her small stature and pimples for breasts she looked about twelve years of age, but acted fourteen and was supposed to be over sixteen. She started to pull on her white corset and I helped lace her up.

'What's all the fuss?' she rattled on. 'We're only handling cocks again. I did all that with my cousin. He showed me just how he liked his balls tickled and his foreskin pulled back and forth until he spurted. I must admit Hermann is a bit broader than my brother. And that Albert! He's a lot to handle.' I smiled, remembering Albert's massive member, and regretted that it had been some time since we had had pleasure together. She grunted as I pulled her tight. Her waist was tiny.

'I think these uniforms are stupid. Might as well wear nothing at all,' she went on, tugging at the bottom of the corset. 'Why do you wear black? You wore red outfits at the start of the term.'

'We've moved on to the next stage,' I replied cagily. 'You'll find out next year.'

'And what are those marks on your bottom? Have you been beaten? Has Madame Thackeray punished you for something?'

'She'll be punishing you if you don't get downstairs now. Off you go,' I gave her a helpful shove towards the door. She grabbed her white stockings and slippers and ran out. I shook my head and followed her more slowly and, I have to admit, rather more reluctantly.

I met my other five companions at the bottom of the cellar stairs. We huddled together sheepishly as we feared what Madame Hulot had in store for us this evening.

'Come on, girls, do not wait around,' Madame appeared out of the shadows in her fierce black leather outfit, carrying a crop. 'We have a lot to do.'

She led us to the central space in the crypt. The chains on the pillars hung down unused but on the beaten earth floor there was a naked young man. He was kneeling over a steel box-like frame with his neck held in a clamp and his wrists bound by steel rings at one end. Rings around his thighs just above his knees held him to the other end of the open box frame. His ankles were also locked in steel rings and held apart by a steel bar. It was obvious that he could not move a limb but that was not the end of his discomfort. A small steel ring was fixed around the rim of his knob at the end of his cock. This was fastened to a chain which connected to the bar separating his feet. The chain stretched his penis beyond its normal length and made his glans look like a dark red plum about to be plucked from the branch. Two wooden battens about two inches square and two feet long rested against the back of his thighs and clamped his scrotum. His testicles were stretched and squeezed into a shiny taut ball. I could not imagine how much this pained him because he was prevented from making any sound other than a grunt by a muzzle of steel and leather that forced his mouth open.

'Take a good look, girls,' Madame Hulot said cheerfully standing at her captive's head. 'This is George, a young man from the village. He is demonstrating an extreme form of the art of restraint. You see that he is unable to move arms, legs or head. What is more, his manhood is stretched and squeezed into an unnatural conformation. His two orifices are open and available.' She walked around to his rear end and gave his buttock a sharp blow with her crop. A livid red mark appeared but he did not, could not, move, and the smallest whimper emerged from his gagged jaws.

'Restraint is all about control. Losing it that is. George has given up all control of his body to his mistress, that is me. Or it could be you.' She pointed her crop to each of us in turn. She bent down and took the glistening sphere of his balls in her gloved hand. I watched and grimaced as she visibly squeezed, twisted and pulled. A cry emerged from George's throat.

'But why, Madame?' Olivia asked.

'Because, handing over control takes all responsibility away from the victim. If you know what their desires are you can withhold them and dole them out a little at a time whenever you wish. The victim is kept in a state of anticipation and will thank you for any attention you give. Now I know that George here has a preference for other men. His cock has never experienced the interior of a woman's fanny. Tonight we shall indulge him.'

She clapped her hands and from the shadows in the recesses of the cellar a man stepped forward. It was Mario, one of the Venus School for Young Ladies team of male workers. He was naked and carried his erect penis like a lance in front of him. He walked right up to the back of the kneeling and restrained boy. Madame held out an open jar to him. He dipped his fingers in and they came out dripping a greasy semi-liquid substance that he smeared on his penis. He knelt behind George and held the tip of his penis against George's arsehole. He thrust. Half his cock disappeared into George's rectum. George let out a grunt. Another thrust and Mario was in to the hilt.

'There,' said Madame clapping her hands with glee, 'as you can see George is used to being sodomized. His arse welcomes cocks. But being restrained he did not know by whom or when or how he would be penetrated. Now, Mario, complete your business.' Mario needed no second bidding. He gripped the boy's hips and began to rock back and forth, his cock alternately appearing and disappearing into the tight hole. After several strokes he froze and his own buttocks and thighs quivered. He pulled back and his flaccid penis emerged dripping semen. A trickle of fluid ran out of George's arse around his stretched cock and dripped onto the floor.

'Thank you, Mario, you may leave us now.' Mario bowed and withdrew into the shadows.

'Now it could be that your future partner is one such as George,' Madame continued in lecture mode. 'Many males grow tired of exerting authority on their families, servants and employees. Their greatest desire is to forfeit control and give themselves up to restraint and punishment and whatever humiliation you can pour down on them. If like George they have a fondness for cock then perhaps you can find boys willing to service them – don't worry, there are many who will – or you can join in yourself.' She stepped aside to a wooden chest and took out a leather-covered box. She opened it to reveal a double-ended dildo in black smooth leather. She held it up for all of us to examine.

'Some of you may have seen an implement like this before.' Natalie and I exchanged a wink, while some of the other girls looked confused. Madame Hulot crouched with her legs wide and inserted one end of the dildo into her fanny. She let out a sigh as she pushed in as far as it could go. She fastened the straps tightly around her waist. When she stood up straight she had a large cock bending upwards from her crotch. She knelt behind George and like Mario pushed the dildo slowly, steadily, smoothly into his arse.

'Now not being a weak male, likely to spurt after but a few strokes,' she went on, 'I can fuck George's arse for as long as I have the energy and the desire to do so. He has no say in the matter. I can keep him here all night, or for days, whatever is my whim. I can withdraw, leave him for a time, come back when he least expects it and thrust the cock up his backside.' She did a few token strokes to demonstrate. The immovable subject of her attentions grunted with each thrust. She stopped and withdrew.

'But tonight it is your turn.' She began unbuckling the straps. 'Olivia, you can give it a go.'

Over the next hour or so we each took our turn fitting the double dildo and thrusting it into the poor boy's rear. When it was my turn I was surprised by the resistance that George's back passage offered. It required a lot of force to invade his hole and push the dildo in to its full extent. When he had been buggered by every one of us he looked exhausted and barely made any sound.

'Don't you think he has had enough, Madame?' Natalie asked.

'Perhaps he has, but don't worry. When he is released he will thank me for all that we have done and he will return to us the next time he wants to give up his male responsibilities. But for now we will just leave him where he is.' Madame escorted us away, back to the cellar stairs.

'Of course this is only one side. I have suggested that your partners may like to delegate their authority to you. But what if they want to be masterful? Perhaps they do not have the authority that they wish for in their daily lives. They can play out their fantasies on you. Tomorrow night one of you will be the subject.' She turned and left us looking at each other wide-eyed.

The following evening I sat on my bed, dressed in my black uniform, but unmoving. I knew the time was going on but I couldn't bring myself to step outside the room. There was a knock on the door and Natalie entered.

'Come on, Victoria, it's time.'

'I don't want to go, Natalie.'

'But you must. Madame will be furious if you miss a lesson.'

'I know but I don't want to be locked to that frame.' Natalie sat by my side.

'I didn't want to at first, Victoria, but I've been wondering what it would be like to give up all responsibility for my body; to have things done to me that I have no control over; to be exposed to the eyes of people that I do not know; to have cocks and dildos enter me without me deciding whether to allow them entry.'

'And your decision?'

'I surprised myself, Victoria. I want to find out. Come on.' She stood and pulled me to my feet. She dragged me to the door, down the corridor, down the flight of stairs and then down the steep stone steps into the crypt. The other four girls were already being addressed by Madame Hulot. She looked at us and frowned.

'So who is going on the frame?' Natalie's hand shot up. 'Ah, Natalie. Good. Prepare her girls.'

I stood back while the other girls stripped Natalie naked and carried her to the frame that sat on the floor, illuminated by candles and oil lamps. Natalie was made to kneel and the clamps and chains were placed around her neck, wrists and ankles. The muzzle was fastened around her head and her jaws were forced wide apart. She looked like the sphinx in that position and I was drawn to the beauty of the smooth white skin of her back and bottom.

'Of course unlike George, Natalie does not have a cock and balls for us to abuse,' Madame said, 'but I do have these.' She held up a number of sprung clips such as are used to hold documents together. She knelt and reached underneath the frame to grab hold of one of Natalie's nipples. With difficulty she squeezed one of the clips and placed its open jaws around the nipple and released it. It snapped shut and Natalie let out a high-pitched grunt. Then Madame pulled on the cord attached to the clip, stretching her small breast into a cone. She tied the cord to the steel frame and repeated the action on the second nipple. Now Madame moved to Natalie's rear. Her legs were splayed wide, revealing her sex. Madame took hold of her left labia between her finger and thumb and snapped a clip on, then pulled the cord so that Natalie's lips were dragged open and again tied the cord to the frame. She did the same on the right side so that Natalie's gaping cunt was revealed to all. Natalie seemed to be moaning but nothing intelligible could emerge from her open mouth.

'Now we'll leave her to settle down for a few moments,' Madame Hulot said. 'Of course this frame is just one way of restraining your subject. Ropes, leather cuffs and straps, steel manacles, they all are of use. You may attach your victim to a fixed point such as a ring in the floor or merely render them immovable and exposed. Your imagination is your only limit. Finding a new and different way to restrain your partner or to expose them in a humiliating fashion is one way of keeping the tension, maintaining their interest. Believe me, with some willing subjects, finding something new and different can be a chore. Over the next few months you will experience many different forms of bondage, abuse, humiliation and degradation, so that when you leave this school you will know precisely what liberties you will allow your future spouses to take and what degree of control you wish to exert or relinquish. It is up to you to learn. Now let us see to Natalie.'

She clapped her hands and this time three naked men appeared, all of them unknown to me and the other girls. Their ages seemed to vary from mid twenties to late forties and their heights and build varied similarly. One thing they had in common was firm erections.

'These are three of our kind neighbours,' said Madame introducing the three men. 'They are of course delighted to assist with our lessons.'

One man knelt in front of Natalie's muzzled head. He inserted his penis into her open mouth and wedged his knob between her tongue and the roof of her mouth. The second gentleman went behind her, knelt and thrust his cock into her open fanny. In one drive he was in so deep that his balls rattled against her pubic bone. At the same moment the first man thrust his penis down Natalie's throat. I winced because I knew that Natalie always gagged when she took a man deep in her mouth. Both men thrust in and out together and quickly came to their climax. They withdrew leaving Natalie coughing and dripping semen from her mouth and fanny. Now the third man stood behind her. He smeared some of the goo proffered by Madame Hulot on his cock and presented it to Natalie's arse. He pushed and the tip forced an entry into the tight puckered sphincter. Natalie groaned. He pushed again and the whole head slipped inside. Natalie cried out. He pushed once more and his shaft slid from view. Natalie let out a cry from her throat such as I had never heard before. The man belaboured her arse until he too came and, withdrawing, left a trail of fluid trickling down Natalie's thigh.

'Don't you think that she has had enough?' I appealed to Madame.

'Perhaps she has,' Madame glared at me, 'but the point

about this game is that it is not up to her, it is my decision when and if to release her.' She turned away from me and looked at the other girls. Her eyes fixed on one.

'Bertha, put on the double dildo.' The big girl jumped to her task eagerly. Soon she was equipped with a massive cock. 'You may choose for yourself which orifice to fill.'

Having seen the enthusiasm with which Bertha had approached the art of discipline I was not surprised to see her position herself to thrust into Natalie's poor abused rear. I think my dear friend swooned before Bertha finally reached her own orgasm and fell back. The black phallus slid out of Natalie's arse and Bertha lay on the earth floor with the cock erect.

At that point Madame relented and Natalie was released from her bonds. I carried her to her room and sent her room-mate to sleep with Lydia in my room.

I bathed Natalie's swollen fanny and arse and rubbed soothing ointment into the marks made by the clamps on her neck, wrists, ankles and nipples. She opened her eyes and smiled at me.

'Thank you, my friend.' She slept while I stayed by her side.

Some hours later while it was still dark she awoke.

'Are you well?' I asked.

'Yes. A little sore, but yes, I am fine.'

'I thought Bertha was going to rip you in two,' I said.

'She is certainly vicious,' Natalie agreed.

'So are you still attracted to the idea of bondage and forced intercourse?' I asked, expecting Natalie to reply in the negative. She surprised me.

'Madame is right, you know. When you are restrained you become detached. My mind seemed to leave my body and I watched while those three men and Bertha used it for their own satisfaction. I had no part to play other than provide the flesh and the holes for them to fill. I have long

200

felt the desire to have intercourse with men of whom I knew nothing and I have wondered what it would feel like to have a cock thrust up my arse. I would never have had the courage to seek out those fantasies but Madame fulfilled them for me tonight. Yes it was painful and uncomfortable, but the feeling of being a machine solely used for the pleasure of others was tremendous.'

'You amaze me, Natalie.'

'I amaze myself, Victoria. Your giggly little friend enjoying being the willing victim of wild, violent pleasure seekers. Perhaps I won't do it again in a hurry, but some time in the future I will willingly partake in the games again. But now, Victoria, please love me.'

Her hands sought my breasts and caressed my nipples, and her lips found mine. Her tongue and mine intertwined. My hands slid down her smooth back to her small round buttocks. She slid down me, her tongue making patterns around my breasts and navel until it reached my crotch. She licked at my quim, exciting such passion within me that I clamped my thighs around her head, holding her while her tongue worked deeper into me. I came with a shuddering suddenness and, flinging the bedclothes off us, leapt astride Natalie and buried my head in her fanny, my nipples rubbing against her stomach. I sucked and chewed at her lips and clitoris and in a short time she too reached her orgasm.

I lay back beside her.

'There. That was satisfying,' she whispered and hugged me tight.

Chapter 17
Victoria's Christmas Dilemma

As the train carried me towards England for the Christmas vacation, I dozed and daydreamed about the term that had passed at the Venus School for Young Ladies. I felt tired and a bit stiff, my nipples, fanny and rear were a little sore and the marks of my most recent beating were still fading from my buttocks and yet I felt more alive than I had ever felt before. Madame Hulot had ensured we experienced as many forms of discipline, restraint and humiliation as she could possibly arrange within the confines of the school and had worked us hard while ensuring that we came to no lasting harm. At first I had been a reluctant participant and was not convinced that pain and discomfort added to my enjoyment of sexual pleasures. On the other hand my friend Natalie had delighted in being bound and restrained, while Bertha had proved to be an enthusiastic and skilful mistress of the whip. Gradually I came to understand the attraction of these unusual pastimes. The ability to hand over responsibility for one's own body to another and the freedom that gave to respond to every stimulus in an abandoned fashion became attractive. Of course the other point of our training was that we could also become the mistresses and apply the punishments and abuse to those who placed their trust in us. My thoughts lingered on my last lesson.

*   *   *

We were down in the crypt beneath the school. I was taken and stripped of the few clothes that I was wearing. A mask was placed over my head that prevented me from seeing and also covered my ears so that conversation was muffled. A hard leather bit was placed in my mouth and fastened behind my head so that I could make no complaints. Then leather cuffs were placed around my wrists and joined to a short steel bar that was in turn connected to a steel collar fixed around my neck. My hands and arms were thus rendered immobile and held against my breasts. A chain fixed to a ring in the floor was linked to my collar. The chain was only two or three feet long so while I could kneel I could not rise to my feet. Having been placed in this position I was left. I do not know how much time passed and I strained to hear any sound but the padding in the mask kept me isolated from my surroundings. For all I knew my classmates and Madame Hulot may have been standing close by the whole time and laughing at my predicament.

After an indeterminate time I received a blow to my left buttock. It was such as surprise that I toppled over from my kneeling position and my neck received a painful yank from the chain. The blow left a burning streak and I guessed it had been made by a cane. Another blow caught me on my right side this time and I deduced from the curving stream of fire that it was caused by a whiplash. I tried to cry out but the gag prevented anything more than a gurgle escaping from me. Now the strokes came fast, first to one side and then the other. Tears moistened the mask covering my eyes and saliva dripped from the corners of my mouth. I tried to wriggle and escape but the short chain, my bound hands and my inability to see or hear where my attackers were meant that I was unsuccessful. However I moved, the cane and the whip found my flesh.

At length the beating stopped. Hands lifted me and placed me astride a man. He held my shoulders in his strong hands, preventing me from resting on him. Other hands spread my thighs and lifted my hips and then lowered me onto his erect penis. My fanny slid down his manhood almost as if I was being pierced by a spear. With his whole shaft inside me I could feel his testicles in my groin. He shifted his grip, throwing his arms around me and holding me tight against his chest with my arms and the steel bar crushing my breasts. He bucked a few times and his moving cock stirred my emotions.

And then he paused, holding me motionless. I felt hands parting my buttocks and something pressing against my anus. It was soft with a hard core. I realised it was a second penis trying to achieve entry. Its owner pushed and I felt my arse being forced open and what felt like a huge log driven into me. The second man continued to push until he had buried his full length in my rectum. I could feel both cocks in their respective channels almost touching each other. Now the man under me began to buck in earnest and my rear assailant pulled out and pushed in repeatedly. Nailed by the two cocks I could not move and had to just ride out the pummelling they each gave me. Regardless of the fact that I was playing no part in the intercourse and was merely a receptacle for the two instruments of pleasure, an orgasm began inside me sending my heart into palpitations, my brain swimming and my limbs trembling. It reached a climax as both men ejaculated. Through my deadened hearing I heard them both emit cries of delight. One pulled out of my arse like a cork from a bottle and the other pushed me off him once his flaccid prick had slid out of my fanny. I rolled across the dusty floor until the chain at my neck checked my motion. I remained there for some time until Madame Hulot returned and released me. Somewhat painfully I returned to my room and examined my body in a full length mirror. My buttocks and thighs were covered with red stripes and my crotch was a sticky, gritty mess of dust and semen.

My train neared Waterloo and I looked out for my father come to meet me. But there was no sign of him. When I descended from the carriage he was still not there. I waited for some time then decided to use some of my own coins to take a cab to our home. The house was dark and no servants came to the door. I waited on the doorstep sitting on my trunk, gradually becoming colder and colder. As the church clock struck eleven, my father appeared on foot. He swayed a bit and I could smell drink on his breath. Despite the cold his coat was undone and his clothing dishevelled. I had never seen him in such a state before.

'Ah, Victoria. You found your own way home then.'

'Yes, Father. Where have you been? I'm cold and tired after my journey.' He struggled to place his key in the lock.

He sniffed, 'You're cold and tired. No thought for me I suppose, your only father.' He pushed the door open and staggered inside. I hurried to follow him. The house felt cold and empty.

'Where are the servants? Why is the house cold? Why are you like this, Father?' He continued along the hallway and up the stairs.

'Gone, gone. It's all gone,' he said to himself as much as to me.

I dragged my trunk over the doorstep and closed the door. Then I hurried up the stairs, following my father. When I got to his bedroom the door was closed. I turned the handle but the door would not open.

'Father, let me in. What is the matter?' There was no reply. I banged on the door a few times and called out again but he would not answer me. Eventually I gave up and went to my room. It was cold but at least the bed was made.

Without undressing I crawled under the covers, curled up as much as I was able in my tight-laced corset and eventually fell asleep.

I awoke as the winter sun, filtered through yellow fog, made a half-hearted attempt to banish the night-time shadows. Yawning and stiff from my fitful sleep I made my way down the stairs. There was no sign of my father in the dining room or his study. I went back upstairs to his bedroom but though I found the door open, the room was empty and the bed unmade. Back downstairs I searched the kitchen. There was no sign of my father or food but for a piece of stale bread. The cooking range was cold and there was no coal at hand. I presumed that my father had already left to attend to his business but I was more concerned with how I was to see to my own needs for warmth, food and hot water to wash. While gnawing at the hunk of bread I walked around the whole house. Many rooms were bare, their furniture, furnishings, ornaments and paintings from the walls gone. Even the bookshelves in the library were bare. What had happened? Had father sold his belongings? Why?

It was mid-morning when there was a knock on the back door. I ran to see which tradesman was calling. I opened the door to the coalman. He was a young man dressed in shirt, jacket and trousers, all covered in a film of coal dust.

'Oh hello. I'm so glad you've come. We seem to be out of coal. I don't know why.'

'It's because I haven't been paid, Miss,' the coalman said.

'Haven't been paid?' I repeated.

'No, Miss, not for months. I'm not to deliver any more until the bill has been paid.' I couldn't understand. Why hadn't my father paid the bill? How had he allowed the household to run out of fuel?

'I'm sorry, I haven't got any money.' The coalman

turned to leave. I grabbed his black hand, 'Oh, please don't go.'

'If you can't pay and the master of the house isn't here, there's no point me staying, Miss. It'll be the debt collectors you'll see next.'

'No, please. I need coal. The house is cold; I need hot water to wash.'

'I'm sure you do, Miss, but there's nothing I can do.'

'Just one bag.'

'Only if you can pay.'

How could I pay my father's bill? I looked at the young man. Beneath the coal dust he had handsome features. I knelt in front of him, looked up into his face and appealed to him to think of a poor woman in the cold. He shook his head. I placed a hand on his groin without thinking and felt a twitch. An idea came into my head. Perhaps one service would deserve another. I undid one of his fly buttons, then another.

'What are you doing, Miss?'

Another and another came undone. He wasn't wearing anything beneath the trousers and his penis flopped out. It was white and clean. I caressed it with my middle finger. It trembled and grew. The head lifted up and the purple knob pushed through the foreskin. I gripped it in my hand, squeezing it gently but firmly.

'Just one small bag?' I asked. I reached out with my tongue and touched the tip. He staggered but I kept my grip.

'What do you mean?' His voice had developed a dreamy, faraway quality. I encircled his knob with my lips and rubbed the ridges beneath it with my tongue. I released my grip on his shaft and cupped his balls, running a finger behind them up the crack between his buttocks. I took hold of his cock with my other hand and leaned back, letting the knob slide out of my mouth.

'I'm sure you can spare just one small bag.' He rocked on

his feet.

'Yes, yes. Just do it.' I smiled and lowered my head again. This time I took his cock deep into my mouth and rubbed my hand up and down the shaft. As I suspected it did not take very long for his climax to arrive. He groaned loudly and his semen gushed into my mouth. I swallowed it hungrily. I made sure every last drop had been licked and sucked from his penis before I released it from my mouth and tucked it and his balls back inside his trousers. I stood up and he hurried to do up his buttons.

'One small bag,' I repeated. He turned to run out to the rear yard.

'Yes, I'll get it. But the bill still needs to be paid.' He went to his cart and good as his word returned with a half hundredweight of coal.

'Perhaps we can repeat our bargain some time,' I said.

'Perhaps,' he replied running off. He mounted his cart and urged the patient horse to get moving.

I managed to get the range lit, which warmed the kitchen. Then I heated some water and undressed in front of the fire to wash myself. I dressed in some looser clothes more suited to working in the kitchen and pondered what to do about food. I did have a small amount of money in my trunk saved from last summer; it seemed that I must go shopping for my victuals. I dressed myself like a housekeeper and went out to the market to buy bread, butter, milk and pies. Back home I was at last able to satisfy my hunger. The rest of the day I spent awaiting the return of my father from whom I hoped to find an explanation for our situation. But he did not return. Late into the night I sat by the small fire in the kitchen keeping myself warm. It was nearly midnight when the front door bell was rung. I ran along the hall and flung the door open expecting to see my father on the step. Instead it was a policeman.

'Good evening, Miss.' He took his helmet off and held it in the crook of his arm, 'I'm afraid I have bad news.' He informed me that my father had fallen from the platform and had been hit by an underground train entering the station. Some witnesses said that he had jumped while others said he slipped. Either way he was dead and I was required to identify the body. The policeman very kindly escorted me to the mortuary where I confirmed the body as that of my father. I only saw his face. The rest of his body was covered by sheets. His chest had been crushed by the train. He looked peaceful lying there as if he was asleep. I almost wanted to shake him to wake him up. The policeman took me back home, said a few kind words and then I was alone again.

The fire had gone out and the kitchen was cold again. I sobbed then as much for myself as my father. What was I to do? I fell asleep, eventually, in the wooden chair in the cold kitchen.

I was woken by the bell ringing and someone banging on the front door. I stirred and hurried to see who could be making such a racket. On opening the door, a gentleman in a frock coat and bowler hat pushed past me and into the hall. He went into the dining room and looked around.

'Who are you? What are you doing?' I demanded. He pushed past me again and went into my father's study.

'Bailiff, Miss. You've got lots of unpaid bills and the courts have given me the authority to assess what items we can confiscate to meet the sums.' He went into the drawing room.

'But you can't do that,' I appealed.

'Oh yes I can.' Now he was in the kitchen.

'But my father only died last night.'

'Sorry to hear that, Miss. Means that I had better work faster before the executors tie everything up for an age.' He climbed the stairs and reached the library. I followed him into the bare room and watched him gaze at the empty shelves.

'Seems someone cleaned it out before I got here,' he went on. He moved on to my father's bedroom. There was just the unmade bed from the night before last, his last in this world. The bailiff finally arrived at my bedroom. He pushed my door open.

'Ah, this is better. Some good stuff here.' He looked at my wardrobe, dressing table, chest of drawers, the pictures on the walls, the full-length mirrors.

'Oh, please, sir. You wouldn't take my possessions.'

'Nothing is yours. It all belongs to the courts. It'll be gone by nightfall.' I collapsed onto the bed in shock.

'What will I be left with?'

'Nothing I should think. Your father's creditors are owed thousands of pounds.'

I felt as if I was bound in cords by the courts. I had no freedom, no control over what was happening to me. Only one course seemed to remain. I took hold of the hem of my skirt and pulled it and my petticoat up to my waist. I revealed myself to the bailiff.

'Is there nothing that will delay you?' I asked.

He looked at me and a grin spread across his face.

'You've lost everything so you might as well lose your honour,' he said, removing his hat and coat, and beginning to undo the buttons of his trousers. He advanced towards me. I shuffled back onto the bed, pulling my skirt and petticoats up to my waist. I opened my legs and raised my knees. He crawled on to the bed between my legs with his erect penis poking out of his trousers.

'You're a right temptress, aren't you, my lady,' he said as he crawled over me. His hot breath brushed my cheek and his cock rubbed against my fanny.

'Guide it in,' he ordered. I reached between my legs, took hold of his penis and placed it between my lips. He pushed and the tip slipped into my vagina. He sighed. He thrust again and I felt the cock sliding deep inside me. He lowered his head.

'Kiss me, darling.' I didn't want to but his tongue found its way between my lips and I tasted its foul flavour. He began to thrust repeatedly.

'Come on, love. Match me.' He held my arms against the bed and grunted on each inward thrust. He came with a gasp and I felt a gush of semen within me. He dropped onto me, his weight pressing me into the bed and stifling my breath. I struggled to breathe and beat against his shoulders. He heaved himself off.

'Careful, lady. You don't want to upset me now, do you?' He stood up and rearranged his dress. 'To show you how much I care, I will put off my return until tomorrow. I am sure you will be able to entertain me then. Good day.'

He left and I listened as he went down the stairs, walked along the hall and pulled the front door closed behind him. I stood up and brushed my skirt and petticoats down. I was disgusted with myself but thankful that I had bought a day's grace. But what could I do? I hurried to my father's study and pulled drawers and cupboards open. Paper after paper spilled out, letters, invoices, nothing that meant anything to me. I was in despair when the front door bell rang again.

I opened the door but an inch and peered around it. I was fearful that the bailiff had returned despite his promise. Instead a slim, smart, young man in a new overcoat was standing on the step with a cane and top hat.

'Hello. Miss Victoria, is it? My condolences regarding your father's untimely death.' He doffed his hat and I saw that he had short, dark hair slicked down and pale features.

'Who are you?' I asked.

'Ah, pardon me.' He presented a card and said, 'Samuel Blenkinsop of Blenkinsop, Blenkinsop and Blenkinsop, Solicitors. I'm the last one by the way; my father and grandfather are the others. We are the executors of your father's estate.' The card confirmed what he said so I opened the door. He stepped into the hall.

'Executors?'

'Yes, we represented your father while he was alive, and we shall handle matters now that he is dead. May we talk?' I took him into my father's study. Papers were strewn over the floor and other surfaces.

'I've been trying to find out what happened but I don't understand it.' He sat in a chair while I grabbed handfuls of papers and dropped them again.

'Ah, I'm afraid your father's business dealings suffered a great misfortune in recent months. Well, he lost a fortune and left a lot of debts. There is not going to be anything left in his will for you once our bill has been paid.'

I told him about the coal man and the bailiff demanding payment.

'I'm afraid there will be a lot of that.'

'But I can't service them all,' I cried.

'Service them?'

I described how I had gotten a bag of coal from the coal man and put the bailiff off for a day.

'You would sell your body for a bag of coal?' There was a look of amazement on his face.

'Not my body,' I replied, 'my skills, my knowledge, my experience. Just like you I suppose with your knowledge of law and wills and I don't know what.'

He laughed. 'Well I suppose you're right. We each have our expertise. What do you want me to do?'

'Help me. Save what you can of my father's estate. I suppose the Berkshire house is gone as well. Leave me enough to set up on my own.'

'And how will you pay?'

I turned away from him, knelt and pulled my skirts and petticoats up. I presented my bare arse and fanny to him.

'This is all I have to offer,' I said, my head resting on the carpet.

Perhaps it was the sight of the white heart of my buttocks, or the pink orchid of my sex. Or possibly it was the faint musky odour that rose from my exposed fanny. From being starchy and distant he became inflamed by animal passions. I looked over my shoulder to see him throwing his coat off, and fumbling with the buttons of his trousers. He thrust his trousers and drawers down below his knees and knelt behind me. His penis was already proudly erect and his commendable testicles dangled between his legs. I turned my head away and awaited the touch of his cock against my quim. His cool hands rested on my buttocks and then I felt his cock, not against my fanny but pressing against the tight puckered hole of my anus. A few months earlier I would have recoiled from this indignity and not believed that a fully erect penis could enter my rear passage, but the last term at the Venus School for Young Ladies had taught me differently. I used my newly developed skill to relax my muscles and so when he applied pressure his knob slid inside me. He let out a long drawn-out sigh as he pushed in further. When he could penetrate no more he paused. I felt as though my abdomen was full, that I was forever rendered immobile by his spike, like a butterfly pinned to a display box. Then he began to pump me. Each thrust was accompanied by an insult, 'you slut', 'whore', 'common hussy'. I took each name and accepted it, for they were indeed true. After innumerable advances and retreats, when I felt that my whole arse was afire, he came and filled me with his semen. When he withdrew it trickled down my thigh.

He remained kneeling, breathing heavily. I got up and let my skirt and petticoat fall, restoring my decency to some extent. I collected a bowl of water and a cloth and, kneeling before him, washed his shrunken penis.

'I'll do what I can, Victoria, but it is not going to be easy. Your father's affairs are in disarray.' He re-fastened his trousers and replaced his coat and hat. 'I will call again soon.'

Christmas was a lonely and dismal affair. Samuel was, however, as good as his word and ensured that I had sufficient fuel to fire the kitchen range, and food enough for my needs. I moved a small mattress and blankets into the kitchen and lived there, spending my time looking through father's papers and trying to make sense of his business dealings, with little success. The bailiff did not return but Samuel did on a number of occasions. Each time he came I offered him my body and each time he took advantage of the availability of my rear orifice. On one occasion early in the new year we were lying on my improvised bed in the kitchen and I was caressing his erect manhood prior to intercourse. I asked a question which had been troubling me.

'Why, when I offer you my mouth and my vagina, do you always choose to sodomize me?'

He turned a little red in the cheeks and there was a pause before he answered.

'My father expects me to marry soon. I would not want the scandal of making you, one of my clients, with child.'

I sensed that was not his whole answer. I stared at him and after a few moments' thought, he went on.

'Also, I like the constriction one feels when one enters an arse.'

'You have experienced others similarly, then.'

'Yes,' he said almost inaudibly, 'at school and university I have been both the active and the passive partner. But please do not speak of it again. My father must never know of my predilection for a tight anus.'

I chuckled, 'I don't think I am in a position to tell tales, Samuel. Come, your cock is ready for the game, fill my arse again.'

I really do feel that despite my apparent subservience to his desires I gained some kind of authority over Samuel Blenkinsop. He became most solicitous about my health and well-being. However, despite his efforts in warding off the creditors and bailiffs nothing could prevent the ultimate forfeit of all my father's possessions. I discovered that the London house had been mortgaged and many of the furnishings already sold to service his debts. Our Berkshire estate would also be broken up. In a few weeks it would all be in the hands of other owners and I would be homeless and penniless. I had to decide what to do and my only thought was to get away. There was only one other place that was anything like a home and that was the Venus School for Young Ladies. I determined to return for the spring term. My fine dresses and jewellery were sold and together with the remaining cash from my summer occupation, I bought my passage to the Austrian mountains.

Chapter 18
Victoria's Term of Servitude

I trudged up the mountain track, my feet sinking into the snowdrifts with a biting easterly wind cutting through my thin woollen coat. The Venus School for Young Ladies could just be seen above through the veils of snow ahead of me. I had used the last of my money in getting to the village and I had nothing left to pay for a sleigh to carry me up to the door of the school in style. However, I did not have a trunk full of luggage to accompany me; I carried just a small cardboard suitcase packed with a few skirts, petticoats and blouses.

With the final light of day fading I came at last to the main entrance to the school and tugged on the bell pull. After a short delay, Eric opened the door. He looked at me for moments before recognising me.

'Victoria, what has become of you?' He opened the door wide, and invited me into the hall. I shook snow from my coat and shoes. Madame Thackeray emerged from her study bedroom.

'Who was that at the door ... oh. Hello, Victoria. We weren't expecting you. You had better come into my office.' I put my case down and Eric made to pick it up.

'Leave that, Eric,' Madame commanded. 'Victoria will not be staying in her accustomed room.' Madame returned to her study and I followed. She sat at her desk leaving me standing in front of her. With the warmth of her log fire the snow and ice in my clothes began to melt and drip onto the carpet.

'What are you doing here, Victoria?' Madame asked.

'I have come for the next term, Madame.'

'But your father has not paid your fees to my agent in England.'

'My father is dead, Madame,' I said, noting that a look of sympathy passed briefly across Madame's face to be replaced by the stern visage that I found unfamiliar.

'I am sorry, Victoria. You must be sad. But who will now pay your bill?'

'No one, Madame. My father's money is all gone and I have no one else.'

'But you cannot be a pupil here without paying. We are a school not a poorhouse. You will have to leave.'

'I have nowhere else to go, Madame.' Tears welled in my eyes and I began to sob.

'Stop your snivelling, girl.' She passed me a handkerchief. 'You know we don't suffer that kind of weakness here. We teach you to be strong, independent women.'

I blew my nose and dabbed at my eyes. 'I know, Madame, I have tried. I've dealt with coalmen and bailiffs and solicitors but I have nothing. I couldn't think what else to do but come here.' There was silence for a few minutes while Madame looked at me, searched my face for the truth of what I said and contemplated. When she spoke again her voice was softer.

'You have obviously had a trying time, Victoria, and it would be hard of me to send you back out into the snow to perish in the cold. I will see what I can do to find you a position suited to your skills and talents, and in the meantime you can be my maid.'

Her words cheered me. 'Oh thank you, Madame. I will serve you with all my energy.'

'There is a problem, however,' she mused, 'we don't have any rooms for maids.' Indeed the men carried out all the tasks around the house under the supervision of Madame Hulot. There were no maids. 'But, there may be a solution.' Madame rose from her seat and walked around her bed to the far end of the room. There was a door which she opened to reveal a small room, a box room, barely more than a cupboard. It was cluttered with trunks, packing cases and other items of luggage.

'This could be cleared and a bed made up for you. It has the advantage of being close to me if I should have need of you. There, that's decided.'

'Thank you, Madame.'

'That is all right, Victoria, but I want you to remember that you are no longer a pupil here so you must not talk to the girls, and nor must you treat the men as your servants.'

'No, Madame.'

'Good. Now collect your case and start clearing out that room.'

The little room that was to become my home was soon empty. It was bare of furniture and as it had no fire of its own I relied on the little heat that spread from Madame's study for warmth. Still, with a mattress and blankets, I expected to be comfortable enough.

Having warmed up a little I stripped off my wet clothes and was hanging them to dry when Madame called for me.

'I shall be retiring shortly, Victoria. Your first task will be to warm my bed.'

I looked around for a warming pan but could see nothing that would suffice.

'With what shall I warm your bed, Madame?'

'Why, yourself, of course. Take your clothes off and get under the covers. I will be back shortly.' She left the room and I hurried to remove my remaining underclothes. I slid under the bedclothes, feeling comfortable for the first time in many days.

I was actually asleep when Madame returned.

'Wake up, girl. Help me undress.' I stirred and slipped naked from the bed. I assisted Madame in removing her silk dress and petticoats and then unlaced her corset. Soon she was naked too. She went to the bed and I began to move towards my little room.

'Where are you going, Victoria?'

'I was going to bed, Madame,' I replied.

'I did not dismiss you.'

I hung my head, 'No, Madame.'

'Then come here. I need some warming.' She lifted the covers and I slipped into the bed beside her. She pulled me to her so my head rested against her firm breasts. I lay still as I was unsure of what Madame required of me.

'Your body is comforting,' she said quietly, 'but my hand needs warming.' She pressed a hand between my legs. Her fingers pulled at my lips until they could slip inside. I spread my legs a little.

'Not too wide. I want to feel the warmth of your thighs on my hand,' she whispered. Her fingers dug further, pushing into my crack. Her thumb found my clitoris and made me gasp. Her fingers were inside me now digging deeper and deeper. She pushed and twisted her hand until her fist was within me. No cock was ever as thick as a balled fist but Madame ensured that I stretched to accommodate her. I felt as if my womb was full and that I was the dummy which she controlled. With her hand motionless inside me she leaned forward and took a nipple in her lips. It was erect because my whole body felt charged with electricity. She played with the engorged nipple with her tongue and closed her teeth on it. I cried and she released my breast but rammed her hand up my vagina hard. I gasped.

'Keep quiet, girl,' she hissed. She took hold of my other nipple in her teeth and bit hard. I struggled to keep silent, clenching my teeth.

'Yes, I see our arrangement is not without its benefits,' Madame whispered in my ear. She pulled her hand from my fanny. 'Go down on me, now.'

I slid down the bed beneath the suffocating covers. She parted her thighs and I crawled between them. A hot and strong sexual odour emanated from her fanny. I extended my head and pressed my nose between her lips. I pushed my tongue into her crack and lapped up the juices. Now it was her turn to moan. She tossed her head from side to side as I worked on her, forcing my face harder against her quim so that I could reach further into her hole with my tongue. Then I moved up and grasped her long clitoris in my lips and began to suck and play with it with my tongue. She thrashed around, sometimes grasping my head with her thighs, sometimes opening her legs as wide as she could, pushing me away while gripping my head in her hands and urging me on. Through it all I kept my grip on her knob until her orgasm began to subside. Finally she released my head.

'You can go now,' she whispered. I crawled out from the covers and went to my own bed to fall into a deep sleep.

The following days fell into some kind of routine. I rarely left Madame's study but waited on her, helped her dress and undress and warmed her bed. Many nights she demanded that I pleasure her and I soon found the moves that brought her to a satisfactory climax in the minimum length of time. I was disappointed that I did not see my former school friends. Madame Thackeray forbade me from mixing with them in the drawing room or going upstairs to their rooms. One evening, however, she sent me to the kitchen to collect a cup of hot chocolate. As I passed the stairs, my friend Natalie was descending with the other girls. They were dressed in black corsets, stockings and ankle boots and obviously on their way to a session in the cellar with Madame Hulot. When Natalie saw me she ran to me and flung her arms around me. The other girls clustered around us.

'Oh, Victoria, how wonderful to see you. How are you?'

'Shh,' I said, 'Madame Thackeray must not hear us talking.'

'She said that we mustn't speak to you,' Natalie whispered. 'She said that your father is dead and that you have lost your fortune.'

'That is so and it is why I am reduced to being Madame's maid.'

'But I miss you, Victoria. I miss our kisses and the touch of your hands on my body. I miss you when Madame Hulot is instructing us.'

I nodded in agreement. 'I know. What are you doing this evening?'

'How to stop a man getting an erection,' Freya said.

'How strange,' I commented, 'why should you want to do that?'

'Apparently Madame has some instruments which perform the task,' Natalie explained.

'Come on. We're going to be late,' Bertha said, urging the other girls towards the door to the cellar stairs.

'We must find a time to meet and talk,' Natalie called out as she was dragged away.

'Yes, we must,' I replied, suddenly very sad that I was not part of the group any more.

They disappeared in a huddle through the narrow door and I continued to the kitchen. Johann was stoking the range. Blond and well-muscled, he was the quietest of the menservants.

'What do you want?' he asked.

'I've come for Madame Thackeray's hot chocolate.'

He nodded to the jug on the hotplate. 'Don't you want something too?' he asked, standing up straight and coming towards me. I poured the hot liquid into the cup waiting on the kitchen table.

'What do you mean?' I asked.

'Shut in that room. You haven't had it for weeks, have you?'

'Haven't had what?'

'This.' He pulled his erect cock out of his flies and stepped closer to me.

'Perhaps I don't want it,' I offered. He grabbed my arm.

'You didn't used to say that. You're not one of the fancy girls now. You don't decide any more.' He pushed me back against the kitchen table, tipping me so that I fell onto my back. He shoved my legs apart and pushed my skirt up to my waist. He grabbed my thighs and pulled me towards the edge of the table, towards his arrow-like cock. I struggled to push myself up on my elbows.

'Why are you doing this, Johann? You have endless opportunities to fuck the girls. Why force me to have intercourse with you?'

'Because I can. You're nothing now. You have no wealth. If you don't do what we say Madame will throw you out.' His manhood was at the entrance of my sex, forcing the doors and barging into the corridor.

'So this is about control, is it? You think you can control me because I'm just a servant now.'

'You're not even a servant. You're Madame's slave. She only keeps you so that she can have her way with you. If you stop satisfying her you'll be out and done with.' He gripped my buttocks and rammed his penis into me hard. I gasped as he pierced me, but forced myself into a sitting position.

'So what about the girls who stroke you, suck you and open their legs for you. What are they?'

'Sluts, devil women, whores of hell.' For a quiet man he suddenly had a lot to say. I felt his penis thrusting deep inside me.

'And what does that make you?'

'Damned. Damned. Damned.' On each word he thrust in and on the last I felt him come, semen filling my womb. He withdrew and sank to the floor sobbing. I slid off the table, smoothed my skirt down and picked up the cup of chocolate. I stepped over him and left the kitchen. I felt a trickle running down my leg.

The next morning, Madame brought me an envelope. On the outside it said simply 'Victoria'. I tore it open and read the letter inside. There was just one line that read 'I am sorry' and it was signed Johann.

'What is it?' Madame asked. 'Who is sending you letters?'

'It is from Johann, Madame.'

'Johann. He has disappeared. Eric says he walked out late last night and has not returned. What have you had to do with him?'

I cried and sank to the floor. Bit by bit I explained how he had raped me and called all the women dreadful names; how he despised us and himself.

'He always was the quiet one,' Madame mused. 'Well, he's gone and we will have to replace him. What it does show is that you must not speak to the men. You must stay in here unless you are accompanying me or Madame Hulot.'

'Yes, Madame.'

My service, or slavery as Johann had called it, became something like a gaol sentence as I was not permitted to leave the room or speak to anyone other than the principal or her deputy. However, I could see no alternative. I had no money to travel anywhere or to provide the essentials for life so I threw myself into my tasks. I served Madame and pleasured her whenever she required it. I came to know every part of her body, where she liked to be caressed, the time to spend sucking on her nipples, the pressure to apply when licking around her arsehole, the precise spot in her vagina where a finger could bring her to orgasm. Often she would strap on a dildo and pump me until we both achieved a climax. Satisfying her needs became the meaning of my existence.

On a few occasions I was not required while Madame Thackeray spent the evening with Madame Hulot. I thought they were talking school business but Madame Thackeray returned flushed and her hair untidy. She did not partake of my services for a few days afterwards. Later I found marks on Madame's body as if she herself had felt the weight of someone's hand, but she never spoke of it and I refrained from mentioning it.

One afternoon in early March, Madame said she had business to attend to and that I was to stay in my little room and close the door. I did as she said but some time later I heard cries coming from the study. I pressed my ear to the door to hear well. There was the swoosh as a cane or crop sped through the air, the crack of the implement on flesh and the cry of the victim. Madame was punishing someone. I opened the door a crack and peered through. It was Lydia, my former room-mate, bent over the elephant stool. Good, I thought, she was often insolent and deserved to be taught a lesson of contrition. The beating stopped and now I watched as Madame Thackeray, herself naked, caressed Lydia's fundament. I felt strange. Of course, Madame always followed the pain of punishment with pleasure. I realised that I knew what was going to happen next and the acid bile of jealousy filled me. When Madame picked Lydia up from the stool and laid her on the bed and began to kiss and caress her small, childlike body, fury grew in me until I could stay behind the door no longer.

I burst out of my cupboard, flew across the room and tried to drag Lydia off the bed.

'No, that's my duty,' I screamed. 'Only I can give Madame pleasure.' I had Lydia by the arms, tugging her, but she was fighting back and kicking out. Madame fell on me with her arms around my waist and dragged me off. She held me up as I shouted and kicked and waved my arms.

'Get, Madame Hulot, now! Go, girl,' Madame cried.

Lydia ran out of the room naked. I continued to lash out but gradually I subsided into sobs.

Madame Hulot rushed in, red in the face.

'What is the matter, Grace?' I had never heard Madame Hulot, or anyone, refer to Madame by her Christian name. Now hearing it, I sagged in Madame's arms.

'The girl has gone mad. I think she feels that only she can answer my needs. Foolish girl. Take her away and punish her.' Madame Hulot grabbed my arms and twisted them behind my back. Madame Thackeray released me and Madame Hulot marched me out of the study, across the hall to the small door beneath the stairs. All the girls had come out to see what the commotion was and they watched as Madame Hulot pushed me down the stairs to the cellar.

She led me to a small room, a dungeon. She flung me onto the dusty floor and went out, locking the door behind her. I lay on the floor and sobbed. A short while later Madame Hulot returned carrying chains and manacles.

'Take off your clothes, girl.' I did as I was told and stood naked in front of her with my head hanging.

'Give me your hands.' I held out my arms. Madame Hulot locked steel cuffs around my wrists, linked together by a few links of chain.

'Kneel!' I knelt and Madame tugged the chain until she could fasten it to a ring fixed in the middle of the floor of the cell. The chain was just a few inches long so I had very restricted movement. I could kneel, I could crouch, I could stand so long as I bent double, but I could not get away.

Madame Hulot stepped back from me and unrolled her long black leather whip. I tried to retreat from her but I was well within her range. She cracked the whip and the lash fell across my buttocks and thighs. Again, and my back felt the fire of her stroke. She used all her skill to land blow upon blow on my body no matter how I wriggled and strained against my bonds. She circled around me seeking her target. Eventually, I could no longer move and lay on the floor while she lashed me from my soles to my neck. I fainted.

I awoke in the dark. My wrists were still bound and my body was still aflame from the whipping. A long time passed before someone entered and laid a bowl of water beside my head. I stirred myself and lapped at it like a dog. The cold water on my cheeks was refreshing. I returned to lying flat on my stomach so that there was no pressure on my wounds. Later still I began to feel less sore and so twisted myself into a sitting position with my legs apart and the ring to which I was attached between my thighs. I passed the time sitting there in the darkness fingering my quim, the pleasure that I gave myself overcoming the pain of my beating and the fear of what was to become of me.

Someone, I could not tell who in the dark, came in and left a plate of bread and cold meat. I knelt and, holding the food in my bound hands, lowered my head to eat. Days passed in this way. A chamber pot was provided for my toilet which was removed from time to time, and food and water were brought to me. I had no way of tracking time other than the muffled sounds from beyond my locked prison of Madame Hulot's lessons. I forgot what the day was.

Madame Thackeray came into my cell carrying an oil lamp.

226

She leant down and held it close to me. The light dazzled me and I squinted at her.

'Victoria,' she said, 'I have found you a position. An acquaintance of mine runs an establishment in Vienna. We'll get you tidied up and pack you off. But if you do not behave you will stay here. Do you understand?'

I nodded. There was nothing I wanted more than to escape from this cold, damp, smelly dungeon. I knew now that I was not Madame Thackeray's first love. In fact in my days of solitude I had realised that Madame Hulot and Madame Thackeray were a couple. Although Madame Thackeray was the principal, it was Madame Hulot, the elder of the two, who was the dominant mistress in their relationship. I had just been a passing fancy and even if I had not reacted to her session with Lydia when I had, Madame would soon have tired of me.

Madame Hulot came in and unlocked my handcuffs. Stiffly and unsteadily I got to my feet and stretched my back. Madame Thackeray threw a blanket over my shoulders and guided me out of my prison and out of the cellar.

I was bathed, powdered, given clean underwear and a simple dress to wear. A rather threadbare cloak and hood were put over my shoulders. I stood in the hallway awaiting my transport.

Natalie ran down the stairs. She threw her arms around me, hugged me and kissed my cheek.

'Oh, Victoria. It has been dreadful what has happened to you.' I returned her hugs, welcoming the comfort of her warm body against mine.

'I'm all right,' I said, 'but you shouldn't be with me.'

'No, Madame has given me permission to say goodbye to you. But it is not goodbye but *au revoir*. I will keep in touch with you, Victoria. I shall not let you come to harm.'

'Thank you, Natalie. I long to be free to hold you in my

arms again. Perhaps that time will come after I have spent a while in Vienna.'

The door opened and Ludwig the carter appeared. 'Are you ready, fraulein?' he asked.

I kissed Natalie on her lips and replied, 'Yes.' I let my arms drop from my friend's waist and pulled her arms from around my neck.

'Till we meet again, Natalie.'

'It won't be long, I promise.'

I turned and stepped through the doors, walked down the steps and mounted the cart. Natalie waved from the doorway as I began my journey to Vienna and a new life.

Chapter 19
Victoria, for Sale

I arrived at my new place of work in late afternoon. It was a former hotel in the style of the Hapsburgs but no longer in one of the fashionable areas of Vienna. I tugged the bell pull and after a few minutes the door was opened by a middle-aged woman in a maid's uniform.

'Who are you?' she asked in the Austrian dialect of German.

'I am Victoria. Madame Thackeray of the Venus School for Young Ladies has sent me. I have a letter of introduction.' I proffered the letter and it was taken from my hand.

'You had better come in.' I was shown into what had been the foyer of the hotel. The maid went into a side room and emerged a few moments later following another woman in a blouse and long brown woollen skirt. She circled around me, examining me. 'So, you are Victoria. I was expecting you. I am Frau Muller. Follow me.'

I followed her into the office. Frau Muller closed the door and sat behind a large desk. I remained standing, unsure what was expected of me.

'Undress please.'

I took off my cloak and laid it over a chair and then unbuttoned my dress. I pulled it over my head and let my slip fall to the floor. I stood in my drawers, my arms folded across my breasts.

'I said undress. I mean completely.' I lowered my drawers and then stood feeling self-conscious about my nudity for one of the only times in my life.

'Drop your arms. I want to see what you have.' I let my hands fall beside my hips. Frau Muller got up and approached me. She grasped a nipple and rubbed it between her fingers. Her hand was cold and I flinched.

'Stand still, girl! Hmm, satisfactory bosom.' She went behind me.

'These marks on your buttocks and back. Have you been beaten?'

'Yes, Frau Muller.'

'Well, you'd better behave yourself or you will get another. Do you understand me?'

'Yes, ma'am.'

'Bend over and spread your legs.' I touched my toes with my hands. Through my legs I could see Frau Muller bending to examine my fanny and arse. With the finger and thumb of each hand she parted my lips and looked closely into my crack. 'Hmm. Not a virgin, but it looks healthy.' She returned to her seat.

'Stand up, Victoria, and put your clothes on. We'll start you on the second floor.' As I re-clothed she explained that the first floor rooms were for the top quality free-lance girls while the second floor was for the house girls. She escorted me up the broad staircase, past the fading glories of the first floor and up to the lower-ceilinged second floor. She opened a door to a room and ushered me in. The room was small with just room for a bed, a small upright chair, a little wardrobe, a dressing table and a washstand with a bowl, a jug of water and a chamber pot beneath it. There was a clock on the wall facing the bed.

'This will be your room, Victoria. You will stay here unless told otherwise. A maid will bring you more suitable clothes. When I bring a client you will do what he says. Do you understand me?'

'Yes, Frau Muller.'

'Good. I am sure you will fit in well here, Victoria. Now undress, wash and prepare yourself.' Frau Muller withdrew, turning the key in the door as she left, and leaving me to contemplate my future. I had become the insults that Johann had flung at me – a whore, a common prostitute. I undressed and hung my poor clothes in the wardrobe and then gave myself a thorough wash using the tepid water in the jug and the bar of gritty hard soap that was provided. The maid entered without knocking and dropped an armful of clothes on the bed.

'You had better get ready quick. The men will start arriving soon,' she said. I sorted through the clothes and dressed myself in a front fastening corset in bright pink with matching bloomers. Over these I put a white petticoat and a bright red dress of poor-quality silk such as may be worn by dancers on stage. It barely came down to my ankles and left much of my bosom exposed. Thus dressed, I sat on the bed and waited.

Not long passed before there were footsteps and voices outside my room. A small window in my door that I had not noticed before slid open and Frau Muller's face appeared.

'Stand, Victoria.' I stood.

'There you are, sir, a fresh young Englisher.' Frau's face was replaced by that of a middle-aged gentleman with a trimmed beard and wide moustache. He looked for a moment and then went away. The window was slid shut.

'She'll do,' I heard him say. 'One hour, you say?' I glanced at the clock which showed twenty minutes past eight.

'That's right, sir. In you go, sir,' Frau Muller replied. The lock clicked and Frau Muller flung the door open. The gentleman, in a formal coat and carrying a top hat, entered. Frau Muller closed the door behind her as she left.

Little was said between us. He removed his coat and gloves and then he sat on the chair and told me to undress. For the third time in a little over an hour I stripped off my clothes. This was where I made my first mistake I discovered later. I should have made the act of disrobing a major part of my act and so taken up a considerable fraction of the hour that the gentleman had paid for. Instead I undressed as quickly and carelessly as I usually did. He was not impressed, but when I was naked he showed a degree of interest.

'Sit on my lap,' he said. I did so and with his free hand he caressed my legs and thighs and then cupped my breasts, feeling each nipple. He lost interest after a few minutes and pushed me off his knees. He stood up.

'Undress me.' This was a task at which I seemed to have some expertise. I helped him remove his jacket and waistcoat and then knelt to undo his garters and trouser buttons. I pulled off his heavy shoes and removed his hosiery. He pushed his trousers down to his ankles and stood before me in his shirt and long cotton drawers. His body, when revealed, showed signs of age. His body hair, like that on his head, was flecked with grey and the muscles in his arms and legs showed wastage. Nevertheless his heart beat strongly and his body carried little excess weight.

I pulled his drawers down slowly, gently releasing his manhood. His testicles flopped out but his penis was lost among the folds of skin. I realised that I was going to have to work hard to satisfy this gentleman. Kneeling in front of him I began to rub my hands up and down his thighs. Then I moved to cup his balls and massaged them gently. There was a flicker of movement and the small pink head of his cock appeared. I bent my head and touched my lips to it. It stirred and swelled and grew a little. Now there was enough of a shaft for me to hold. I gripped it in my hand and I felt it respond, stiffening as the blood rushed into it. The circumcised head was now a healthy mauve and had lost its dull, wrinkled appearance. I encircled it with my lips, caressed it with my tongue and sucked. I drew a gasp of pleasure from its owner and his legs wobbled. I continued to massage his balls with one hand, grip the shaft with my other and suck on his knob. All the time his penis grew and became harder.

The gentleman muttered something and sat down on the bed pulling his cock from my grasp. He lay back and beckoned to me. I climbed astride him and lowered myself slowly and carefully onto his now quite considerable manhood. He sighed as he entered me. Although he was nothing like as large as Eric, Hermann or Albert, he filled me and I rejoiced at the feel of a cock pressed deep in my fanny and his balls between my buttocks.

I began to ride him, bouncing up and down, hindered somewhat by the springiness of the old bedstead and mattress. The oscillations of the bed did not quite match my movements as sometimes as I raised myself up his penis almost dropped out and at others we bounced together with his cock locked into my channel. He was breathing deeply now and flexing his legs to provide extra impetus to the thrusts. He came quite suddenly with a little whimper and subsided immediately. There was just a little trickle of semen from his penis which quickly retired to its nest within his scrotum.

I stretched myself out alongside his prostrate form, wondering what to do next. Soft snores indicated that I would possibly not be called on for much. He slept on until it was gone nine of the clock. I wondered what I should do as his hour was nearly up. At ten past I nudged him and he stirred.

'I think perhaps you had better get dressed,' I suggested. He looked at the clock and was not at all pleased to find his time had nearly passed. He began to dress, muttering and accusing me.

'I didn't pay for an hour of your company for you to let me sleep, young woman.'

I apologised but suggested perhaps he did need the rest since he had fallen into slumber so readily after our intercourse. He had the grace to admit that the lovemaking had been pleasurable and relaxing, then placing his top hat on his head, he left.

I got up washed myself and dressed yet again. I hoped that I might have the opportunity to look around outside since my door was now unlocked but almost as soon as I was fully clothed Frau Muller arrived with my second client. I had learnt some important lessons from my first customer and so took longer to introduce myself to the gentleman and to remove my clothes with more of a flourish. This man was shorter and stout with a bald head. He was more aggressive and once we were naked he threw me onto the bed and fell on me, forcing his cock into me with little attempt at foreplay. He did not fall asleep after his first orgasm and ordered me to feel and suck him into readiness for a second round.

After his departure there were three more guests to entertain until, shortly before dawn, I was at last able to fall into a deep sleep myself.

And so my life as a whore began. It continued day after day with sometimes three or four, sometimes eight or nine, clients a night. Some old, some young, all reasonably wealthy; some clean and considerate, others smelly, grubby and unpleasant to bed. The routine of handling and sucking cocks, of being fucked in both channels, being on top or underneath or approached from the rear became tedious and a chore. Only occasionally did a gentleman trouble to make my experience a pleasurable one. I never saw a single coin from my clients and never knew how much they paid for my services. That was always handled by Frau Muller. I rarely saw any of my colleagues because if we weren't working we slept and when we weren't working the door to my room was locked. Plain but wholesome food was delivered to my room three times a day and the elderly maids emptied the wash bowl and chamber pot and refilled the jug with hot water. Once a week I was allowed to the bathroom for a bath. That was the highlight of the week when I was allowed half an hour to wallow in hot water and to soap myself all over. But each week after my bath, Frau Muller would examine my body and approve me for another week of hard labour. I reflected on the turn of events that had brought me to this life, but with no money and no apparent prospects I could see no reason for trying to escape.

I had been working at Frau Muller's establishment for three to four months when late one afternoon she sent a maid to escort me from my room to her office. There was a large window in Frau Muller's room and I looked out on sunshine and flowers and people walking by in summer dress. I felt tired and bored with the endless coupling. Frau Muller sat at her desk and ignored the summer scene.

'I've had some complaints, Victoria.'

'Complaints, Frau Muller?' I couldn't understand who could be complaining about me.

'Some of your clients have said you are listless, not energetic in bed and not giving them enough attention.'

I was horrified. 'But Frau Muller, I always try my best.'

'That may not be enough. You have looked a little, what shall we say, uninterested, lately. That's the trouble with you girls born with everything. You don't have the determination to improve yourself like some of my girls have. I think you need some sense knocked into you to wake you up and realise what you are here for. It's not cheap keeping you fed and clothed and there is the upkeep of this building to consider.' I couldn't respond because as far as I could see every pfennig that I earned went into Frau Muller's pocket. 'So, you'll spend a few days in the basement. See if that galvanises you into action.'

'The basement? What is that, Frau Muller?'

'You'll see.' She rang a small bell on her desk and very quickly a maid entered.

'Take Victoria to the basement.' She looked down at some papers, leaving the maid to urge me to follow her.

We crossed the foyer but instead of taking the broad stairs up to the bedrooms we descended a narrow set of concrete steps and entered a narrow corridor. Small gas lights at widely spaced intervals did little to disperse the darkness. On each side of the corridor there were doors. I tried to glance inside as we passed but they were dark. At length the maid stopped and pushed a door open. It swung slowly as if it was very heavy. I stepped inside. It was small, barely four feet square, with bare concrete walls and floor. There was no light.

'Take your clothes off,' the maid instructed.

'What? Here? Now? This is no more than a closet.'

'Do as I say.' Her voice sounded threatening and despite her being older I was not sure I could fight my way past her. I undressed. She gathered up my clothes, stepped outside and closed the door. A heavy bolt was rammed through. I was left in the utter darkness with barely enough space to crouch down. There was nothing to do but wait.

I don't know how long it was, it may have been one hour or five, but eventually I heard sounds of people in the corridor and rooms. The bolt was pushed back and the door opened. I got to my feet. Two maids filled the doorway.

'Turn around,' one ordered. I turned and my arms were grabbed and pinioned behind me. A rope was passed around my wrists and tied tightly. Then a leather blindfold was placed over my eyes and secured behind my head. Hands pulled me out of the closet and pushed me along the corridor and then to the right into some other space.

'She's yours,' the maid said and then I heard her steps and those of the other maid moving away. A door slammed. I stood, straining to listen. As my ears became attuned I picked out three or four sources of sound – breathing, soles of shoes on the concrete floor, a match being lit.

'Well, my fellows. Think she will do?' The voice was that of a young man, English perhaps. There were calls of agreement from three other locations.

'Well, let's set to it,' the first voice said. I was immediately aware of the four men closer to me, their breath on my neck, my back, my breast and thigh. A hand caressed my left breast going round and round in a spiral until it reached my nipple. It was squeezed, hard, and I yelped.

'Oh, so she is real and not a mannequin,' an American voice said. The others laughed. There were other hands sliding up and down the inside of my right thigh, circling my buttocks and untying the rope that bound my wrists. I thought I was to be freed but instead my hands were lifted up above my head and encircled by tight leather cuffs.

'They're fastened,' the first voice called and I was yanked up by my arms. I cried at the sudden tearing of my limbs. The lifting stopped with me standing on tiptoes. If I lost my balance I swung with all my weight taken by my wrists.

'Let's warm her up, guys,' said the American. There was a pause while I swung and struggled to keep my weight on my toes, then a fiery slash down my left thigh. Another caught me across my right buttock, another across my stomach and another on my right shoulder. Despite the pain and strain in my wrists I wriggled and swung, trying to avoid the blows that were coming at me, but they were on all sides. All my actions did were to make them laugh and compete to land a blow. At first I was able to make out crop burns, cane strokes and whiplash, but after several blows they all felt the same. My whole body became a bonfire of pain.

At last it stopped and I was left swinging from my wrists. Through my pain I could hear the men breathing heavily.

'Best get her down,' said another voice, with a French accent. The tension on my wrists was released and I fell into a crumpled heap, but I was not left to recover myself. Two men lifted me and moved me forward until my knees made contact with a padded stool. I was made to kneel on it and while two men held my body, another pulled my ankles apart and locked them into some device that prevented me from moving my legs. Then I was bent down, my hands drawn back and my wrists fastened next to my ankles. I was now completely immobile, unable even to rise. My flesh still burned from the beating but at least my arms were no longer being stretched and my knees were cushioned.

I was left untouched for some time but I could hear men around me drinking, smoking and chatting. I imagine they were also looking at me and deciding which portion to take, which cut of meat would give the most pleasure. The pain in my flesh passed down through several levels from unbearable to smouldering, but my back and shoulders began to ache from the unnatural position in which I was crouched. And then the touches began again. A finger traced a line across my back, obviously following the weals of my whipping. Another smoothed the inside of my legs. Then a finger traced along the crack between my buttocks. It paused at my anus and tentatively prospected the force necessary to gain entry. It travelled on, entering the moist fastness of my fanny. Despite my pain and indignity I found myself trembling at this intimate touch. I felt my lips swelling and the finger moved more slickly up and down.

'Look at that,' the English voice said, 'she likes it.'

'Well, she is a hooker, of course she likes it,' the

American said.

'Surely all women would be excited by a finger in their quim,' the Frenchman commented.

'Not my wife,' the Englishman retorted.

'Have you ever touched her?' chortled the American.

'I wouldn't dare,' the Englishman responded and all broke into laughter. The finger, however, didn't stop and now began to push deeper into my vagina. I so wanted my clitoris to be rubbed or sucked but it was ignored. I tried to speak but only a gurgle came out of my mouth.

'She's trying to say something,' another English voice said, younger and lighter in tone.

'Well, you'd better stuff something in her mouth and stop her,' said the first Englishman.

'What?'

'Do I need to tell you?' The men laughed. A hand grabbed the hair on top of my head and pulled it up. As he did so, the head of an erect penis pressed at my mouth. I resisted at first but the hand pulled my hair harder and involuntarily my mouth opened. It was filled by the plum-sized tip of a cock. The man rammed it in and unusually I began to gag. I struggled to breathe through my nose but he kept his manhood pushed deep to the back of my throat. While my attention was focused on breathing and coping with a mouth full of cock I felt another penis driving into my fanny. He didn't approach gently but thrust in his full length in one powerful movement. The force pushed me forward driving the cock in my mouth further down my throat. I tried to free myself but my hands and feet were too tightly secured to allow any movement. The two men fucking me timed their thrusts almost as if they were watching each other over my back. The one in my mouth ejaculated first. The semen trickled out of my mouth and down my chin. As his erection subsided I gasped for breath. Then with one final brutal thrust the second man came, filling my cunt with his juice.

No sooner had he withdrawn than his place was taken by the third man who rubbed his swollen cock head up and down my crack before aiming for my arsehole. This time I screamed as he achieved entry and got a slap across my face for my trouble. The cock stretched my arse taut and his vicious movements felt as though I was being torn apart. He achieved his orgasm and was in turn replaced by another, presumably the fourth man. He entered my vagina still slick with semen from the first entry. With the extra lubrication he took longer to come, riding me like a buck until, with a gasp, he shot his load.

And so it went on. By the time all four had had their pleasure of me the first was ready to resume. There was barely a pause when I did not have one or other of them in arse, fanny or mouth and sometimes two at once. As each one took his turn the others laughed and commented and clashed their glasses. Each of my orifices was as sore as my beaten flesh when they finally desisted.

I think the four men left but I still remained bound on my podium, the muscles in my arms and legs and shoulders steadily becoming stiffer and filling me with excruciating pain. I don't know how long it was before someone, a maid I presume, finally came and undid my bonds. She helped me off the stool but I was shaking and unsteady after being in such an awkward position for so long. She said no word of sympathy and offered no other assistance but retied my hands behind my back. Then she supported me walking down the corridor to the tiny closet where I had been kept earlier. I curled up on the floor and slept fitfully.

I was awoken by the door opening. I was dragged out and carried to another room where I was flung over a waist-high stool not unlike the elephant in Madame Thackeray's room. My ankles were pulled apart and fastened.

'There, she's not in much of a state to respond,' said a

female voice, 'but you can have what fun you like with her.' There were a variety of mumbled comments. The door slammed shut and a few moments later a cock forced its way into my sore fanny. I cried as I was fucked but no one seemed to pay any attention to me. One after the other came and had their pleasure, although what pleasure it can have been fucking what was almost a slab of dead meat, I don't know. My awareness of what was happening broke up into stabs of pain and rhythmic thrusts and periods where I lost any sense of my own body at all.

Eventually everything stopped. There was silence and I wondered whether I had died.

Chapter 20
Victoria Finds Her Goal

'Victoria, is it really you?' The voice sounded familiar but came as if in a dream in my semi-conscious state. I woke up enough to realise that I was still flung over the stool like a sack of turnips, my ankles bound to the legs, my wrists tied behind my back and my fanny open and exposed like a gaping wound. Every part of my body was sore or ached from the beating and fucking I had received.

'It is. Oh, please, please, release her, quickly.' The French accent finally triggered my memory – it was my dear friend Natalie from the Venus School for Young Ladies. Fingers pulled at the bindings and at last my ankles and wrists were freed. Arms pulled me from the stool and laid me on the cold concrete floor. I opened my eyes to see Natalie looking down at me.

'What have they done to you, Victoria? Where do you hurt?'

'Everywhere,' I muttered and fainted.

I awoke to the delicious feel of clean, smooth cotton sheets caressing my breasts and buttocks, my head resting on a soft down pillow and my body supported by a feather mattress. Mentally, I examined myself. Parts of my skin still tingled, there was a lingering soreness in my bottom and my arms felt a little stiff, but otherwise I seemed to be approaching my normal self. I opened my eyes. Natalie was looking down at me. Her worried frown turned into a broad smile.

'Oh, you are awake. You have been sleeping for a whole day. How are you, my love?' she said.

'I think I am quite recovered. Where am I?' I looked around the room at plush decorations but anonymous works of art.

'The Imperial Hotel,' Natalie replied.

'In Vienna?' I was not sure if I had been transported from the city during my state of unconsciousness.

'*Oui*, we're staying here until you are fit to accompany us to Paris.'

'Paris? Us?'

'My Uncle Pierre and I. We would like you to come to his home for as long as you wish.'

'That's very kind, but I do not want to be a burden ...'

'*Non*, my love, you will not. Uncle Pierre has a proposition. He would like to commission you to be his model for a set of photographs.' I recalled Natalie's tale of when she had been the subject of her uncle's photographic hobby.

'You mean his *special* photographs which he sells.'

'That's right, but this time I shall organise it properly and you will be paid.'

'Well, I don't seem to have any other offers of employment and I presume my position at Frau Muller's emporium has been terminated.'

'That dreadful woman. Uncle Pierre had to get very firm with her to make her release you. But, come, let me help you take a bath.'

She held my arm as I took shaky steps to the bathroom. I sank gratefully into the hot water. While Natalie soaped my body she talked about her Easter vacation and the summer term at the Venus School for Young Ladies; how Madame Thackeray refused to say where I had gone until the day of my eighteenth birthday just before the end of term.

Strangely my birthday had passed without me noticing. Natalie and my classmates had been worried and determined to find me. How horrified she was when she had discovered what had happened to me.

When I was towelled dry and lying on the bed, Natalie rubbed soothing creams into my abused skin. Her gentle fingers circled my breasts, my stomach and, by instinct, slipped between my legs. Lightly, she caressed my lips and carefully opened them up. Her creamed finger slid up and down my crack. She found my clitoris. I sighed.

'That is not hurting, is it?' she asked.

'No, my dear, it is wonderful. So few of the men paid any attention to my desires. You are re-kindling my attraction to pleasure.'

Very softly she rubbed my little knob and gradually feelings that I had almost forgotten began to run through me; a little tremble in my stomach, a knot of desire in my breast, a growing and delicious tingle in my fanny. I came to orgasm with a gasp of joy. Natalie planted a kiss on each of my nipples.

'There now. Sleep again and you will recover fully.' I did indeed drift into a pleasant slumber.

Over the next few days, I recovered quickly and the marks of the crop and cane and whip faded from my body. I ate well, dressed in the fine clothes that Uncle Pierre had bought for me and we even went outside the hotel and looked at the famous palaces of Vienna. Uncle Pierre decided that I was fit to travel so we took the train to Paris and arrived at his house.

We soon got down to the business of the photographs. Uncle Pierre imagined me in the role of Greek goddesses. There was no subterfuge. I knew exactly what Uncle Pierre wanted and he agreed to say what he wanted in each picture. We began with me as an imperious Hera, with a bared breast. Then I was Ariadne, the hunter, with the fur of a small animal barely covering my body. Next I was the newborn Aphrodite, emerging fully grown and naked from the clam shell. For each set of photographs, Uncle Pierre was most concerned for my comfort but had me adopt a variety of poses. Not once did he attempt to touch me although he came very close with his cameras on many occasions. Afterwards I looked at his prints. Some pictures were chaste, but most, designed for his male clientele, showed my private parts from one angle or another.

After each day's posing Natalie and I played and chatted. Having completed her two-year course at the Venus School for Young Ladies, I wondered what she would do in the future.

'Get married, I suppose,' Natalie replied.

'After what you have learned, will that satisfy you?'

'Oh, I shall be very careful in my choice of a husband and make sure that he is willing to learn how to pleasure me.'

'Will one husband be enough? Beatrice has a number of patrons to ensure she gets what she wants.'

'Hmm. That is a thought. Perhaps I shall take lovers. But what about you, Victoria? What will you do?' I had thought about that question a lot but had found no answers. Perhaps Uncle Pierre's photographs would open a career in that direction.

The next day I was playing the part of Europa, seduced by Zeus. This involved my adopting various postures to indicate the ecstasy of lovemaking with a god. I lay on my back on a couch with my head bent back over the edge, arms hanging down by my side, knees raised and thighs wide apart. Uncle Pierre moved around with his camera tripod, taking photographs from this angle and that. He approached my side to take a close-up of my breasts. Then he moved to the foot of the couch and photographed my quim.

'Are you going to do to me what you did to Natalie?' I asked.

He flustered. 'What has Natalie told you?'

'Everything. If you want me excited for this last picture then I need some preparation.' He did not need any more encouragement but crawled onto the couch and placed his head between my legs. To be honest, I did not need much stimulation as the thought of photographs of my sex being sold in the streets of Paris excited me enough already. Nevertheless the touch of his tongue on my clitoris and in my vagina soon had me rocking and bucking. At the peak of my orgasm he withdrew and flashed his magnesium lamp. As he replaced the glass plate in its black envelope I got off the couch and approached him.

'Now for your reward,' I said.

'Pardon?'

'My thanks for taking me in and looking after me.'

'It is nothing.'

I knelt in front of him, my nipples rubbing against his trousers. I unbuttoned his flies and helped his expanding penis escape. I licked along its length, top and bottom, leaned underneath and sucked his balls, then licked back along the shaft to the purple knob. I ran my tongue around it and rubbed against the little hole. Uncle Pierre was already gasping and his legs were shaking. I opened my mouth wide and engulfed his head. I pressed my lips around it and sucked. He was throbbing and I could feel his semen starting to flow. I sucked hard just as the flood gushed into my mouth. I chewed and swallowed. There was the sound of running feet on the marble floor.

'Victoria, you have a … oh!' I released Uncle Pierre's penis and turned to see Natalie standing by my side. 'I'm sorry, I didn't mean to interrupt.' Uncle Pierre had gone bright pink and was hurriedly doing up his buttons. 'Don't be embarrassed, Uncle, I knew that Victoria would pleasure you when she felt the time was right.'

'You girls. You never cease to surprise me,' he mumbled.

'What was it that made you run?' I asked.

'Oh. A letter just came for you.'

'A letter?' Who could be sending me a letter? I took the envelope from Natalie and noted that it had travelled to Austria before finding its way to Paris. I tore it open and pulled out the letter. The letterhead said Blenkinsop, Blenkinsop and Blenkinsop, Solicitors. I started to read, gasped in amazement, sank to the floor and read it all again.

'What does it say, Victoria? What is the matter?' Natalie was worried.

'It is amazing,' I said.

'What is amazing? Tell us,' Natalie demanded.

I got up and sat on the edge of the couch.

'It is from Samuel Blenkinsop, my father's solicitor and executor of his will. When I last saw him at the New Year he thought that all my father's fortune was gone but it seems he was wrong. Apparently the Berkshire estate was put into a trust for me before he made his losses. The estate is mine. Of course a lot of the furniture and paintings and other things were sold, but the house is still there for me to use.'

'That is wonderful news,' Uncle Pierre said. 'You are a woman of substance after all.'

'What will you do?' Natalie asked.

'I'm not sure but I am going to give it a lot of thought in the next few days and write some letters if I may.'

Indeed a germ of an idea had entered my head as I read Samuel's letter through a second time. I thought about it, then discussed my plan with Natalie and Uncle Pierre. I wrote my letters and received encouraging replies. So, some ten days after receiving my news, I returned to London, staying in a smart hotel, with Natalie as my companion and Uncle Pierre as escort. We met Samuel Blenkinsop and set various arrangements in motion. A couple of weeks passed in a fever of activity as my plans developed, until at last we were able to take the train to Reading. We hired a coach to travel the last few miles to what was now my country estate. The first view of the rose-pink stone of the house made my spirits lift with joy.

For over a year the house had been closed up, empty and musty, but in the last few weeks a team of workers had opened it up, let in the summer air, made essential repairs and begun simple re-decoration. Not all of it was as yet habitable but now it was time to take on a permanent staff and prepare the building for its new use. While the tenanted farms would provide a little income, considerably more was needed to maintain the estate and enable me to live the life that I desired.

I decided to carry out interviews in the library. The shelves were still empty but with the blinds raised, the room was light and comfortable. I sat at a desk trying to feel as mature and authoritarian as possible. I called for the first interviewee to enter. He entered carrying his cap in his hands but stopped mid-step when he saw me.

'Victoria!'

'Hello, Bill. It's Lady Victoria now, or ma'am, if you please.'

He flustered, and bowed his head, 'I'm sorry, ma'am, we did not know who was taking over the estate.'

'That was the intention. Now, I know of your ability with the fillies, both equine and human, but do you think you could perform another job for me?'

'Anything, Vic … my Lady. It has been a difficult time since your father closed up the house and disposed of his horses.'

'I'm sure it has. So will you be my head footman?'

'Head footman? I'm not sure what the job involves, ma'am.'

'Let me explain. Drop your trousers.'

'I beg your pardon, Miss.'

'I said, drop your trousers.' I got up from my seat and walked around the desk while he fumbled with the string that held up his battered and threadbare trousers. They slid to the floor. I stood in front of him.

'And your drawers.' He complied, his hands shaking. His penis was small and shrivelled but his testicles hung low, garlanded in hair. I touched the buried tip of his cock.

'Are you still seeing that scullery maid?' I asked.

'Which maid? Ah ...' The memory of our last meeting came to him. 'Well, not her, no.' He looked worried.

'I'm sure there are others. Don't worry, Bill, I have forgiven you. But I remember how much you like this.' I caressed his cock and it quickly grew, rising to attention. I pulled on the foreskin and his wonderful plum of a knob appeared. I rubbed the tip gently with the finger and thumb while massaging the shaft up and down with my other. Bill rocked on his heels and whimpered quietly. He came in my hand. I held it up and in front of his face licked the semen from my palm.

'There. That was good, wasn't it?' I explained my plans to him and the part he had to play.

Soon we had maids cleaning and preparing rooms, cooks in the kitchen and gardeners clearing the grounds. Natalie ran from room to room ensuring that the new furniture and furnishings were arranged correctly. Uncle Pierre instructed Bill and the other young men that I had selected in how to perform their duties and I supervised and worried that things would not be ready in time. At last, the day that I had planned for arrived. By mid-afternoon most of the servants had returned to their homes and Natalie and I were clothed in our fine dresses.

A carriage drew up and Bill did a good job of escorting

the three guests into the drawing room. I rose from my chair to welcome them.

'Beatrice, it's so lovely to see you again. Theophilus, you look most handsome. And Amelia, that dress suits you so well.' The four of us, together with Natalie and Uncle Pierre, embraced and began chatting. Bea related that trade in Brighton was good and that all her rooms were now occupied; Theophilus confessed to making regular visits to Bea's establishment but his career in the bank was on the rise; and Amelia announced that she was now living all the time as a woman while managing her inheritance.

Soon, a cab delivered Samuel Blenkinsop. He was introduced to everyone. I made sure that he and Amelia sat together and got to know one another. I was made to recount my story of the last year, my trials after my father's sudden death and my recent reinstatement as a lady.

At last, when it was nearly time for dinner, a carriage pulled up. Bill opened the main door but I hurried out to greet my last guest. He stepped down on to the gravel and opened his arms as I ran to him and flung my arms around his neck. He kissed me chastely on the cheek.

'I was so sorry to hear about your father,' I said.

'It was a shock but at least he saw me married and ready to take over the business.'

'How is your wife?' I asked.

'Very well, and perfectly happy staying at home, looking after our baby son, while I travel the country visiting our factories. It is wonderful to see you again, Victoria.' I took his arm and guided him up the steps and into the house. My guests stood waiting for him to be presented.

'May I introduce Sir Gilbert Stebbings, industrialist and benefactor.'

Everyone wanted to talk at once but I was able to usher us through to the dining room for dinner. We sat around a circular table and engaged in conversation. I was delighted to see Bea and Uncle Pierre giggling together like old friends; Natalie was being sweet to Theophilus; Samuel had a hand on Amelia's thigh and on more than one occasion he whispered something in her ear that made her smile and blush. Bill supervised the maids serving the food and remained standing behind me when I dismissed the other staff. I coughed to clear my throat and get my guests' attention.

'I am so glad that you could all come this evening and join in our venture.' I looked around at smiling faces. 'Two years ago when I started at the Venus School for Young Ladies I had few if any thoughts for my future. I have learned such a lot, in particular about my desires and those of other men and women.' Bill coughed behind me. 'One thing I have learned, particularly in the last seven or eight months, is responsibility. Whatever happens in the future I am going to be responsible for what happens to me.'

'Hear, hear!' cheered Theophilus.

'I also learned that I have a talent for pleasing other people, men and women. I would like to pass that talent on to others. If two frauds like Madame Thackeray and Madame Hulot can run an internationally known school, then, with help, I am sure I can too. With my dear friend Natalie by my side,' Natalie smiled and nodded to me, 'and the support and advice of our trustees, Gilbert, Theophilus, Samuel and Amelia, and of my good friends, Beatrice and Pierre, I am sure that we can make a success of the Victoria College for Ladies.'

'Named after the Queen?' Bea asked.

'Perhaps,' I replied. 'Our school will offer a modern curriculum covering all the arts and sciences and will teach our young women how to be independent citizens.'

'Hurrah,' Natalie cried.

'And, of course, with the help of Bill and the other boys, we shall introduce them to the arts of pleasure so that they

251

too can be fulfilled.'

My audience, including Bill, applauded and whistled and hooted. Gilbert stood up and signalled the assembly to hush.

'May I say on behalf of the other trustees that I am sure that our investment in this new venture will be a sound, nay, a rewarding one. Victoria taught me a great deal when we met not so long ago in Venice and there is nothing I would like to do more than support her. So let us drink a toast to Victoria's College.' Everyone stood up with their glasses and drank the toast.

'Thank you all,' I acknowledged their congratulations. 'Now I think the entertainment can begin. Your rooms are prepared so set to it.' I turned to Bill, 'Is your little maid waiting for you in her room with her legs wide apart?'

'I hope so, my lady.'

'Then get your cock out and go to her.'

'Thank you, my lady.'

Bill hurried out closely followed by Uncle Pierre with Bea on his arm. Natalie tugged at Theophilus' elbow, urging him to move while Samuel and Amelia exchanged a kiss on each other's lips before setting off arm in arm. Gilbert and I made our way to my new bedroom with its thick carpet and low divan-style bed. I pulled on his bow tie and began to unbutton his shirt.

'When you left me in Venice, I had no thoughts that we might meet up again.'

Gilbert skilfully undid the tiny buttons of my bodice. 'Nor I, but you have been in my thoughts every day, including my wedding day. This is my dream come true.'

With a bit of shuffling we were soon standing naked. His smooth chest rubbed against my nipples and his hard rod poked my stomach. I caressed his firm buttocks.

'Mine too,' I said.

252

More great books from **X**cite...

Naughty Spanking One
Twenty bottom-tingling stories to make your buttocks blush!
9781906125837 £7.99

The True Confessions of a London Spank Daddy
Memoir by Peter Jones
9781906373320 £7.99

Girl Fun One
Lesbian anthology edited by Miranda Forbes
9781906373672 £7.99

Sex and Satisfaction Two
Erotic stories edited by Miranda Forbes
9781906373726 £7.99

Ultimate Curves
Erotic short stories edited by Miranda Forbes
9781906373788 £7.99

Naughty! The Xcite Guide to Sexy Fun
How To book exploring edgy, kinky sex
9781906373863 £9.99

For more information and great offers
please visit
www.xcitebooks.com